HOOK

THE UNTOLD STORIES OF NEVERLAND

K.R. THOMPSON

Hook © 2018 K.R. Thompson
2nd edition

All rights reserved under the International and Pan-American Copyright Conventions. No part of this book may be reproduced or transmitted in any form or by any means, electronic or mechanical, including photocopying, recording, or by any information storage and retrieval system, without permission in writing from the publisher.

This is a work of fiction. Names, places, characters and incidents are either the product of the author's imagination or are used fictitiously, and any resemblance to any actual persons, living or dead, organizations, events or locales is entirely coincidental.

1

BAD FORM, INDEED

*A*n eternity passed before Big Ben tolled five bells. They were heavenly peals to Archibald Jameson, who began to wonder if time had somehow gotten stuck or if the gigantic clock across the square was broken. Stretching out his long legs, he stood up from the desk and scooted around the corner, taking care not to bump the towering mountain of paper at the edge. Naturally, it was the largest stack in the entire room—the work that he had yet to finish. If he was even a fraction as meticulous a man as his father—the very man who left him the shop— he would have stayed, locked the front door, and remained into the wee hours to finish the work, however long it should take.

But he was not his father, and he had no intention of pretending to be so. While he was very good at running the print shop, it wasn't something he enjoyed. It was only what he must do to ensure his survival. Remaining any longer than necessary just wasn't going to happen as far as Archie was concerned. His inheritance should have been a blessing since he was the youngest of four sons. Without the steady work the shop provided, he might as well have lived out on the street, begging for what scraps could be found. To him, the feel of the paper and smell of ink felt like a prison where he was trapped day in and out. His release came in daydreams. As he pondered another life or another world, the work piled up before him. He spent hours upon hours each day, dreaming of adventure, of places and people that always made those in his life seem dull in comparison. Those daydreams made his life bearable.

But even the daydreams wouldn't hold him there once Big Ben chimed its fifth peal. He never stayed a second longer than required.

He blew out lamps and turned over the sign in the window, then pulled on his frayed, black frock. He took one last glance around, then slapped on his hat and stepped outside. Chilly air greeted him as he pulled the door shut, listening to the muted sounds of the doorbell. He turned the key in the lock and jiggled the knob.

Odd, he thought. The tinkling sounds he heard earlier sounded nothing at all like the brass bell on the frame of that door. Odd, indeed. Perhaps it was the remnants of his latest daydream, for the door had never sounded that way before. Still pondering the bell, he turned and rammed into a young boy, who let out an audible *oof*, as he landed on the side of the street.

"I do beg your pardon," Archie said, offering his hand to help the boy up. The lad flashed a smile, showing a unique set of small, pearly white teeth, before he took Archie's proffered hand and replied, "Quite alright." Without waiting for Archie to say anything more, the boy took off, disappearing around the bend.

Hunching over against the cold wind that sent leaves dancing about his legs, Archie shoved his hands deep into his pockets, and made his way down the bricked street, no longer in the rush he was in moments before.

"Mary, I don't see how we can afford to keep her." The booming voice was startling. Archie glanced up at a window, which was open in spite of the chill. "Let's see, two pounds nineteen…"

"George, dear…"

"Now, Mary, hold on a moment. I have the tally right here. Do you think we might try it for half a year on say, five five three? Only half the year, mind you. Oh, drat, I forgot to figure in colic."

The voice of the man and his wife argued back and forth as Archibald stood, rooted in place, wondering at their strange conversation. As this was his normal route home, he walked by No. 27 every evening. He half-hoped this financial dispute might possibly involve their dog. If it did, he would be more than willing to step up and offer to solve their financial dilemma. He lived alone and the thought of the trim Newfoundland he had seen carrying in bottles of milk from the front steps bolstered his spirits.

The talk of colic, however, kept him from knocking on the front door.

"Shall we say one pound? Yes, that is what I'll put down. But what of mumps? I've heard that can be quite taxing. I daresay that should be twenty shillings there. Don't give me that look, Mary."

It was at this point a sharp cry of an infant pierced their conversation and Archibald was quite certain that Nana the Newfoundland was most assuredly not the topic of money, colic, mumps, and their current distraught state. He shook his head, wondering about the sanity of the Darlings in No. 27 as the silhouette of a woman he presumed to be Mary shut the window and the voices muted.

Poor Nana, Archibald thought, to be stuck with people such as that.

He didn't even want to think about the child whose fate rested on the odds of her contracting whooping-cough and so he openly wished the inhabitants of No. 27

would not be so lucky as to have any additional offspring. He voiced exactly that, and in that same instant, heard that funny peal of bells again. This time it sounded suspiciously like laughter.

He spun around, searching for the source, and saw a crone of an old woman who stepped out of No. 31. She heard his wish and didn't agree with his rather bold assessment. Archie was sure she hadn't laughed a day since she had been born, and moreover, he was certain that glorious day of her arrival had been at least a century earlier.

"Well," she puffed up, looking much like a wrinkled, ancient bullfrog before she croaked, "I never!"

"Yes, madam. I should hope for precisely *never* as it seems the most promising period of time," he smiled and bent, giving her an elaborate, low bow to thank her for her agreement. "For to wish them more mouths to feed, when one seems to be their undoing, would be bad form, indeed."

The old woman gaped at him, mouth working like a fish out of water. Then, she clamped it shut in a fierce scowl, and proceeded to slam the door with as much vigor as her frail limbs could muster.

Archibald smiled to himself, silently touching the brim of his hat in mock farewell before he spun, leaving the occupants of both No. 27 and No. 31 to their own devices and ignorance. He continued his stroll down the street in much better spirits, knowing that he bested the old woman and possibly even the Darlings without their even knowing it, though he was certain his sentiments would be relayed by their observant neighbor.

Ah, well. They should have known better than to trifle with something such as a child. A small victory, but a victory nonetheless if it caused them to think of someone other than themselves.

The breeze picked up and proceeded to burst insistent, frigid puffs that threatened to dislodge his hat. He clamped one hand on top, squishing it down around his lean face as he resolutely lengthened his stride and marched on, determined to make it home before the storm set in.

He'd almost made it to the corner, to the place where he normally made the left on N. Westburl, and then a right onto 43rd, followed by a various assortment of other long deviations that would get him safely home, when a large crack of thunder shook the air. He decided that just this once he might consider taking the most direct route, albeit dangerous, foreboding, and possibly life-threatening. He stopped right on the bend of the street, uncertain for a fleeting moment, until the next jolting crack of thunder made up his mind for him. He headed straight along Market Street, which followed the length of the

Thames River, hoping that the seedy individuals who lurked around the pier were as mindful of the storm as he, and would not cause him trouble on this particular evening, for even though he was quick-witted and could talk himself out of most troubles, sailors tended to be a harder breed of people. They were a sharp and cunning lot, and Archie did not know if he could outsmart anyone else that day, and didn't wish to press his luck.

He made it past the pier, hesitating just long enough to glance at the small boats tied to the dock. There were obviously people about, and so far he had been lucky enough not to encounter any of them.

But one final ground-shaking crack and the tinkling sound of bells changed it all. The clouds overhead clashed and he ran for the shelter of a nearby tavern, barely escaping the torrent of rain.

Archie had never been in The Captain's Keg before. He stopped just inside the door and let his eyes adjust to the dark, smoke-filled room. He realized that not only had he run into the very people he wished to avoid, but that he also had a new problem.

These men weren't just sailors.

He was ready to run back out and take his chances of drowning in the street, when he heard the same tinkling of bells from earlier. This time, it sounded like mocking laughter.

Well. He might very well be losing his mind, but a coward he was not.

He straightened to his full height—all six feet and four inches of it—and removed his crumpled hat with a flourish, tucking it under his arm. He walked proudly down the three steps that led into the heart of the tavern—to a bar, teeming with pirates.

A couple of heads turned at his arrival and those who met his solemn, blue gaze were quick to drop their eyes back to their drinks. His spirits lifted, Archibald nodded to himself more than to anyone else in particular, a slight smile playing on his lips. He was holding his own.

Still erring on the side of caution, he scanned the length of the bar, finding three open seats. Two were between rather burly, shifty-looking blokes with tattoos. The third seat, on the end of the bar, sat beside an elderly gentleman with longish white sideburns, a round belly, and spectacles to match that sat precariously upon a rather bulbous nose. The gent on the other side was scrawny, his clothes in tatters, thin face in a scowl as he stared at a leaflet of paper before him. Even though he sat still, there was a nervous energy that pulsed off the small man. He gave Archibald the impression of a jittery, starving squirrel. Archibald decided his best chances lay between the old man and the squirrel and so he took his seat, nodding in a genial fashion to the old man, whose watery blue eyes barely gave him a passing glance. The squirrel didn't acknowledge his presence.

"What'll it be, mate?" the barkeep asked.

Archibald bit his lip to keep from laughing. Every drink in the tavern was the same yellowish liquid. Why the bald man standing behind the bar bothered to even ask such a mundane question was beyond him. Perhaps he was daydreaming again. He did do that a lot and at times it seemed real. "'Tis all ale, is it not?"

"Aye, but will it be single or double ye'll be havin'?"

Archibald lifted one finger and waited for his drink.

"Ye'd have much better luck with rum, I should think," the old man said as he stared down into his own glass, "The ale's watered down. Not fit for a fish to drink, it isn't."

One dreg out of the glass, and Archibald was quite certain the gentleman was more than right. It tasted like something poured from an old boot. Not that he regularly drank from old boots, mind you. Thank heavens he hadn't ordered twice the amount of the vile stuff. Deciding it better not to even bother asking for the rum, which was most definitely hidden beneath the counter and out of sight, he tossed a couple of coins onto the scarred wooden bar, and sat looking down into the remnants of his glass, listening to the patter of rain on the tin roof.

A strange thought came. For a bar filled with pirates, it

was most unusual. It was rather quiet, an odd comment here or there, but otherwise there was nothing but silence. Surely they weren't all sitting around listening to the rain. Archie couldn't figure it out. But he knew one thing: these people weren't living up to his expectations of the loud, fearless persons he always thought pirates to be.

The squirrel on his left shifted around on his stool, staring even harder at the parchment. Sweat popped out on a face that was now a color that reminded Archie of the paper in the print shop, a colorless, pasty white. Good for paper, not for squirrels.

"Well?" a low, deep voice rolled out from a dark corner and broke the silence, startling Archie. "Give us the news then, Harper."

Ah, well now. Things may get lively yet, Archie thought, casting a quick look to the corner from where the voice rumbled. It was too dark to see the man who sat against the wall, but Archibald got a good look at the pair of worn, dark leather boots propped up on the table, and the curling wisps of cigar smoke that floated up to the rafters.

"It says a r-roy, royy…" the squirrel named Harper stuttered, the paper shaking in his hands.

"Ach! The man canna read it anymore than the rest o' us." A complaint hurtled from one of the tattooed blokes at the opposite end of the bar.

As if he were getting more anxious, Harper tried again, his voice in a near squeak, "A royy-alll..."

Archie spied the lettering, and against his better conscience, whispered just loud enough that Harper would hear, "A royal pardon is offered to those pirates who surrender on or before the fifth of September, this year of 1718." He waited as Harper relayed the message, then continued, "Being limited to crimes committed before the fifth of January. All other crimes, committed after such date, will be considered for a death of hanging."

Archie sensed the old man on the other side of him shuffle about, as if he were searching for something on the insides of his pockets, but Archie's attention was fixed on the squirrel he saved. Harper turned and gave him a toothless, yet thankful, smile and set to guzzling the contents of his glass as quickly as possible in an effort to calm his shaking nerves.

"Well, that counts us out, lads," a dark chuckle came from the corner, "No pardon for the likes o' us, I fear. We all be hanged."

"Aye, but they must catch us first. I won't be finding me neck in a noose," a shout rang out, followed by the murmur of agreement from all the others as they lifted their glasses in salute.

Feeling rather in-tune with the pirates, Archibald picked up his glass as well and toasted the luck of the now boisterous lot, draining the last contents of his glass. Some small part of his brain noted that while the ale was vile before, it also became bitter the longer it sat. The bitterness left as soon as he noticed it, having been replaced with a rather calming sensation.

Pirates truly weren't a bad lot, he thought sleepily, just people like everyone else. They were only misunderstood. He turned to convince the elderly gentleman on his right of exactly that, when the darkness came and took over. The last thing he heard was the old man chuckle, singing,

"Yo-ho, me mateys, yo-ho…"

* * *

"Careful now, lads, mind the poor lout's head, aye? He'll be having a dreadful headache come morning without any extra bumps ye'd be givin' him along the way."

The voice was familiar—rather achingly so—though Archie couldn't quite seem to get his faculties in order to remember who the owner of the voice was. The few times he could open his eyes, nothing at all made sense. It all came and went in blurs with distorted figures he couldn't quite make out. The darkness came and went, so in the end, he figured it better to keep his eyes shut for the time being and try to concentrate on other things, foggy and confusing as they might seem. He thought he was being dragged along the rough boards of the pier, and while that familiar voice seemed to care about the condition of his head, his legs and backside seemed to be another matter entirely of which the man cared not a whit as they bumped him along each splintering plank. Luckily, the drug slipped into his drink deadened the pain, and he only registered the faint, odd pricks and scrapes where the wood had its way with his flesh.

"He's got hair like black candles, he does," a crackling voice snickered by his head.

"Aye, Smee, are we taking this poor soul aboard for his long locks? Did the cap'n order you fetch him a wifey, then?" another voice chimed in, followed by raucous laughter, and a low retort from the man named Smee that Archibald couldn't make out.

"A good bit heavier than he looks," the first voice by his head huffed, "Slow ye down a bit, Murph. I'm losin' me grip. Oh drat, there he goes."

And those were the last words Archibald ever heard on the shores of bonnie England as his head hit the pier and the darkness crept over him once again.

2

SHANGHAIED

*H*is head felt ready to burst into a million pieces at any given second. In a futile effort to keep it whole, Archie clamped both hands on top of his aching skull and gritted his teeth. It would help if the room didn't feel like it was tilting this way and that. Back and forth, back and forth. Well, it served him right consorting with pirates, he thought ruefully. A most dreadful sort they were and the tavern was no better. He'd know next time to take his chances of drowning in a rain-filled street than to step foot in that particular establishment ever again, or anywhere else where the word *keg* was sported as part of the name. Yes, better drowned than drunk. A lesson learned the hard way, but still he learned it. That's all that mattered, though he made a mental note not to share this knowledge with any other living soul. He'd take it to his grave with no one the wiser.

Eyes still shut against the thumping of his head, Archie rolled to one side and sat up, hands still holding a throbbing brain in his skull, lest it decide to pound its way through his eyeballs. There was one thing of which he was certain—he hadn't felt this terrible in his entire life. But he didn't have time to sit and feel sorry for himself, the print shop would have to be opened soon, there was work waiting for him. He was already farther behind than he cared to admit. He could feel just as miserable there as he could here—wherever here happened to be. He loosened his hold on his head in an experimental way to make sure his brain wouldn't escape him, then rubbed his hands against his sore eyes and slowly opened them.

"Good day." The old man from the bar nodded from his perch on a bench in the corner of the room. He peered at Archie from behind his spectacles as he whittled on a small chunk of wood.

Well, at least there was only one old man, Archibald reasoned silently to himself. He expected to be seeing double at this point. The problem was that the room still seemed to be moving this way and that. Back and forth, back and forth—with a slight sloshing sound he attributed to his drunken brain, slogging about in his head. He must have gotten too drunk in the tavern to make it home and be sleeping the remnants of his terrible evening off somewhere. The hangover would explain the tilt of the room.

"I'm sorry I cannot wish you a good day as well, as I don't agree with you on how well this day has begun," Archibald noted wryly, gripping the edges of the cot in an effort to still his roiling stomach which decided to revolt at the pitch of the room. "Due to the current state of both my head and belly, I must also disagree of your earlier assessment of the ale."

The old man shook his head. "Nay, 'twas most certainly watered down. Never had a drink in that tavern that wasn't. Take a wee nip from that jug there near yer feet. It'll settle yer spirits a bit. May help yer head, too."

Archie bent over and picked up the small brown jug and pulled the cork. It didn't take more than a single sniff to tell him what the contents were. He frowned at the old man.

"I fail to see how taking yet another drink will solve my present situation as it 'twas ale that got me into my current predicament."

"I told ye ye'd fair better with rum, and so ye shall." The eyes behind the spectacles glared at him as if daring him to contradict him any further.

Deciding to humor him, lest the old man have a heart seizure, Archie took one mouthful of the rum and was in the process of swallowing, when the old man added,

"After all, as this ship's doctor, I should know what I gave you."

Instead of spewing alcohol everywhere, Archie choked, part of the alcohol burning its way down his windpipe. He hacked and wheezed, feeling sicker than before, as he realized the constant moving of the room was due to the fact that his current location was the belly of a vessel at sea.

"I'm-on-a-ship?" Archibald spat the words out between coughs before he managed to get his breath and his thoughts in order.

"Aye," the old man said, putting his hand up to ward off the impending onslaught of questions. "The cap'n gave orders to bring any man able to read or write aboard so here ye are. Stroke of luck to have one such as ye to sit beside me as Harper stuttered about on that paper, I should think. We'd still be sitting there if ye hadn't helped him. Though I admit, I had strong doubts ye'd finish that ale. We appreciate the toast to our livelihood, to be sure."

No good deed will ever go unpunished, Archibald thought as he stared at the man who looked more like someone's sweet grandfather than a dark, conniving pirate who abducted men for their ability to read.

"You will release me at once," Archibald's voice dropped octaves as he found his bearings and the courage to stand and tower over the old man. He knew he had at least a foot on him and more than a good forty years of youth in his favor.

"Free to go where ye will," he shrugged, looking up to meet Archie's cold gaze with his own, "though I doubt it be far. Ye see, we've been at sea two days now. As I didn't think ye'd drink much more of the ale, I dumped the whole vial of drug in that glass. I'm afraid I gave ye quite the dose that knocked ye on yer arse. Be sure that I extend my most humble apologies. But we be far from any shore, unless ye'd be a mighty fine swimmer..." The sentence trailed off as another shrug followed the first and something dark flitted just under the surface of those watery, old eyes. For the first time, Archie wondered if maybe he'd underestimated the old pirate. There was something sinister that lurked under the façade of the slightly amused look on the man's face as he fiddled with a knife that looked more lethal by the second. Snowy white hair, arthritic, knotty fingers, and spectacles aside, Archie was sure that the man was more than capable of slitting his throat should the need ever arise, and being as he still didn't have his sea legs under him, he decided odds were *not* in his favor. Carefully, he backed to the cot and sat.

As if reading Archie's mind, the old man nodded, "Aye, that's right, lad, just settle ye down now. I'm thinking we might be starting out wrong. Let's introduce ourselves proper, eh? Name is Artis Smeeson, better known to the lads aboard as Smee. I'd be ship surgeon, occasional cook, and pirate in general for whatever else need be done." He gave a small mock bow, not bothering to stand from his comfortable seat on the bench. "At yer service, o'course. And you'd be?"

"Jameson." Archie didn't feel obligated to reveal his entire name. As far as he could tell, all the pirates went by a single name anyway. "Which ship am I on and who is her captain?"

"We be on the *Queen Anne's Revenge*."

The simple sentence made Archie even weaker in his knees. Thankful he was sitting down, he managed to whisper, "That means her captain is..."

"Edward Teach," Smee said. The dark smile that painted his bearded face never reached his eyes.

Archie bent over and buried his head in his hands. Not only had he the misfortune of becoming shanghaied in a tavern, and woken up on a pirate ship while losing two days of his life, the ship he happened to be on was under the management of the most notorious pirate of the seven seas. Undoubtedly, he was the same man in the corner of the tavern that Archie had never gotten a good look at, but for two worn boots and cigar smoke. Archie was ready to crawl under the cot upon which he sat. Throughout all his daydreams, never had he imagined something like this, and most unfortunate was the part that it was reality. There wouldn't be any waking up from it. What would become of him on a pirate ship out at sea? There was no telling. With a small smile, he realized he wouldn't ever be going back to the print shop. That thought made him happier than anything had been able to do in a long while. He was free from the obligation of everything in his life. There wouldn't ever be a need to daydream again. Adventure had found him.

He was sailing with Blackbeard.

"Smee, the cap'n wants you up top. They-they've spotted a sh-ship," the stuttering voice of the squirrel Archie had saved called down from a dark corner in the room. Archie squinted and barely made out the form of a small set of wooden steps.

Smee sighed, scooting off the bench as he called out, "Aye, Harper. I'm on me way." He shot another look at the man sitting on the cot. "I'll send him down with a bite. Food might help ye see the situation in a better light, eh?"

Archie gave him a slight nod and watched as the old man made his way up the steps, then listened as he gave orders that food be given to the "poor lout down in the hold." He rolled his eyes. He'd never been called a lout in all of his twenty-three years, but he supposed there was a first time for everything, and so he decided not to hold it against the elderly, kidnapping, old coot of a pirate. After all, being on a pirate ship—or any ship for that matter—

was a first for him. While a small part of his mind still held back in trepidation as his life had been toddling along in a dull manner thus far, there was a small part of his heart that was glad for his perceived misfortune.

He decided that finding out as much as possible about the ship and her crew would be in his best interest and so he stood up, still wobbling more than he cared to admit, and inspected his surroundings more closely. He was in a small room with many kegs spread about. He bumped one and heard a slosh, and then he smelled a faint, familiar scent. After a quick count, he knew that the thirty-some odd barrels surrounding him contained rum. But other than the barrels, his cot, and Smee's bench, the hold was sparse. It was too bad he hadn't the mind to ask the old man for more than just the names of the ship and her captain. He was still pondering what little information he possessed, when a slight form appeared on the steps.

"Good to s-see you a-awake, s-sir," Harper stuttered, not meeting Archie's gaze as he thrust a small loaf of bread out in front of him.

"Yes," Archie agreed. He, too, was pleased to be coherent. But instead of giving a flippant reply to the slight, nervous man who obviously felt responsible for his current predicament, Archie smiled and took the loaf, adding the warmest, most sincere thank you he could manage.

It must have worked, as Harper returned his smile, and settled on the bench across from him, watching as Archie tore into the loaf with more enthusiasm than he thought was possible. The fact that he was oblivious to his hunger, and also that the bread was fresh, made it the best thing he'd eaten in his entire life.

Within a few moments it was gone, followed by another swallow of rum and Archie felt his spirits somewhat restored. He turned his full attention on Harper, now intent on gleaning as much information from the man as he could.

"My name is Jameson. Pleased to make your acquaintance."

"Harper. Jonathan H-Harper," the man stuttered slightly.

Archie smiled. "Well, Mr. Harper, I thank you kindly for that bread. It was wonderful."

"Welcome, sir." Harper replied, still watching Archie warily, though he seemed at ease and his stuttering temporarily ceased.

"Might you tell me a bit about this ship and where we might be headed?" Archie asked in such a genial manner one might have thought he inquired to the state of the weather outside.

"Oh, aye, sir. We be on the *Queen Anne's Revenge* with two hundred souls aboard under the watch of Cap'n

Blackbeard. We be headed toward the Americas, I'd suppose."

"You'd suppose? You aren't certain?"

"No, sir." Harper shook his head, sending a thatch of brown hair down into his eyes, making him seem very young. "I've only been here a couple months longer than you and the cap'n doesn't tell us much as to where we're goin', but I've heard talk among the crew that he wanted to get back towards the Americas. S-something about a Lieutenant Maynard who wants his h-head on a s-spike."

"Well that would seem to be reason enough to leave in a hurry, I should think," Archie mumbled. It would also account for the lack of cargo. He looked up at the squirrel of a man who stuttered again and shifted about on his seat. His face was younger than he had first thought. The perception of age came from the lines around his mouth, which was due in most part to the absence of teeth. But his eyes were as clear and brown as summer honey, and right now they regarded him with the curious caution of a child.

"So, Harper, is it?" Archie smiled as the squirrel nodded. "Might I be so bold as to ask your age and why you're on this ship?"

"Sixteen. I'd be here for the same reason as you. But instead of drugging me like they did you, Caesar saw me looking at a paper and thought I was reading, so he swatted me with an oar as I walked by." He pointed a finger to his mouth of missing teeth.

Poor wee bugger, Archie thought, catching glimpses of a few teeth broken close to his gums. To be abducted for your ability to read and write was bad enough—but to be kidnapped by a crushing blow from an oar when you could barely eek out a few simple sentences on a decree? That was most assuredly the worst luck, especially if you had your teeth intact to begin with. He wondered what would happen to the boy in front of him if the captain realized his literary skills were rather lacking. Those few remaining teeth would be doomed for sure. Well, one could hope things wouldn't go that far. But if any of the rumors Archie heard of the dreaded pirate Blackbeard were anywhere close to being accurate, he was an even rougher character than his crew. And his crew? Well. They weren't a tame bunch by any means, if the kidnapping old man and the oar-wielding Caesar were any example. Yes, there was more than sufficient reason for the boy in front of him to stutter.

"This Caesar fellow sounds rather..." Archie frowned as he searched for an appropriate word. "Disturbing."

"Aye, you could say that," Harper's voice dropped to a whisper so low that Archie strained to hear him. "Black Caesar's his name. He'd be Blackbeard's bo'sun. And he's got a soul as black as 'is skin so his name surely fits. Take my word; you don't want to cross 'im. He'll gut you and hang you from the yardarm faster than a wink. Pure evil, he is."

"I shall do my best to follow your advice," Archie said.

"There were women."

"I beg your pardon?" Archie focused on the squirrel again, wondering if the boy had all of his faculties in order, or if the oar had taken more than his teeth.

The brown eyes that looked back at him glazed over, remembering as he repeated. "Women," his voice came out in a low hiss, "he trapped over a hundred of 'em on an island. Stole 'em off ships that were passing through. He'd go off on raids, leave 'em locked up on his island with nothing to eat. Lots of 'em starved… died. They say his island is cursed, haunted with the souls of them women. They run him off. Only thing Caesar's 'fraid of is evil spirits. That's the reason he joined up with the cap'n—to get away from 'em."

"And your point is?" Archie said, mentally hop-scotching, trying to keep up with the boy.

Harper tried to give him a carefree shrug, but the tense hold of his shoulders only hunched him forward, making him look even more defenseless. "I just wanted to warn you. Caesar's an evil man. A cursed, evil man."

"Evil. Got it." Archie gave him a quick, solemn-faced nod which earned him a small, toothless smile. It was then he realized he still hadn't gleaned very much information from the boy in front of him other than that he was, indeed, only a boy, that their destination was rather vague, and that there was one pirate in particular (other than the one who drugged him) he should keep an eye on.

He didn't get to quiz the young man any further before shouted curses rang out overhead, and feet pounded across the deck, shaking a cloud of dust down from the beams over the cot. Looking rather alarmed, Harper jumped from his perch and flew up the steps faster than Archie thought possible.

Well, no time like the present, he reasoned to himself as he stood from the cot, thankful that the teeter of his walk was due in most part to the rocking of the ship. The sun glared down at him from overhead, blinding him as he made his way up the stairs. It took a moment for his eyes to adjust to the scene around him. He gripped the railing on his right side, as crewmen whipped around him in a flurry of activity.

"Ship off the port bow!" Came a bellow from overhead.

Archie gripped the railing tighter as he looked up to see the man who shouted, standing on a small landing, high up on the mast, pointing at a small ship that bobbed along, a miniscule white speck on the deep blue sea.

It was at this next moment Archie found himself wondering if perhaps the print shop might not be a safer haven than where he now stood as he spotted the man described by Harper as pure evil.

"All hands to quarters! Let out the main sail!" The dark-skinned man barked orders as he stalked around the deck, a whip clutched in his hand. Faint blue lines swirled around his bare chest and arms, moving much like the ocean's own tide. His muscles flexed while he delivered blows here and there, whip cracking on the backs of those too slow to do his bidding.

Archie stared at him, completely fixated on the man with blue tattoos. So entranced he was, in fact, that he hadn't even realized that in return, he gained the man's attention by standing there—until it was too late.

"Harper!"

"A-aye, s-sir?" Harper materialized out of thin air, stuttering worse than before.

"Take 'im with you and show him the ropes before I hang him from 'em!" the man snarled, sending a row of golden hoops swaying in his ears whilst giving Archie a rather disconcerting view of white teeth that had been filed to points. "Every man earns 'is keep on this ship. Off with you, before I take the skin from yer back."

"Aye, s-sir," Harper mumbled, jerking Archie along to the rigging on the side of the boat as Caesar's whip cracked on another pirate, "C-come on, then. We-we have to go up top and let o-out the sails."

Archie followed the boy to the side of the ship, to a confusing web of ropes that hung from the mast to the deck.

Well, isn't this lovely, he thought as he sighed in despair. He was by no means enthusiastic where heights were concerned. It wasn't so much that he feared being so high up in the air, it was just that he had never been farther up than a simple ladder could take him. Oh, who was he kidding? He hadn't been this afraid in his entire life! A fall from such a height would mean a quick and certain death, and that was one occasion he wished to avoid. He half-wondered if his chances would be better facing the sting of Caesar's whip.

Harper zipped up the rigging, climbing as if he were born a monkey. Archie gulped, then gripped the ropes, and started his perilous ascent. His feet slid around in the rungs and the rope bit into his hands, but still he held fast, making slow progress as he wished to be at the top and be done with whatever it was he was supposed to do to make the sail billow out into the wind.

"Ach, ye fool," the disgruntled pirate below him complained. "Hurry it up, then! That ship'll be gone all way to Africa afore ye crawl yer arse up there."

Several more complaints were issued by the line of men behind him on the rope before Archie made it to the enormous beam, still holding onto the ropes for dear life.

He ignored the cursing pirates beneath him and let out his breath. Yes, now it would be much better. All he had to do now was follow Harper and figure out how to let out that blasted sail.

As he watched, Archie learned that the climb up to the mast was the easiest part of the task. Harper grabbed hold of the beam, bare feet walking easily out onto a single rope stretched beneath the mast with nothing at all holding him fast. He turned and gestured for Archie to follow his lead.

He has to be joking, Archie thought as he stared at Harper in disbelief. They wanted him to walk out on a single rope with nothing to keep him from falling? It was fool's errand. Pure insanity. The squirrel had obviously lost all of his marbles.

"Hurry ye up, ye yellow-bellied coward," the pirate below him snarled, apparently in a hurry to join Harper for their suicidal walk along the mast.

Well, all the pirates below him were insane, too. Every last one of them nuts, Archie concluded. He hadn't joined a pirate ship. Nay, 'twas a circus.

"Your shoes." Harper pointed to the buckled, black leather on his feet. "Take 'em off. Should've done took 'em off first thing. Be quick now and throw 'em down."

"Aye, before we throw ye down!" the man below him threatened, grabbing hold of Archie's feet and jerking off his shoes before he could object. Luckily, he had a good hold on the ropes before his feet were pulled from beneath him. Two hollow thuds sounded as his shoes landed far below him on the deck. Archie wondered if that was the same sound his skull was going to make when he landed between his shoes.

A rough hand grabbed hold of the seat of his breeches and shoved him upward, pushing him the last few inches until he found himself on the same foot rope as Harper with the pirates behind him, pushing him along, leaving him no choice but to follow the boy. He gripped the rough rope with his bare toes as he clung to the beam in front of him. He was surprised when he didn't slip. He scooted along after Harper, ignoring the sharp twinges as the rope cut into his tender flesh of his feet. It was much easier walking on this single rope with no shoes, than it had been climbing up the rigging with the slick-soled leather on.

"Aye, that's good then," Harper said as they reached the center of the mast, "Now we loose the sail. Untie the reef points."

Archie watched a full second as Harper grabbed hold of one of the leather ties that bound the sail around the mast. He was quick, and within a second, the first was untied and he moved on to the next one. Archie's fingers found the tie in front of him and untwisted the leather.

With the quick work of the pirates on either side of him, it took merely a moment until the canvas sail came free and caught in the wind.

"Hold fast." Harper instructed, motioning to the thick, wooden yard as Archie felt the lurch of the ship as the wind hit her sails and they began their pursuit of the white speck on the sea.

"Hoist the colors," came another order from below.

Archie looked down at the quarterdeck to the frightening sight of the captain of the *Queen Anne's Revenge*, dressed in his finest. Archie watched as he turned, looking every inch a pirate king, from his fine-feathered hat to his boots. The sound of the flag being raised registered dimly in his mind as the captain turned his black gaze up to the mast.

Seconds later, Archie's view was blocked by a black flag depicting a skeleton spearing a heart with one hand while toasting the devil with the other. But in those few seconds before, he spotted the fuses lit in the black beard that sent wisps of smoke about the captain's head, and saw no traces of mercy in the dark eyes that met his.

Archie wondered if maybe the flag's bones weren't toasting the captain himself.

3

WE SHALL HAVE TEA

Archibald was most impressed with the *Queen Anne's Revenge*. Within moments of climbing back down the rigging, the Dutch fluyt came into sight, bobbing along close enough that he could see the panicked faces of her crew scurrying about on her deck in vain efforts to flee.

And very well troubled they should be, Archie reasoned. It was quite sensible of them to be so. The Dutch ship was by no means small, but the *Anne* made her look like a small, inadequate dinghy in comparison. With three giant masts whose sails were taut in the wind, she was swooping in on the smaller ship at an impressive speed. Then, of course, there were forty guns on board, add in three times the hands on deck (and ferocious hands they were, to boot), and a captain who looked as if he had just surfaced from the depths of hell on a mission to consume the soul of the merchant ship. Yes, if those Dutchmen were in their right minds, they were terrified.

Archie stood out of the way, and tried to look as unassuming as possible as a variety of menacing pirates whipped around him. If he was lucky, they would ignore his presence and he wouldn't be pressed into another task that would leave him weak-kneed and bereft of any more odd articles of clothing. Namely, his shoes that he still hadn't been able to find. He hoped that he wouldn't need them anytime soon. But if he were going to be forced to engage the enemy in combat, he preferred to have them on. It wasn't that he minded standing on the smooth wood of the deck in his bare toes. The truth of the matter was that he felt if fate should decide he would meet his end this day, he wished to have all that he had come onto this ship with, however little it would be.

That included his shoes.

He craned his neck, trying to spot them between the various bodies that ran about. At least it didn't appear anyone had stolen them. Nearly all the feet he saw were bare, save the captain in his booted splendor.

He spotted one shoe near the quarterdeck, and so he eased himself along until he reached it and snatched it up, feeling somewhat better. As to its mate, he gave up hope of ever finding it, and resumed his task of looking as inconspicuous as possible since he gained the attention of a couple of swarthy-looking lads while on his quest to recover that one shoe.

"Fire a warning shot off her bow, if ye please, Mr. Moreau," the captain folded his hands behind his back, looking every part the crazed gentlemen with fuses lit in his beard as he addressed someone on deck.

"Aye, Capitan," the man spoke with a definite French accent. His black, curl-covered head was bent over an enormous cannon as he peered across the sea, carefully gauging the distance so as not to accidentally blow a hole in the other ship.

After all, what kind of warning would they be sending if they sunk yon ship with the first blast? Archie smiled to himself as he wondered if that particular scenario ever happened.

But he didn't get to see it occur this time, because seconds later, after he gauged his distance, the curly-headed man jumped back, yelling his order, "Fire!"

The hot linstock touched the cannon and it fired, recoiling several feet back to be caught by several ropes so as to keep it from rolling across the ship and squashing those so unfortunate to be in its path. The most unfortunate of all, being Archie, who seemed to be in adventure's way once again as in that instant he happened to spot his other shoe through the cloud of grey smoke, a few feet away near the cannon.

Forgetting his previous goal of looking invisible, he was close to his shoe, when a whip cracked the air and a deep voice bellowed, "Ye had yer warning."

Archie looked up to see Caesar, arm raised to lower the whip on him when the man who ordered the cannon's blast stepped in Caesar's path, catching his arm with not a second to spare.

"The man has not signed the book," he said in a tone that dared Caesar to contradict him. "So until the capitan says otherwise, he does not get treated as part of the crew. Strike him and you shall break the code. Then you'll face *me*."

Caesar never uttered a word as he lowered his whip. He glared at the man for a moment, then turned, taking his fury to the other end of the ship where several other pirates felt his wrath.

"Here you are, *mon ami*." The man smiled at him, handing him the shoe. "I am Philip Moreau, at your service."

"Thank you, sir," Archie said, "I am Archibald Jameson." This man, he decided, was worthy to know his full name.

"Well, Mr. Jameson, might I suggest that you take greater care once you have joined us that you do not attract the end of Caesar's whip. It carries a most terrible sting."

Archie nodded. He had no intention of being Black Caesar's whipping boy.

"Mr. Moreau." The captain's black eyes found his first mate. "If you are finished distributing pleasantries and footwear, would you be so kind as to join me on the quarterdeck?" He turned to look at the fluyt, which offered surrender upon the cannon's blast; a white flag now flapped amongst her sails. "Company, we'll be havin' soon."

"Y-you follow m-me." Harper materialized at Archie's side as Moreau left to follow his orders. "C-come on. They'll be boardin' her s-soon." He led Archie away from his spot near the quarterdeck.

Luckily, this time he wasn't required to go up and tie the sails. The news of Mr. Moreau's assessment of his current position of guest, and not pirate, traveled through the crew and he was left alone, safely at the bottom of the mast as he watched Harper and the others scale the rigging in record time.

Archie felt the ship slow as they neared the other vessel. She was a smaller ship, with two masts and a tiny, defeated crew that stood on deck, looking extremely depressed. It was obvious she was a merchant ship from the small smattering of guns that she sported. Though there was more cargo space, there would not have been much of a defense, had they been so foolish as to decide to do battle with the *Queen Anne's Revenge*. The fluyt was an oddly built ship, larger at the bottom where she held her cargo, then tapering upward to a smaller deck. The wooden figurehead of a mermaid with flowing hair and open arms was mounted on the ship's bow, her body poised as if she had sprung from the sea to greet them.

Jolig Roger. Archie spotted the name on her bow and racked his brain for the small bits of Dutch language that lingered there. The *Jolly Roger*, that was it. He suppressed a smirk. Her crew looked anything but jolly as the *Queen Anne's Revenge* drew alongside and grapnel hooks were thrown to her deck, catching her railings and drawing her fast.

There weren't but a handful of sailors aboard, and though they didn't appear the least bit happy, they also didn't seem anxious to be boarded. At least they had sense enough not to offer any resistance.

Their captain came to the railing and waited as the ships were secured. He was a short, portly man with a balding head and a dour expression, whether from being boarded by a pirate crew or just his usual appearance,

Archie wasn't sure, though he was betting on the latter. The man came forward, scowling for all he was worth, and approached Blackbeard without an inkling of fear. He thrust his sword out toward the captain with the still-smoking beard, hilt first, giving Blackbeard complete control of his vessel and crew, without uttering a single word.

The smoldering, black eyes of the captain regarded the man for a moment before taking the gleaming handle. Then he smiled, and addressed his first mate, "Mr. Moreau, if you'd be so kind as to send for Mr. Smee. As the lads check yon bonny ship and her cargo, the good captain here and meself shall take our tea on the deck."

Archie felt his jaw drop. Never before had Archie heard of any pirate offering a merchant captain teatime as his cargo was being confiscated. No guns fired, save for the single warning shot. No one had even so much as drawn a pistol or sword. The entire chain of events went so smoothly that Smee was pushing a small table to the center of the deck, befitting it with a pristine white cloth, cups of tea, and small biscuits.

Archie was beginning to admire Blackbeard more and more. The man looked fiercer than anything Archie had ever seen, but there was also cunning and wisdom behind those black eyes that made him believe if there were ever a pirate ship to be on, this was it. He made himself a promise in that moment. He would do everything in his power to be as much a pirate as the man who sat, with the fuses still lit in his beard, taking a dainty sip of tea with his captured prey.

He spotted Harper on his way to the *Jolig Roger*, and decided that he would offer his assistance. He was now more than ready to be a full member of the crew—so long as they didn't make him climb up the rigging every five minutes. He paused just long enough to chuck his shoes behind a coil of rope so he would be able to find them again, and then ran to catch up with the squirrel, who had made it onto the deck of the Dutch ship.

"She's carrying sugar." A triumphant Harper grinned at him over the casks and sacks that filled the hold. "She's plumb full of it!" His voice ended in a happy squeak and the squirrel hopped from one foot to the other, giving Archie the impression that they found gold instead of the multitude of sweet granules that surrounded them. He resisted the urge to dance around too, less perhaps it wasn't that big a deal, but from the wide grins on the faces of the pirates around them, it seemed obvious that it was valuable cargo indeed.

"There will be no need in moving all this." Moreau appeared, face creased in a wide smile as he took in their cache. "I will inform the capitan we will take the ship with us as we go. Take her crew aboard the *Anne* and put them in irons below her decks. Move lively, lads, lest they change their minds about being so hospitable in giving us their lovely sweets."

Several pirates scurried from the hold, eager to imprison the merchant sailors while Moreau turned to Archie. "So do you wish to take your share of our plunder and join our crew under the black flag?"

"Yes." The statement was simple, but held all the power that a single word possibly could as Archibald had never wanted anything so much in his entire life.

They left the *Jolig Roger* and Moreau disappeared for a moment, then came back with a large leather-bound book in his hands with a detailed picture of the *Queen Anne's Revenge* embossed on its cover.

"The ledger of all souls aboard," he explained, taking the book to the small table where the two captains sat, warily regarding one another over a small porcelain teapot. "If you would excuse the intrusion, mon capitan," Moreau waited until the dark gaze of Blackbeard fell upon Archibald, "This good fellow wishes to become one of the crew." He set the book and a quill with ink amongst the plate of biscuits, then backed up and gave Archie a firm shove toward the table.

"So ye want to join me crew." Blackbeard sounded

bemused. "Why should I let ye? Are ye carpenter or sailmaker, per chance?"

"No, I am a cook." The lie slid off Archie's tongue so easily it surprised himself, but it was the only thing he could think of that might keep him off the rigging as a pirate.

"A cook that reads, now that's a rare find, I should think. Thank me lucky stars, I should, as fate has smiled so sweetly on me this day." The deep laugh that rumbled from Blackbeard in response to his own joke not only startled Archie, but also seemed to unnerve the Dutch captain whose hand shook as his teacup clattered to the saucer. "What be yer name, lad?"

"Jameson."

"Well, Jameson, make your mark and join our merry crew." Blackbeard shoved the book toward him.

Archie took the quill, noticing the marks happened to be a line of *X*s, as if the majority of the crew couldn't so much as sign their name. He dipped the sharp edge into the ink, and at the bottom of the page, changed his life forever.

His ears registered the strange tinkling of bells again, though his brain didn't recognize it as he stared down at the name he had written.

A. Jameson.

Blackbeard glanced down at the book before shutting

it with a quick snap that caused the Dutch captain to jump in his seat. Handing the book back to his first mate, Blackbeard smiled, a small gleam of white teeth hidden beneath his beard.

"Welcome to the *Queen Anne's Revenge*."

4

SO NOW YE ARE A PIRATE

The week that followed was grueling. Never had Archibald figured that the job of cooking for a few pirates would be so difficult. Simply getting the oven the correct temperature was almost impossible. Then, of course, there was the fact that he didn't know exactly how to cook anything past the basics for a simple tea. Feeding a crew of over two hundred was by no means a piece of cake. Not that he had cake to give them, anyway. That particular item was above his skill level and would never grace his menu as long as he was cook. His crewmates were lucky to get burnt stew, which they ate for quite a few meals in a row. Naturally, this caused a few of them to mumble various curses and threats as he scooped out their rations, should he not improve his culinary skills quickly and to their liking. The fact that he was taller and looked more imposing than those dissatisfied souls seemed to be the only reason they had not made good on their threats thus far, but Archie wasn't fool enough to think he would be able to intimidate them much longer. After all, if anyone forced him to eat the slop he had been calling food, he would have been more than irate himself. Something was going to have to happen—and soon—before he ended up being tossed over the side of the ship as fish bait.

He was in the process of stirring yet another pot of sludge, wondering if perhaps he should have lied about knowing how to make sails or build ships, when Smee came hobbling into the galley.

"Ye can't feed the poor louts the same thing day in and day out," he advised. "It gets 'em in an awful mood, ye see."

Archie sighed, deciding it was time to confide his secret with someone. And if there was anyone on board that would be an acceptable ally, it was the old man who knew how to drug people. "I am not a cook," he told Smee solemnly, giving him the full effect of the truth as he stared him straight in the eye.

"Ye don't say!" Smee feigned shock, placing a gnarled hand over his chest as if in the beginning throes of a heart seizure.

"Yes, I do say." Archie nodded sadly. "I haven't a clue how to make anything more than a simple pasty for tea."

"I don't think ye can even make that." Smee smacked the burnt chunk of flour named the "pasty" on the side of the table, as if expecting to dent the wooden leg. "I'm thinkin' ye best tell the cap'n that ye aren't cut out for cook duty."

"So he can feed me to the fishes? I think not." Archie folded his arms across his chest, unwilling to contemplate telling Blackbeard the truth of the matter.

"Aye, well. Ye can't keep going on the way ye are. The crew will murder ye before the cap'n has the chance," Smee observed, then sighed, "Suppose I best show ye a thing or two then? Else ye might be layin' at the bottom of the sea soon."

"I suppose I could use a bit of your help." Archie nodded.

Smee hobbled to the pantry and looked in. "Why haven't ye given the lads their bread ration? There be plenty in here."

"It would seem we have a bug infestation," Archie noted as he walked over and took a chunk of bread and showed it to the old man, pointing out the small black creatures that wriggled there.

"Ach! 'Tis naught but weevils." Smee shook his head despairingly and picked up a plate, smacking the bread hard enough that the little beasties fell free and crawled about on the flat surface, "Any sailor knows there be nothing to fear from a weevil. A bit of extra crunchy meat you may not see mayhap, but nothing that'll kill ye."

Archie watched in disdain as the old man took a bite of the bread. He wrinkled up his nose. He had considered himself a pirate ever since he signed that book, but apparently he wasn't as much of one as he thought. Of course, at the time, he didn't realize eating bugs was a requirement.

"All right then, laddie. What say we fix 'em up something worth eatin', eh?" Smee collected an odd variety of items from the pantry and started banging around with pots and pans.

Archie watched in amazement as the old man bustled about, demonstrating full knowledge of the galley with its cantankerous oven. He stopped long enough to hand the crock full of stew to him. "Here. Throw this overboard, aye?"

Archie turned to do as he was told, the old man's voice carrying after him. "The pot, too. It's ruint."

He made his way up the steps and across the deck, chucking the pot into the sea, much to the crew's delight.

"Maybe he's giving up as cook," he heard one pirate say hopefully.

"Aye, me bowels haven't been the same since he came aboard," another chimed in as he made his way back down to the galley.

In the few moments he was away, Smee was busy and the pot that started to bubble smelled enticing. Surprisingly so, Archie noted, for it being cooked by a man who had just eaten bug-infested bread.

"Here, cut these up." Smee thrust an armload of potatoes at him and handed him a knife. "Make yerself useful instead o' standin' there gawking at me."

By the time Archie finished chopping up vegetables, the aroma from the galley attracted the attention of several of the crew. They were, undoubtedly, curious and hungry for something other than Archie's sludge.

"Get gone," Smee ordered, "It will be done soon enough. Ye won't be dyin' of starvation if ye wait a bit longer."

Begrudgingly, they left, though one pirate in particular gave Archie a look that chilled him to the bone as he moved to the door. Something wasn't quite right with that one. Something crazed flitted below the surface of his eyes, something... not... sane. Archie felt the hair on the back of his neck rise up on end as the man muttered, "Finish him... can't cook... should just finish him here and now. Better off without 'im."

"Move if ye would, please." Smee gave Archie his sweet, grandfatherly smile, oblivious to the pirate who muttered just outside the doorway.

A strange request to be sure, Archie thought, but he

switched places with the old man more for the reason of putting distance between himself and the door than to appease Smee.

A moment later, the mutterings got louder and the pirate burst into the galley, a knife gleaming in his upraised fist. He faltered upon seeing Smee and the old man spun around, neatly planting his own knife between the man's ribs. There was a sickening, crunching sound as Smee pulled the knife out and the blank look of the dead settled itself on the face of the would-be assailant as he fell to the floor in a heap.

Smee set to wiping his blade off on the edge of his apron, and then gasped as he saw the pot on the stove boil over.

"Curse ye for a fool, Jake Awbry," he said, glowering as he stepped over the corpse that had landed near the oven. "Leave it for ye to be the one to ruin a decent pot o' soup."

Archie stood with his mouth open, watching as Smee went back to stirring the pot as if nothing out of the ordinary had just happened.

"Ye could go and grab one of the lads and get Jake on out of here," Smee said in a conversational tone as if the man below him were merely drunk instead of dead. He turned and looked at Archie. "Well, go on then! It's not like he's going to walk himself out from under me feet, now is he!"

Fumbling, Archie made it around both cook and corpse, and had the good luck of running into Harper. Relieved that he found someone he knew, he stopped the squirrel.

"Do you think you might be able to help me a moment?"

"I know less about cooking than you, if that is possible," Harper said in an odd moment of clear speech.

"It isn't cooking that I need your help with."

"I beg to differ. You couldn't cook an egg if the chicken were to lay it in the pan for you." Harper grinned. "You need all the help you can get."

Of all times for the boy to become friendly, this wasn't the time Archie hoped for. "I need bloody help moving a dead body."

"Oh, really? Who is it?" Harper craned his neck to see around Archie. Then he spotted the dead face by Smee's foot. "Jake Awbry. Can't say I'm sorry 'tis him. What did you do? Kill him with your cooking?" He snickered, following Archie back into the galley.

It took several heaves, loud expletives, and odd grunting to get the dead maniac up to the deck. Luckily, no one said a word to them as they dropped his body unceremoniously in a heap by the mast and headed back below decks; Archie to the galley, and Harper disappearing to wherever he had been going to begin with.

The soup wasn't burnt, so that made it the first meal in over a week that hadn't been scorched beyond recognition. It was too bad Archie couldn't take any credit for it. Smee handed him a platter with filled bowls, then took another himself laden with bug-eaten bread. "We'll take this to the captain's quarters first. Best we let him know about Jake so he can sell 'is effects and send the money to 'is widow."

Archie was astounded by the complete lack of remorse. By the old man's tone of voice, one would have assumed the pirate died peacefully in his sleep instead of being knifed to death, never mind the fact that there was a woman somewhere who didn't yet know her dear, although insane, husband would soon be lying in the darkest corners of Davy Jones' locker.

"Well, come on, then," Smee urged, as if noticing the slow progress of the lad in front of him. "Soup's no good cold, ye know."

Cold or no, it is a definite improvement from what they had been eating, make no mistake. There was no way anyone was going to complain about the temperature of this meal, Archie thought, not bothering to change or lengthen his stride. They would get there soon enough without any help on his part.

They crossed over to the hold and climbed the steps, with Archie moving even slower than before. Smee huffed and grumbled under his breath, until the very last when he went quiet. That moment of the old man's silence unnerved Archie even more as he heard nothing but the sounds of the ocean and creaking of the ship. After twenty-three years of life, he discovered he still hadn't mastered the art of walking. At least not where the *Queen Anne's Revenge* was concerned. Nervousness and the tilting vessel were his undoing as he stumbled, barely catching his footing before he landed headfirst in the captain's door. Fate, however, was smiling down on him and the soup stayed mostly in the bowls with the exception of a few splashes on the wooden platter.

"Saint Brendan!" Smee scowled at Archie. "Why on earth do I bother to help ye, I'd like to know."

Archie didn't bother answering him, though he pondered why the old man would invoke the patron saint of whales to protect lukewarm soup. Surely his stew hadn't been that bad. He was still frowning at the current state of events when he heard the strange tinkling sound again. He hadn't heard it since that fateful night he stepped in the tavern. Nevertheless, there it was. The sounds of bells, laughing at him again.

He jerked around to see if Smee had heard the tinkling sound, too. It was plain from the dour expression that stretched from one fuzzy white sideburn to the other that he hadn't, although it did appear he was considering to finish the job Jake Awbry had set out to do if Archie didn't soon knock on the door.

"Will ye be comin' in today, perhaps? Or do ye plan on standing guard at me door for the rest o' the night?" Blackbeard's voice grumbled at them from inside his quarters.

Not bothering with a polite knock, Archie gave the door a shove with his elbow, carefully balanced his platter, and entered.

Blackbeard took a deep breath and smiled, white teeth gleaming in his beard. "Smee, ye had mercy. Smelled your soup all the way through the floorboards, I did."

"Aye." Smee returned the smile genially, as if he regularly bestowed his good graces on the most unfortunate of the crew.

A map depicting the various stars lay unrolled on the table. Ignoring the two pirates, Archie set his platter on the far side, safely away from the paper and inspected the map, tracing various dots with his fingertips.

* * *

BLACKBEARD WATCHED THE COOK, WHOSE HEAD WAS BENT over the table. His long, black hair hid his face from view, but his fingers moved along as if they knew the paths of the sky by heart. There was rarely anything he missed, especially when it came to his crew. He knew each of his men well, their attributes and their downfalls. And while he was generous to a fault, there was also a reason he was known as the scourge of the seven seas. It was a title earned through sharpness and cunning, the same attributes that kept him out of the clutches of the British Navy thus far.

As he eyed his newest crew member, he was certain the man didn't have a clue how to cook. He had known it since the first meal he had been served, when half of his men spent the night with their bums on chamber pots, the other half vomiting over the railings. It was no wonder the man in front of him made so many enemies in such a short time, but still the man showed grit in not giving up, continuing to serve the same, awful slop defiantly, day after day.

Blackbeard's stomach gave a queasy turn at the thought of the man continuing to prepare his meals, so he asked hopefully, "Know something of the stars, do you, lad?"

* * *

"Yes." It was truth this time. Simple truth. Archie had been in love with the sky for as long as he could remember. As a child, he would lay under the twinkling stars, memorizing their names, tracing the patterns of their constellations with his fingertips pointed at the sky.

"This one right here." He pointed at one of the largest dots. "This is Regulus. There are five other stars in its group." He traced them with his finger, showing that they made a sickle shape, a nearly perfect hook. "They are at their brightest now; but they will disappear during the autumn months and stay hidden until the following spring."

Blackbeard nodded, more than pleased with this display of knowledge. "Well, Mr. Jameson, what say ye to being my navigator instead the ship's cook?"

"Well," Archie was rather taken aback by the offer and tried not to look ecstatic. "I do appreciate the offer, but the crew may have need of my culinary skills if we are to survive, I'm afraid."

The two small sections beneath Blackbeard's eyes—the only places not swamped by hair—became as red as two tiny poppies, as if he were attempting not to laugh outright. A slight snort escaped him as he said, "I think ye'll have naught to worry about, lad. I'm sure we shall survive just fine without your ministrations."

"There be a slight matter that happened in the galley a bit ago," Smee interjected.

Ah, yes. Here it comes, Archie thought. He had just

gotten a chance to break free from his prison and before he could accept, Smee was going to ruin it all.

"The matter being Jake Awbry, I would suppose?"

The man must know all that happened aboard his ship. The pirate hasn't even been dead long enough to get cold, Archie thought, surprised.

"Aye. He came at us in a fitful rage, he did." Smee shook his head in a knowing way. "I had me back turned for the soup and yon lad was peelin' praties. Jake was nearly on me when the laddie sunk a knife in him. Saved my life, he did."

If Archie was speechless before, now he was dumbstruck. That was in no way how he remembered the chain of events, though now he was certain that Smee was an Irishman, for no one else ever mentioned potatoes as praties to him before.

"Is that so, then." Blackbeard's gaze rested on him.

It seemed more a statement than a question, so Archie didn't even nod his head. Admitting to being a murderer was much different than admitting to be a cook. Maybe it was possible the captain didn't know every single detail on the boat after all. There were only himself and Smee as witnesses, but he still wasn't going to say a word unless he was asked a specific question.

"Well, then. It seems the crew should think themselves lucky that none others took the same path as Jake Awbry."

Blackbeard shrugged. "Ye start in the morning as my navigator, Mr. Jameson."

Just like that, Archie's days in the galley ended without a word said on his part, neither accepting nor denying a thing, for which he was extremely grateful. Nevertheless, later on, once they were safely away, Archie turned to Smee for answers.

"Why did you say I killed Jake?"

"Ye needed a roughness to ye, lad." Smee smiled, though it didn't reach his watery eyes. "You dealt a single, sure stroke that felled a man to his death. The men will accept ye as one of their own, no doubt. They'll be thinkin' twice afore they cross ye again." He watched as Archie mulled over this latest bit of information, and some dark thought showed in his eyes. "Aye, that's right, lad. So now ye are a pirate."

5

THE FIRST RULE

*D*eath at sea was disconcerting. Archie wasn't sure if he came to that conclusion by the body sewn mummy-style in the sail at his feet with an added two cannon balls to sink the corpse to his watery grave or by the fact that the wind picked up and smacked at the ship as if it were angry with them. The waves grew taller. It felt as if the ghosts of the deep had arrived to ferry the dead man to the underworld—and impatient ghosts they were, to boot.

"N-not to s-speak ill of the d-dead and rush old Jake's last r-rites, but might we hurry this a-along?" Harper asked, watching the approach of the blackest clouds that Archie had ever seen.

"Aye," Blackbeard agreed in a doleful tone, looking up

at the sky as he stood up on the quarterdeck to officiate the makeshift funeral. Thankfully, there were no lit fuses in his beard this time, but rather he had befitted his long tresses with black silk ribbons. It must have been proper attire for mourning, by the captain's way of thinking. He cleared his throat, then rumbled, "Jake Awbry was a good pirate. Quick on the rigging and always kept a weather eye from the maintop. May he find good fortune in the hereafter." He stopped for a moment, as if to make certain that was all that he could say nice about the man, and nodded to Archie and the others who surrounded the corpse.

Well. That was short and sweet, Archie thought as he helped pick up Jake who hadn't been dead long enough to even get stiff. They hauled him to the edge of the ship, pausing just a moment to raise him high enough to clear the railing and toss him over into the waves. The ocean swallowed him as if it had just risen for the occasion. A streak of lightning crossed the sky at the exact second the body hit the water.

"Sell his effects later, aye?" Blackbeard yelled over the thunder. "Here she comes, lads. Prepare to weather the squall!"

The *Jolig Roger* bobbed along a short distance behind them, following the same plan of action as they reduced their sails, checked the ropes on what cannons they could reach in a short amount of time and held tight, ready to ride out the storm that bore down on them in fury. Buckets of rain smashed down, sending men sliding all over the slick wood. Several fell and went rolling, smacking into cannons and masts until they all were able to take cover from the storm.

It lasted moments, moving off as quickly as it had come; then the sun came back out as if nothing at all had happened out of the ordinary. The only proof that anything had occurred were the bruises on the sailors and a quickly drying deck.

The entire experience was unnerving. Archie decided to construct his own set of rules at this point, beginning with the first. Do not die at sea, pirate or no.

"Mr. Smee, if ye would like to resume the sale of the deceased's effects before we cast off and leave this forsaken place, ye may," the captain said, before turning to address Archie, "Mr. Jameson, once ye are finished here, chart our path to Madeira, if ye'd be so kind."

Archie nearly passed on the auction of Jake Awbry's meager earthly goods, which seemed to contain naught but a clay pipe and a well-used stack of playing cards. He was starting to leave and make his way to the chartroom when a fencing sword caught his attention.

"All right, ye cheap-hearted buggers." Smee scowled, obviously not impressed with the forthright good nature of his fellow crew. "Ol' Jake has a widow, ye know. Best ye think of that and dig deep in yer pockets. Who wants to start the bidding?"

Nonplussed at being called names, several pirates crossed their arms over their chests, unwilling to be badgered into offering the slightest bit for the small collection of goods. There wasn't anything there worth having. The pipe was cracked, the cards were so worn that their ink was faded, and the sword was standard issue for a gentleman, but gentlemen they were not. These men preferred thicker blades, things that would not take such precision and care to hack down their enemy. None of them wanted the thin rapier.

Save Archie.

He searched about his person, coming up with the solitary coin left to his name.

"Here." He handed it to Smee. "When I receive my share of our cargo, I shall give you more to send to the Widow Awbry."

"Aye, take it and be merry." Smee traded the odd lot of stuff for the coin, pleased enough with the arrangement.

Archie made his way to the maps and settled down. The storm hadn't moved them very far off course from the island Blackbeard instructed him to find. They should be there in a few days if they didn't run into any other squalls or strong headwinds. He informed the captain of his findings and relayed the message to the crewman who signaled the news and headings to the *Jolig Roger*, then made his way below decks to his bunk amongst the casks of rum to inspect his new belongings more closely.

There wasn't a whole lot his father insisted upon, but luckily enough, fencing classes for all four of his sons was something he took seriously. He considered it an essential part of becoming a gentleman in their society, so every week for hours each evening, the four brothers would take their lessons, regardless of whether they wished to or not. All became skilled with a rapier, though the most proficient had been the youngest brother. Archibald took to his lessons with a vigor his siblings lacked. For his brothers, it was something their father required of them to gain their nobility. Nothing more.

But Archie was different.

Archie mastered his swordplay for the love of feeling the thin rapier in his hand. It was a strong, light weapon that would wear any opponent down if used properly. He practiced for hours to obtain that skill.

Now that his weapon of choice lay in his hands, he felt safe for the first time since he had woken up on the *Anne*. If anyone else should dare attack him, they would take their place beside Jake Awbry in the murky depths of the ocean. Smee may have given him the reputation he needed to survive, but now he had what he needed to back it up.

He grinned, his blue eyes sparkling and dancing with mirth.

Oh, yes. He was a pirate. Let them come for him now.

6

WHAT'S IN AN ISLAND?

They arrived at Madeira three days later, much to the crew's delight. The joy was contagious as they made their way to the island. Blackbeard even looked pleased, a jaunty blue ribbon braided into his beard as he stood at the head of the first longboat being rowed ashore. Several boats followed behind him, with the majority of both crews, dressed in their finest and hauling quite a bit of sugar in a tug behind them.

The thirty-odd hands that kept the *Jolig Roger* afloat and unharmed seemed more than ecstatic as they now could get rid of the Dutch sailors who had been chained below decks. The Dutchmen were the ones who didn't look happy, though they did seem to be relieved to be breathing fresh air again.

Madeira was a Portuguese island, and though it was a

free port, it was a haven for bandits who did not raid or engage any Portuguese ships. Blackbeard knew this well, so Madeira became one of the last safe places where he and his crew could come and go at will without the British Navy at their throats, though they all knew it was a matter of time before it would come to an end. Her Majesty's Navy had a strong dislike for all pirates, but their greatest hatred seemed reserved for Blackbeard himself, the only brigand who always managed to elude their grasp. One naval officer in particular, Lieutenant Maynard, made it his solitary goal in life to track the notorious man down, swearing to stop at nothing until he saw him hang from the end of a noose.

But for now, the worries of Her Majesty's British Navy were the farthest things from the crew's minds. They were free men, ready to release their prisoners, unload their cargo of sugar and take their profits, and of course cause whatever mischief their hearts desired. That in itself was enough to raise their spirits, though the majority of them looked forward to the spirits they would find in bottles—and the wenches who would bring those bottles.

"I'm gettin' me a t-tattoo," Harper announced as they rowed to shore in the longboat.

"Ah. Well, that is wise, I suppose." Archie nodded. Most of the crew inked their skin. If it gave the lad the boost of self-confidence he needed to quit stuttering, Archie was all for it. "What do you have in mind? I might wish to accompany you."

Harper looked at him through narrowed eyes, as if he were unsure whether his friend was jesting or if his words were true.

Archie rolled his eyes. "I am being quite serious." And he was for the most part, though he had no desire whatsoever to get his own skin marked. By his logic, if he stayed with Harper for most of the time they were on this island, he may not attract as much trouble than if he stayed with any of the other more disreputable persons that shared this longboat. He looked around at the hands rowing. All seemed pleased, to be sure, and were certain to be engaging in some sort of boisterous activity soon enough, but the old man sitting in the corner worried Archie the most. Unlike the other crew who were more than happy to share what adventures they planned, Smee sat silent, looking darkly happy to see the pier come into sight.

Probably looking forward to kidnapping some other, unsuspecting poor soul, Archie thought. He wasn't going to stick with the old man and be the one who required to haul the new, unconscious sailors aboard, especially since he knew that they needed quite a few more men to join their crew so as to be able to sail both ships.

He turned to the squirrel. "So what tattoo are you considering?"

"I'm thinking about a... a w-woman." The stutter was worse.

Archie couldn't hide his amusement. "Any woman in particular? What about Boggs? You know, you could always ask him about the woman on his stomach. She's quite a grand sight."

The pirate in question was a very large man who more or less rolled like a ball instead of walked. The woman tattooed on his prominent belly was quite large and round, much like a female version of Boggs himself, scantily clad, with bosoms that quivered whenever the man belched, which occurred frequently.

Harper's face turned red and he closed his mouth in a tight line, refusing to say anything more on the subject of tattoos and ignored Archie, focusing instead on his rowing as they neared the dock.

Blackbeard set out toward the marketplace to secure a buyer for their cargo. He hadn't been gone long when he returned with a thin man with birdlike features who followed behind him to inspect the sugar. The man took a pinch, rolled it between his fingers, and tasted. He nodded to Blackbeard, sealing the agreement to buy the load as he handed him a sack of coins. As he left, he yelled something to the dockhands who came running from all directions to help unload the boats.

Once the sugar was packed onto wagons, Blackbeard

distributed the shares of their profit, then gave them a dark smile as he told them to "go have their fun" with a reminder to meet back in a week's time, else the *Queen Anne's Revenge* should sail without them.

Pirates scattered in every direction, though the majority headed for a long, grey building down the street. The enormous picture of a frothy, foaming tankard on the side of the tavern was visible all the way to the pier. They were going to be drunk before the hour was out.

They'll still be in the same place until next week, Archie thought. He had no desire to repeat his previous adventure with ale, so he caught up with Harper as he made his way down the dirt-packed street.

"I've never been here before," Harper admitted with an awkward smile. "I'd been to several of the smaller islands hereabouts, but never on Madeira. What shall we spend a bit of our monies on, Jameson?"

"Well, I suppose our first duty would to be to find you a woman." Archie grinned.

Harper's face turned red all the way to his shirt collar.

"For your tattoo," Archie added to alleviate the lad's discomfort, though he couldn't help laughing. "I forgot to ask you where you are going to put this woman. Will it be someplace that will cause me embarrassment?"

"No," Harper said, still smiling, though his face turned

a bit sad. He pulled something from his pocket and handed it to Archie.

Archie looked down at the worn drawing in his hands. A beautiful, young girl with cascading, black curls and large almond-shaped eyes smiled out at him. The picture was creased from the numerous times it had been tucked into Harper's pockets for safe keeping.

"This is the woman I want. Her name is Mary. I've known her since we were babes. I've loved her my whole life." His brown eyes misted. "I was on my way to ask her to marry me when Caesar hit me with that oar and brought me on the *Queen Anne's Revenge*. I guess it was luck."

"I beg your pardon?" Archie looked at him, dumbfounded, wondering if perhaps he hadn't meant to say, "bad luck."

"She comes from a rich family. My family was poor, just my mum, my little brothers, and me. I didn't have anything to offer her. She wouldn't have married me—I know that now. But now that I'm a pirate, I'll have a chance." Harper was talking to himself now more than to his friend, who was silent, listening to make sense of his story. "If I keep sailing with Blackbeard and save my share from our plunder, she'll marry me one day... I know she will."

He turned his hopeful face toward Archie and

repeated, "I know she will. She'll have to marry me then, won't she?" Realizing he was asking for an answer that only his Mary could give, Harper took a deep breath, and added, "She's pretty, isn't she?"

Archie's smile was genuine as he looked at his friend, who still held on to hope in spite of life's injustices. "Yes, she is, Harper. She's beautiful." He handed the drawing back. "So we are off to get a tattoo of young Mary then, are we?"

"Aye, I'm always fearful I shall lose this as it's all I have of her," Harper nodded, tucking the picture into his pocket. He held out his arm, patting the inside of his forearm as the future location for the tattoo. "Right here, this way she will always be in me arms until I hold the real Mary again."

So the two pirates made their way down the market street in search of a tattoo shop, finding odd things here and there that caught their attention along the way, including a tailor whom Archie decided to visit once the matter of re-creating the Mary girl had been resolved.

They were nearly to the end and had yet to discover any shops that specialized in inking when a woman carting baskets of fresh bread walked by. They queried her and found that the best artist had a small booth set up in a back room of the tavern, so back they went, retracing their steps back to the very place Archie tried to avoid.

While the tavern was lit adequately, the small room where the artist made his living piercing the flesh of willing patrons was ablaze with lanterns.

A good idea to be able to see who and what he's stabbing, I suppose, Archie thought, though he preferred not to watch as the burly man assembled his supplies in front of him and Harper bared his arm on the scarred wooden table. Still, he felt he owed the squirrel his presence and support, so he sat in the farthest corner and waited as the artist lifted his needles up to inspect their sharpness.

I do hope the man has talent, Archie thought. The possibility of getting a likeness of someone who resembled Boggs's dream woman instead of a young, innocent Mary on Harper's forearm was rather unsettling. Not to mention it would be most difficult to explain to Harper's beloved if some other strange woman happened to be stuck forever on the arm that ached to hold her. That is, if the poor lad should ever be lucky enough to see his Mary again.

Nevertheless, the artist did at least appear to know what he was doing as he studied the photograph and then inspected the curved, hard muscle of Harper's arm before he set to his slow, painstaking work.

Archie sat until his bum started to fall asleep. If time was any indication of the man's skill, Harper would have an exact replica of the real Mary etched in his skin at the same time that Archie passed on of old age.

Shifting his weight from cheek to cheek alleviated some of the pins and needles prickling at his rear, though his legs were long since numbed from being curled beneath the stool upon which he sat. He was certain hours had passed since they entered the tiny cubicle. Many, many hours. He leaned back and tried to stretch as inconspicuously as possible.

Harper was watching and seemed to notice Archie getting antsy. "Might ye do me a favor, Jameson?"

"Yes." Anything. Name it. Archie tried not to look too uneasy.

"A drink from the bar, if ye would." Harper rooted around his pocket with his free hand for a coin.

"No bother." Archie jumped up from his chair. "The drink is on me. I will return with it presently."

He left the room, bouncing on the balls of his feet in an effort to restore his blood circulation, and walked into the bar, full of drunken and disorderly pirates. Chairs were being thrown about in one corner as two of his fellow crewmates were busy knocking one another over in the attempt to win the affections of one plump tavern wench. Another corner held Blackbeard with his boots propped up on a small table, seemingly giving legitimate interviews and hiring for new positions in his crew whilst Smee sat a few feet away at the bar, waiting and willing to give the illegitimate interviews and drug the ones that refused the captain's nice offer. Either way, they were sure to have the souls they needed to sail both ships.

Archie took the long way around the room, avoiding the old man as he dodged the lively crowd and made it to the opposite end of the bar and ordered two drinks.

Naught but ale again. Archie sighed. He wasn't sure what he hoped for, but the pale liquid that flowed from the keg wasn't it.

But beggars could not be choosy, he thought, and as soon as the tankards were filled, he threw the money on the bar and grabbed them, heading back the way he came, neatly avoiding Smee, though he ran directly into the path of a rather elderly tavern wench, who seemed set on earning his money as she tried to lead him upstairs. Archie's eyes widened in horror. The woman had to be as old as his own dearly departed mum, but the similarities ended there. His mother wouldn't have ever been so bold as to grab a stranger's privates.

Aghast, Archie yelped and backed up, drinks sloshing, as he tried to get away from the woman's clutches.

"Ye look a mite lonely, lad." She grinned, giving him a great view of her discolored teeth.

"No! No! I'm not! I assure you, madam." Archie wracked his brain to find a way out. There was no way he was going anywhere near her, much less anywhere *alone* with the ancient wench. Inspiration struck him. "I am so sorry, my dear." He gave her a slow, disarming smile, causing the icy blue of his eyes to sparkle. "I have a future engagement with another lass over in the back room. I just came out to get her a drink. If I had known there were more stunning specimens of femininity about, I would never had acquired her services for the evening. 'Tis assuredly the worst luck as I've already paid her." He watched the woman's eyes narrow and read her thoughts before she offered to accompany him and the phantom woman he had concocted. "I do apologize, my dear, that I am such a poor man that I can't afford to hire you both, 'twould have been a marvelous evening with two such lovely lasses, I'm sure."

Realizing there was no money to be made from him, the old wench gave him a curt nod and went on her way, zeroing in on her next prey that looked to be in the vicinity of where Smee sat, sipping his ale, unsuspecting of the feminine wiles that were heading his way.

More than relieved to have eluded certain tragedy, Archie rushed into the back room, where Harper looked startled at his sudden appearance.

"Your drink, sir." Archie plopped the tankard on the edge of the table, and then sat back down on his bench, not caring if he sat there until his entire body deadened.

There was no way he was going to leave that room again until they left it for good.

As luck would have it, he didn't have to wait for any other body parts to fall asleep. A few moments later, the artist finished his work and patted the speckles of blood from Harper's arm.

The moment of truth, Archie thought, watching his friend inspect the new Mary on his sore arm. Harper studied the ink for a moment, looking at the silhouette of his love through the blotched and bloody skin of his forearm. Then he grinned, his eyes lighting up with sheer joy.

"Look!" he exclaimed, showing his arm to Archie. "Beautiful, isn't she!"

The woman that smiled back from the battered skin looked remarkably like the girl in the drawing. Archie uttered a quick prayer of thanks under his breath to any deity of body art who might be listening and gave Harper a warm smile. The lad paid the artist, still grinning from ear to ear.

They made it through the tavern without any more proposals of indecent nature, though they did manage to catch the attention of the old wench, who looked up from her perch on Smee's lap. She gaped at the two pirates hurrying by.

She probably thinks I fancy lads, Archie suppressed a laugh as they stepped out into the cool, night air.

"You know, we should go back in there and get a room for the night," Harper advised, looking at all the closed shops around them. "There might be vagabonds about."

Archie burst out laughing so hard that tears sprung to his eyes. The hearty laughter echoed down the empty road, bouncing against the vacant buildings. Still chuckling at the dour expression on Harper's face, he explained, "I do believe that we are the most vicious miscreants this island will ever see. We have nothing to fear, my friend. We *are* the vagabonds. Who would dare take on two of Blackbeard's faithful crew?"

Harper looked less than convinced, so Archie added, "I see lights up at the end of the street. I believe we would favor better a good bed at an inn rather than a rough cot in the tavern, wouldn't you agree?" He noted the serious expression, the lines drawn deep around Harper's toothless mouth, so he added solemnly, "I promise to keep you safe, lad."

Harper rolled his eyes at the promise and set off down the lane, not bothering to wait for Archie as he ran towards the welcoming lights of the two-story house. The squirrel was quick on his feet, arriving on the porch of the inn in record time. Then, he turned and waited for Jameson before he set to knocking on the door.

The woman who opened the door wore a frumpy-looking hat that fell down to her eyes. "Yah? What want?" she demanded, lips turned down in a ferocious scowl.

"A room, if you please, madam," Archie made his way up the steps, an imposing figure backed by moonlight.

"Hmm?" The woman leaned back to look up at Archie. She peered at him from beneath the hat, obviously not impressed. She turned and looked at the little toothless man who stood near Archie, and scowled as if she didn't care for either of them to so much as stand on her porch, much less in her establishment. "Two rooms, yah?"

"Most certainly, madam. I have no intention of sharing my bed with yon wee bugger." Archie grinned at Harper as he dropped some coins in the woman's open palm. She pushed back her hat and stared at the money with a wide grin, as if changing her mind about the two gentlemen who wished to rest in her abode, and opened the door wide for them to enter, and then took them upstairs to settle in.

Archie bade Madame Frumpy Hat and Harper a good night, leaving them staring at him in the hallway as he shut the door in their faces. He was tired and more than determined to get a good night's rest in a real bed, even if he bordered on rudeness.

Kicking off his shoes and pulling off his clothes, he crawled into the bed, blissful sleep taking over the second his head hit the pillow. He slept the sleep of the dead, never moving nor hearing a thing until the next morning when the sun streamed through the window to play on his face.

He awoke refreshed and renewed, ready to explore the island and have his own adventures. He met Harper on the way down the stairs and the two left to find their breakfast, stopping just long enough to secure Archie's room for the rest of the week.

"I think I'll be going back to the *Queen Anne's Revenge* tonight, so I won't be needin' a room," Harper announced, looking down at his scabbed arm as if the tattoo was his only reason for coming to the island.

"How did you sleep?" Archie asked, wondering if the preference to sleep on the ship came from a rough night at Madame Frumpy's or from the need to save his hard earned money.

Harper shrugged. "Slept fine, I suppose."

Ah, he was saving up for Mary, Archie noted. He decided not to embarrass the lad and he let the subject drop. After all, who knew? Maybe one day Archie would find someone for whom he would wish to provide. Perhaps there would be a reason to save his coins one day.

But not yet. Right now, his money was burning a hole in his pocket. He was ready for some breakfast and more than ready for a trip to the tailor shop he spotted the previous day. He was in dire need of clothing. His own simple attire was ruined from being drug across the rough planks of the pier the day Smee shanghaied him. The slopchest on the ship hadn't contained clothing he preferred to wear. The pants were baggy and ill-fitting and the canvas shirt chafed everything he had. Oh yes, he might make that tailor a rich man by the time the week was done, but by golly, he would have clothes that fit before they cast off into the unknown again.

They found a girl selling bread on the street corner and they ate. Harper left afterward, anxious to save his money and be back aboard the ship, and so Archie was left to himself as he made his way to the tailor.

Archibald never cared about his clothing before his days as a pirate, but now that he had a chance to purchase whatever he wanted, he found himself being fitted for finer clothes than he imagined.

"I have a nice blue over here." The tailor pointed out a bolt of fabric. "'Twould make a good coat."

Archie fingered the cloth, noting its sturdiness. "Yes, I'll have two made of this."

"What of the red behind it?" the man asked, sounding hopeful. "I would sell it to you at half the price of the blue, should you take some of it. It hasn't sold well, and I need rid of it to make room for the more popular colors."

The bolt of oiled silk was as bright as blood. Archie bit his lip as he tried to keep the look of distaste from showing on his face. It wasn't a color he would ever pick, but then again, he *was* a pirate now. He thought of Blackbeard and the smoking, beribboned beard that struck terror in every man who sailed the seven seas.

One never knew when one might have need of strange attire. He smiled. "Yes, two great coats in the red as well, if you please. And I'd like lots of brass buttons on the front—large ones—if you have them."

The tailor's eyes widened, whether from calculating the profit he was making from buttons or from the odd request of not one, but two, splendid red coats, Archie didn't know. The man started measuring, taking note of Archie's height and girth, and set to planning out the young pirate's wardrobe. Shirts of billowing white, black, and blue fabric with thick lace cuffs were ordered, along with several pairs of breeches, a half dozen silk waistcoats of various colors, and a few neckerchiefs edged in lace.

He was going to look quite the dandy, Archie realized with a smile, his order completed.

His visit finished with the tailor, Archie stopped by the next shop and purchased a new pair of shoes now that his new position of navigator allowed him to more or less stay off the rigging.

Another shop, which sold hats, caught his eye from across the street. Every man should own a respectable hat, he concluded, as he opened the door. A bell jingled as he went inside. Hats of every possible size lined the shelves, though one in particular caught his eye.

"'Allo." The man behind the counter greeted him. "Might I be helpin' ye?"

"Yes," Archie said, pointing, "I'm interested in that hat on yon shelf."

"Ah, a fine choice." The man took the hat down and handed the black pirate's hat to Archie for his inspection. Two great feathers, one white and the other black adorned one side. Archie settled it on his head, looking at his reflection in the mirror on the wall.

"It will do well." He smiled, taking the hat off as he turned to pay.

"Will ye be havin' anything else?" The man gestured to the opposite wall where wigs made of yak and human hair rested on fake, wooden heads.

Archie shook his head. His own dark locks would serve him well enough. He was a pirate after all. A newly converted, dandy of a pirate mayhap, but still a pirate, nonetheless. Besides, he doubted that Blackbeard would give him time to powder his wig before they went into battle. He grinned at the thought as he laid his coins on the counter, "No thank you. The hat will be more than enough."

* * *

The next few days were paradise. Archie spent his days exploring the island, though he didn't buy much else in the stores since he'd given the tailor most of his money. Through his strolling about, he discovered that Madeira's main source of trade was wine. The grapes were grown on the island, the juice put into casks and then sold to the vessels that came into port. If the ship were to keep the wine in its hold for a long journey, the rocking of the boat would age it while giving it an exquisite taste, making it the best money could buy.

It was a great investment, Archie decided as he bought a cask, ordering it to be taken to the dock when he found that Blackbeard purchased a few dozen barrels to be placed in the belly of the *Anne*. Archie doubted that the captain would allow the wine to replace the rum, should their rations ever run out. Blackbeard might be a cutthroat pirate, but he was a savvy businessman, too. The crew wouldn't be allowed to drink his profits.

They can keep their rum. I shall have my own wine. Archie smiled to himself, though he made certain to mark the wooden cask as his own.

He meandered down Market Street, deciding to stop in at the tailor and check on the progress of his clothing. Luck was with him and he walked out of the shop looking like a different person, smartly dressed in his dark blue coat and new breeches with several paper-wrapped parcels containing the rest of his order, tucked under his arms.

He spotted Harper running about in the middle of the street in an obvious, frantic search for something. Worrying about the lad's strange behavior, he shouted, "Harper!"

He turned at the sound of his name, and looked at Archie twice before recognition dawned on his face, followed by instantaneous relief. "Jameson, I've searched the entire island for you. We have to go. We're casting off with the tide."

"What are you talking about?" Archie asked. "We have two days before we set sail."

"No, the cap'n is giving orders for all hands aboard. That's why I came looking for you. A Swiss merchant ship docked last night. Mr. Moreau found out from a tavern wench who found out from another wench who found out from one of the crew that there is a British naval ship, not two days behind it. Rumor is Lieutenant Maynard is aboard, and that he's a-comin' for Blackbeard." The words came out in a rush, then Harper paused just long enough to take a breath, and continue, "I went to the inn first. The old woman gave me your things, but she wouldn't give back any of your money, so everything is in the longboat but us." The last word ended in a nervous squeak. Harper eyed Archie anxiously as if he realized that there was a possibility that the finely dressed man next to him might not want to return to the ship. After all, he didn't look like a pirate anymore.

"Right then, I suppose we must be going," Archie set off with his parcels toward the dock, infinitely happy that the tailor had such impeccable timing.

Relieved, Harper gave Archie the rest of the news, "We've been assigned to the *Roger*."

Archie stopped in his tracks and whirled to face him. "We've *what?*"

"You are to be her navigator. I'm to be on the rigging." Harper shrugged. "We are under the watch of Mr. Moreau as her captain, so all is well enough..." he paused, then clarified, "All is *nearly* well enough. Smee is aboard as surgeon along with the new cook he persuaded to join, plus a few other lads, and... Black Caesar is bo'sun." His face scrunched up in displeasure at the last pirate's name.

Lovely. Archie frowned as they arrived at the dock where a handful pirates were getting into the last longboat. He didn't recall signing the book to be a hand on the *Jolig Roger*. If he'd had the choice, he would much rather have stayed on the *Anne*. At least there he wouldn't have to worry about Caesar trying to flay the skin from his back as Philip Moreau seemed to dislike the demon of a man as much as he.

A single cask sitting on the dock caught his attention

and shook him from his black thoughts. There sat his wine. "That goes with us," he told Harper, gesturing with his chin as his arms were still full.

"Jameson, have ye done nothing but shop?" Harper complained, grunting as he rolled the cask that weighed more than he did.

He made it to the edge of the dock, where Boggs sat in the longboat. The big pirate reached over and pulled the cask onto the longboat as if it weighed nothing.

"Thank ye," Harper thanked him, breathless, as he hopped in, turning to give Archie a hand with his new wardrobe.

"Is this all o' us?" Boggs asked as he unwrapped the rope that secured them to the pier.

Harper shot Archie a grin, "Aye, we have our navigator. To the *Jolig Roger*, we row!"

7

A BIT OF FAIRY DUST

Smee scowled. "I wish ye would keep yer cursed pixie from meddlin' about in me quarters and thievin' all me things. Me needles are missing now, before that 'twas the buttons on me breeches. How am I supposed to sew up any blasted wounds on this ship with me needles gone, I ask ye? And with me pants around me ankles to boot. Best ye tell her to bring 'em all back 'fore I catch her and treat her as the thief she is!" He made a fist and smacked it soundly on the table in front of Archie as if in a vain effort to squash the source of his agitation, but he only managed to cause Archie's tankard to flip off to the floor. As luck would have it, the cup was empty or Archie's temper would easily have matched Smee's.

The old man has surely gone mad, Archie reasoned to himself, wondering if perhaps the pirate hadn't been sampling some of his own concoctions before administering them to the crew in his position as doctor of the ship. "I haven't a single earthly idea of what or to whom you are referring," Archie said calmly, looking up into the eyes that looked ready to cut down anyone deemed guilty. "Would you care to at least give me a hint?"

"The pixie that has followed ye about since the first I saw ye, though if I knew she'd be after ye the whole time I'd never have brought ye aboard to begin with," Smee's voice raised an octave, his face turning red. "Pixies are naught but trouble!"

"Right. They most certainly are," Archie decided to agree, or at least give the impression he was in accord with the man, however insane he might be. "I shall tell her at once she must return those needles and buttons, else I shall banish her forever."

"Ye tell her if she doesn't bring 'em back, I'll…" Smee broke off, raking his finger across his throat in a threatening motion.

As if it would be possible to slit the throat of something as small as a pixie, Archie reasoned silently. To do so, he would have to kill said pixie with one of the needles she had supposedly stolen, which would take more skill and precision than Smee possessed in his knobby, arthritic fingers. Archie sighed. "I'll tell her. You have my word." And he would, he decided, even if it meant talking to himself with no one listening. It wouldn't matter, he consoled himself, his sanity couldn't be any worse than any of the other pirates on the ship.

"Aye," Smee said darkly before he turned and stomped off. "Ye best do that."

Archie waited until the crabby pirate left, shutting the door to the map room much harder than necessary, before he settled his head in his hands and let out a long sigh. "Why must I always attract those whose wits have escaped them?"

The strange tinkling sound laughed at him. Archie's head shot up, searching for the source, but saw nothing out of the ordinary. There were always small things that shifted to and fro with the rocking of the ship, so he watched each of them in turn, waiting for something to appear. Two rolled maps moved a few inches either way, trapped between his measuring instruments.

The weighted lanterns on the walls moved in time to the rhythm of the *Roger*, balancing the flames inside their glass sconces as they swayed to and fro, light flickering against the paneled walls.

The room was quiet following Smee's departure, but for the tankard bumping against the table leg every few seconds. Archie bent over, picked it up, and set it down on the table.

Now there was silence but for the creaking of the ship

and the waves that lapped at her sides. Archie waited a full minute, wondering if perhaps the sound was just a figment of his imagination and if he wasn't every bit as crazy as the old man who just left. He decided to finish it then, once and for all. After all, he *had* just given Smee his word to warn "his pixie" against thievery and at least now there wasn't anyone around to hear him make a fool of himself.

Archie cleared his throat. "You do realize it is not considered good manners to take what is not yours, don't you, my dear?" He wasn't sure why he considered this figment of his imagination female, but since it was his own personal moment of insanity, he continued, "'Tis also bad form to not show oneself when being spoken to."

To his utter surprise, the bell sound chimed thrice more, very slow, barely audible, as if to make tones of apology. A light splash of gold-colored dust covered a small spot in the center of the table when a small blonde head peeked out from its hiding place behind the tankard.

"Well, hello there." Archie smiled in spite of the mixture of feelings that bombarded him. Relief that he wasn't crazy and fear that maybe he was indeed insane and having hallucinations were two of the more prominent, but the strongest was the surprise that he managed to be so convincing as to shame the pixie into showing herself.

"You have nothing to fear from me," he promised her. Yes, the tiny figure was most assuredly female, he noted. She was a small thing, no bigger than his little finger, with wispy blonde tendrils caught up in a knot at the top of her head and large, guileless eyes that watched him with steady caution. She wore sewn leaves, fashioned into a small dress of sorts and shoes made from dandelion tufts. And she was real, he decided. Even in his wildest daydreams, he never would have been able to concoct shoes made of such delicate flower fluff.

"My name is Archibald, though you probably know that," he said softly, so as not to spook her. She was coming out from behind the tankard, seemingly trusting enough, though her eyes stayed on him. "I must say I've never met a pixie before, so I'm quite pleased to meet you. Might I have the pleasure of knowing your name as well?"

The pixie folded her slender arms behind her as her face flushed. She looked down at her feet and shook her head.

Feeling terrible that he embarrassed her, as it seemed the poor pixie was nameless, Archie retraced his steps and tried a different approach, "You know, I think I may know the perfect name for such a lovely pixie as yourself. Would you like to hear it, per chance?"

Well. That got her attention. The pixie's head popped up in anticipation of hearing what he had to say next. She gave a shy smile, daring to come a few inches closer, small golden dust puffing up from her shoes with each step she took.

He smiled back. "I think the name Bell would suit you wonderfully as your voice reminds me of the light, beautiful tones of bells. What do you think?"

The pixie eagerly nodded as her shy smile turned into a happy one.

"Well then, Miss Bell. I am most pleased to meet your acquaintance." He gave her a small, elegant bow which seemed to please the pixie to no end. She clapped her tiny hands, an enormous smile painted on her face, then dipped into a deep curtsy of her own.

"Well now, since we are friends I do have a bit of a question for you," Archie said, and then shook his head as many more questions popped in. "I do apologize, but I seem to have quite a few questions. The first being why would you follow someone like me about? Of course, I am most flattered."

The pixie shrugged, making odd bell sounds as if she wasn't sure herself or perhaps following him was the product of sheer boredom. Either way, Archie didn't know what she meant, as the tones only sounded like music to a song that he didn't know. There was a most definite communication gap between himself and Miss Bell.

It was possible their relationship was going to be somewhat one-sided if all he could ask her were simple yes-or-no questions solved by the shaking of her head either one way or the other, Archie thought, but still he decided to try a few queries, hoping she wouldn't take offense. After all, with luck they might be able to sort some kind of system out.

"One of my fellow crewmates wanted me to ask and see if perchance you might know the location of his needles and buttons?"

A definite, slow nod, though the pixie didn't look happy to admit it.

"Might you return them? The poor fellow is in a terrible state. He's quite old, you see, and gets very high-tempered when his things go missing," Archie urged.

She didn't bother an answer, but rather flew to the corner of the room, sprinkles of gold dust following in her wake. She lighted on a rolled-top desk and tugged open the small drawer in the upper corner, one that Archie had never used.

She pointed in the drawer and waited as Archie came to look. There in the drawer, was a collection of buttons, needles, spools of thread, odd bits of ribbon, a small pair of scissors, a few coins, and a bent nail. The only thing the hodge-podge collection had in common was that each stolen item in that drawer was shiny.

It was apparent Miss Bell had an attraction to bright objects. Archie watched as she stared longingly into the drawer.

"You must return these things," Archie advised her. "You can't keep them."

The pixie turned toward him, a questioning look on her face that asked—*all of them?*

"I'm afraid so. They must all be returned," Archie said sympathetically, watching the pixie's full bottom lip pop out in a pout. She crossed her arms over her chest for a moment, making Archie wonder if he was going to have to take the loot and redistribute it himself, though he wasn't sure who the owners were.

Finally, she picked up one of the needles that stood as tall as she, and flew to the door, waiting for Archie to open it.

The second a crack opened in the doorway, she zipped out of it, gold dust flying everywhere. Archie waited for her to return for another item to take back.

Moments passed.

Worrying that Smee might have caught the mischievous pixie and skewered her with the needle, Archie set out to see if he might save her from whatever tragedy that may have befallen her.

Smee's quarters were the farthest from the map room, so Archie began his trek, inspecting each spot he passed through as inconspicuously as possible, which was not an easy feat by any means.

He walked by the captain's quarters, noting that Moreau was poring over a book at his table. All was quiet there with no sign that the pixie ventured that way. He traveled onward, navigating his way down the narrow steps and through the crew's sleeping quarters.

There was no sleeping happening in this place. Fiddle music played happily while the majority of the crew danced around to the tune. The boards under their feet thumped, causing the entire floor to bounce.

'Twas a wonder the entire ship wasn't bopping up and down in the water and an even greater mystery that he hadn't heard the boisterous lot up in the map room. There wouldn't be any need in trying to sneak around this bunch, Archie decided, so he walked through the throng of dancing pirates, dodging the drunken stomps of one man in particular who seemed to have consumed more than his single ration of rum. Archie was doing a good job of evading him and had almost gotten around him when he got jostled from behind and bumped into the pirate.

The dancing continued uninterrupted as the man kept his same clunking pace of trying to stomp holes in the floorboards. It took Archie another minute to get clear of the dance floor. Then he realized that the drunken man was none other than the one who reported his needles and buttons stolen.

At least one button was still amiss, as Smee's breeches kept inching down only to be pulled back up every few seconds as he kept his rather ungraceful dance steps in time with the music.

On the upside of things, it didn't look as if he murdered a pixie. With that thought in mind, Archie left through the door behind him, taking the long way back to his quarters, still looking for evidence of Miss Bell along the way, but not finding any trace of her or the stolen wares.

He was nearly back to his cabin when a dark figure blocked his path. Black Caesar loomed up in front of him, one of the very few pirates whose height was greater than his own.

"What might ye be skulkin' about and searchin' for, Black Caesar has been wondering? A small golden fairy, perhaps?"

The mention of Miss Bell startled Archie, and he began to worry again of the fate of his tiny friend.

"She might have stayed on Madeira when we cast off days ago," Caesar said in a thoughtful way, gauging Archie's reaction. "But more like she's aboard the *Anne*."

The fact that Caesar hadn't seen the pixie returning her wares that night managed to ease Archie's fears and gave him the extra boost of confidence to look the bo'sun in the eye as the man continued to speak.

"Just as well she never shows her face aboard this ship," Caesar growled. "'Tis bad luck to have a woman aboard, fairy or no."

"Well, since she isn't here, we have nothing to worry about." Archie hoped his tone of voice would discourage further discussion as he pushed past Caesar, shutting the door to the map room behind him with a solid thump.

He waited a full moment until he heard Caesar move off, grumbling under his breath. When silence enveloped him, he let out the breath he was holding and slumped against the door. He had the nagging suspicion that he and the bo'sun would have it out sooner rather than later. The man always seemed to watch his every move, waiting for the opportunity to find fault in his ability as navigator. After all, if something should ever happen to Moreau, then he and Black Caesar, being of equal rank, would both be eligible for the position of captain. The votes cast by the crew would determine who would take the place at the helm of the *Jolig Roger* should Blackbeard or Moreau not be near enough to appoint such leadership themselves. Archie didn't know who the crew would vote for in such an instance, though he would be willing to place a bet that Caesar would find ways to ensure his place as captain, should the opportunity present itself.

Perish the thought. May Moreau have naught but a long and fruitful existence on this earth. Archie offered a silent prayer to protect the captain.

He opened the drawer of the desk and found it empty. Every last button and scrap of ribbon were gone, with no sign of the pixie anywhere to be found.

The thoughts of everyone seeming to know about her, while he himself was oblivious, was disturbing. After all, he'd been in pirate status for nearly a month now, and though he'd heard that tinkling sound a couple of times, this was the first occasion he had seen her. Though he hoped this wouldn't be the last time, Archie wished that she would remain elusive, for the two pirates who bore her ill will would make good on their threats should she be so unfortunate as to be spotted by them ever again.

May she stay hidden, wherever she may be, he thought as he climbed into his cot, falling into a deep sleep filled with dreams of gold dust and shadows.

8

ENCHANTED WATERS

The fog fell upon the *Jolig Roger* in the wee hours of twilight like a mysterious blanket dropped upon a slumbering child. None of the hands on deck saw it coming. It appeared suddenly and was so thick that they couldn't see anything past the boat's railings, and could barely make out one another on their own deck.

The wind was dead calm with sea that was eerily still. As the waves ceased, the ship quit rocking and sat on an ocean as smooth as glass.

Philip Moreau stood on the quarterdeck of his ship, listening to the silence as a small part of his gut told him this was no ordinary fog. While the sight was picturesque, it was also unnerving. There was magic in the mix and something was going to happen soon.

His crew appeared in the same frame of mind as

himself, as each of them cast nervous glances over their shoulders. There were a scant few on deck at this hour, the rest having not yet risen from their wild night of rum and fiddle music.

"We be in enchanted waters, Cap'n," a dark voice intoned as Smee appeared beside him like a ghost. Moreau found himself resisting the urge to jump out of his skin. The doctor of the ship enjoyed his night the most of all, making him the last person Moreau expected to see before noon. Moreau never thought the old man stealthy enough to startle him—rum sloshing in his blood or no.

"'Tis only a fog, Mr. Smee." He sighed, then added truthfully, "But I must also admit I feel something amiss. Pass the word to wake all hands, but tell them to walk softly. We must be ready for whatever comes our way." Moreau gave his quiet order and watched as the old Irishman disappeared below the decks to rouse the others from their drunken slumber.

The *Roger* had yet to catch up with the *Queen Anne's Revenge*. In his haste to flee the island, Blackbeard hadn't waited for his other ship, as if he assumed Moreau would catch up to him within a few days' time. It was an inaccurate assumption. So far there wasn't any sign of the *Anne* and her frightened capitan. Moreau found himself wishing that Blackbeard had waited. Two ships to battle the unknown may not hold any greater odds, but it would have made him feel better in these quiet moments when the loudest sound to be heard was the pounding of his own heart.

Moreau had been on the sea for most of his life. He began as a lad of eight years old, hauling powder to the cannons, earning his first title of powder monkey. In the following eighteen years that he spent on various ships, he acquired many more titles, though none so grand as the one he held now. He worked hard for a long time, and was proud of his command of the *Jolig Roger*, but with that title came the responsibility of watching over every soul on the ship. He wondered if perhaps that was the reason for his unease. After all, he had seen many foggy mornings that bore no ill warnings and he wasn't one to scare easily. Still, he was a man who trusted his instincts and right now he was certain that he had never felt such a feeling of foreboding from a calm sea.

Something was coming for this ship, and the deep feeling of dread that lay in his bones told him that whatever it was, it came for him.

Meanwhile, below decks, Smee was swatting sailors from their cots, informing them to be quiet and mind whatever manners they possessed, however few they may be. The groggy pirates hit the floor, cursing. The majority of the crew slept in hammocks or cots, easily within his reach to flip them out on their heads should they not rise on his command. Four pirates had the luck of having private quarters and all were awake and on their way up to the deck, with the exception of the navigator, whose quarters lay the farthest away.

Harper volunteered to go wake Jameson, and at Smee's nod, set off toward the map room.

* * *

Awakened from his deep slumber by the tense silence, Archie stumbled from his quarters. He was bleary-eyed, but somehow he managed to sheath his rapier to his side without skewering himself and made his way to the door. Though he never heard the partiers across the ship, he had gotten accustomed to the creaking boards above his cot and the muffled curses of those on deck.

The silence was so unnerving that he jumped, smacking his head on the doorframe as Harper materialized out of nowhere. He was too quick-footed, Archie decided, cursing under his breath as he rubbed the sore spot on his forehead that was in the beginnings of forming a knot. He managed to glare at Harper as his eyes watered.

"'Tis a fog." Harper hissed at him, not bothering to wait for Archie to berate him, as he started toward the deck.

"Smee says it's magic water we're in. We're to get up top, Moreau's orders."

"Well, that can't be good," Archie said, following Harper up the steps.

"Be quiet," the boy whispered, looking over his back to scowl at Archie. "Do you wish to wake the dead?"

Moreau motioned Archie to join him on the quarterdeck and gave his orders to his waiting crew. "Ready the cannons."

Archie joined his captain, watching the crew load the cannons and roll them into place. Ready for whatever the silence and fog hid from them, the crew of the *Jolig Roger* waited. A few torturous moments passed, and then someone began whistling.

"Find him," Moreau hissed to Black Caesar, who nodded and stalked down the length of the ship, whip clutched in his hand.

Smee stood beside Archie, a deep scowl lining his face. "Bad luck," the Irishman muttered so low that Archie barely heard him. "'Tis always bad luck to whistle up a wind. The man is a fool."

Black Caesar made a complete circle, checking each man as he passed. He returned to Moreau, hands up in a shrug. He hadn't found the one who dared to break the silence.

The nervous whistling continued and the crew became

even more anxious. Moreau frowned, listening to the haunting, ghost-like whistle.

"It doesn't come from our ship. We are not floating in this cursed fog alone."

Archie watched different decisions pass across his captain's face. Seconds later, one settled itself permanently. He turned to Archie, "You shall have command when I am gone, *mon ami*. There is another ship out there that bears the man whistling that tune. I shall take one of the boats and find her. With a bit of luck, we may board and find them surprised."

Archie nodded. "Yes, sir."

Moreau leaned closer, fixing him with his brown eyes, "If anything—*anything*—should go amiss, blow them out of the water."

"Aye. You have my word."

Moreau took off across the deck, gathering eight of the crew along the way. The creaking of the ropes that lowered the longboat was the only sound that mixed with the haunted whistle.

Moreau turned, giving Archie a slow, final nod as they set off. The words replayed in Archie's head. You shall have command when I am gone.

Surely he meant to say "in my absence," Archie thought. The captain's words had such a sense of finality that he wondered if perhaps Moreau thought his plan ill-fated and decided to bequeath his command to his navigator in the event of his impending death.

No. To think such things is pure folly. Moreau would be back presently. My command will be a short one. Archie shook his head, clearing the strange thoughts from his mind and set to watching the men in the longboat row. A slight noise beside him caught his attention.

Harper stood at the cannon nearest to him, shifting from one foot to the other. Normally in the rigging, this was the first time Archie noticed the squirrel pressed into the duty of gauging one of the ship's guns. While all the other cannons were gauged upward, Harper's was pointed down at the sea.

"All is well," Archie whispered to his friend in hopes to ease his worry and didn't mention that his cannon seemed to be pointing in the wrong direction. In the event that there happened to be a whistling sea monster of some sort, Harper's cannon would be in the prime position to do the most good. Archie smiled at him, and then turned his attention back to Moreau as the fog enveloped the small boat. The tension amongst the crew doubled.

"Be ready to fire." The warning was whispered down the line of cannons. Uneasiness had every man waiting, ready to blow their charge in an instant.

A sudden wind stirred as if in response to the whistle that picked up in cadence. The quick burst of warm air cleared enough of the fog that the longboat appeared. They were just short of engaging their surprise attack on the merchant ship that floated near them. A single flag, striped in yellow and red, fluttered in the breeze, giving the only color in the bleak scene, and revealed the man who had done the whistling. Standing below the flag, stood the Spanish sailor that stirred the wind. He stopped in mid-tune.

Time passed slowly for one grueling second, as both crews stared at one another in shock. Realizing the extreme danger they were now in, Moreau managed to fire a single shot in the same instant that Archie screamed his first command.

"Fire!"

A bright crimson stain spread across the chest of the man who had done the whistling, and he fell into the sea. Moreau's shot found its mark, but in return, the merchant sailors returned a volley of shots and peppered the longboat. No one was left standing, though from a couple of strangled cries, there was one or two who might be saved if someone could get to them. A body lay floating, face down, near the longboat. The curly, dark hair and familiar clothes marked him as one that wouldn't be saved. Moreau was dead.

I'm captain, Archie thought numbly as the *Roger's*

cannons fired and set his ears to ringing. These are my men and this is my boat now.

"Your orders?" Harper yelled as the last cannon fired. Bits of wood flew around them. Their first shots hit the merchant ship.

"Fire at will!" It seemed like a good order, but then, Archie hadn't ever commanded a ship before. As his message was relayed down the line, he watched his men as they began to load the cannons and ready for another shot, and then he turned his attention to the other ship. They managed to catch the merchant ship off guard with their first blast, but now the men scurried about on her decks in an effort to ready their own cannons and return fire.

We need to board that ship, Archie thought. If we could take another longboat, victory could be ours. Moreau's instincts seem sound, and if I'm wise, I should follow his lead.

Another cry echoed across the water from the first longboat and sealed the decision. There were survivors that needed rescuing, too.

"Bring any man not on the cannons to the longboats," he ordered Caesar, who hadn't moved since Moreau had left. "We're taking that ship." At that, Caesar smiled and set off across the deck. Archie turned to Harper. "The ship is yours until I return, my friend."

He received a toothless smile in return and then set off for the boats.

Two longboats settled into the water with Archie at the head of one, and Caesar at the other. "Go and rescue anyone you can," Archie told him as they began to row away from one another in an attempt to be harder targets for the merchants. But Caesar didn't stop by the first boat, choosing instead to disobey and head straight to the merchant ship, leaving Archie and his crew to work harder and backtrack to the longboat that still bobbed amongst the floating bodies.

"I'm glad he follows orders. I don't know what I'd do without him." Archie cursed under his breath as he decided to ignore the longboat that held Caesar and focus on what remained ahead of them in the water.

Six out of the nine men were dead in the ocean, floating about like bits of driftwood as they bumped against the boat, coloring the water red with the blood. One man was dead in the longboat. The last two moaned in agony beside him.

As luck would have it, Smee was one who jumped into Archie's boat. The ship's doctor was taking note of their wounds as another volley of cannon fire flew over their heads.

"Best let me and a few other lads row this other boat back to the *Jolig Roger*," the old man said loudly to be heard over the shots, "They be dead men if they stay out here much longer and I can't help 'em while Harper is blasting his cannons about over me head."

Archie nodded his consent and Smee and five others got into the other longboat and started to row back as quickly as they could.

A loud groan erupted from the merchant ship, and a few waves caught at the longboat. "Hold steady, lads," Archie said, looking at the massive ship ahead of them as it creaked and settled lower into the water. A gaping hole barely showed at the surface of the water, proving there was unseen damage below. Only one cannon had been aimed so low to have made that hit. Harper's shot was sinking that ship.

Archie grinned. He planned on making Harper a permanent fixture on the cannons from now on, since he was giving them the upper hand in this battle.

From the clashing sounds of metal he heard, Caesar and his party had boarded and were making progress of a sort. There hadn't been any more cannon fire from the merchant ship. Harper must have noticed it, too, as he ceased to order the crew to fire any other shots, though it was possible he had spotted his own party trying to board the ship and didn't want to blow holes in his own people. Either way, Archie was happy the boy had the faculties to stop blasting the cannons.

It's appreciated, Harper, I assure you, Archie thought as he sent a final look over his shoulder to the *Jolig Roger*. He grabbed one of the ropes on the merchant ship and began climbing. He couldn't think of a worse outcome than to be shot by his own ship on the first day of becoming its captain.

He pulled his way to the deck and was rewarded by the sight of several merchant sailors holding their hands up in surrender. Caesar was stalked about on deck, snapping his whip on any in his path, treating the merchants much as he did his own crewmates, while his own men battled the few who refused to back down.

Archie pulled out his rapier and stuck it into the belly of one seaman who was running at him with a sword poised over his head. It made a strange sucking *thlunk* and jarred his hands as it sunk into the man's body. It was an odd sensation, not the hard feeling of the thin metal as it sunk into flesh, but rather the taking of the man's life. For many years, he practiced, but it had been exactly that. Practice. Never had he killed another. Fortunately, he didn't get to ponder the meaning of life much longer as another merchant came screaming from above him on the quarterdeck. He jerked the rapier out of the first man and barely had enough time to slide it into the next one.

The second body fell to the ground at his feet. His hands becoming accustomed to the force that it required to pull the rapier free, he jerked and spun around, the fine point of his weapon aimed at the throat of the man behind him.

The man was holding his own rapier out, hilt first. "Go on, take it. We surrender," the merchant captain said in halting English. When Archie didn't move, the captain took a step back and thrust the gleaming handle at him again as if he were worried that Archie would rather skewer his neck than accept his surrender.

"Tell your men to stop fighting," Archie said, never taking his eyes off him. He heard the clank of steel and knew the battle wasn't over quite yet.

The captain was sweating, tiny drops of perspiration popped out on his forehead, as he shouted. Archie translated the Spanish in his head, "Stop. We are surrendering." A few curses were mumbled from the merchants. Not all wished to give in to the pirates, but none disobeyed their captain.

"We accept your surrender," Archie said, taking the rapier from the captain. "Now, in case you haven't noticed, your ship is sinking, so I shall make my terms quickly. You and your crew can either join us, or we can leave you here." As the captain's pallor turned chalky, he added, "In a longboat, of course."

The captain's lips clamped tight in a thin line, as if he were thinking over his slim options. Then, he spoke, "I shall tell my men, but I will stay in the longboat. I will not join such people as *you*." The pointed glare Archie received, made him feel as if he were the most depraved human in existence, which felt nice for once.

Archie grinned. He was pleased that he had been recognized as a pirate, and a good one, at that. "Spread the word, no harm befalls any who wishes to join or stay. One longboat for each party, divide them as they wish," Archie ordered Caesar, who gave him an even better glare than the captain had. The look wasn't as appreciated coming from a subordinate. Archie's voice dropped octaves. "I am your captain and you will obey or suffer the wrath of your own whip."

Caesar didn't answer, only stalked off with his hands clenched at his side.

"Cap'n, you might have a look at her cargo." Boggs rolled up suddenly, looking out of breath. "This ship is sinking faster, and there be more bodies to worry with than just the crew."

"What cargo are you speaking of?" Archie set off after Boggs, who led him to a grate covering the hold. Dozens of dirty, starving faces stared up at him.

"Indians," Archie muttered in awe. "Their cargo was Indians?"

The ship creaked and rocked further to the side, causing him to slide. Catching his footing and his wits,

Archie said, "Boggs, get them out of there. They are coming with us. We aren't leaving them to drown."

"Aye, Cap'n," came the reply as Boggs flipped the grate open. The Indians were hesitant at first, but then began to scramble out as the water began sloshing around their legs.

"I wish to take my effects before she sinks." The captain of the merchant ship appeared at Archie's elbow. "They are in my cabin, I will return in a moment."

The man's eyes shifted uneasily as if he were hiding the truth. At Archie's nod, the captain set off in a near run and disappeared below the deck.

"Follow him and see what he's up to," Archie whispered to Boggs, and then kept his watch as the longboats filled.

Moments later, the captain reappeared, followed by a knife pressed in the small of his back. Boggs followed him, looking smug. "This 'un was going after his gold," he said, handing Archie an ornate, wooden box.

Archie nearly dropped the thing it was so heavy. Setting it down on the deck, he flipped the lid. Hundreds of Spanish medallions sparkled in the midday sun.

"There be a barrel of silver dust down there, too." Boggs shrugged. "I sent one o' the lads after it. Dunno why anyone would make dust out of silver, but it's there just the same. It be worth something, I suppose."

It took two more longboats to carry the Indians, the barrel of silver, and the newly joined crew back to the *Jolig Roger*. One longboat stayed behind, holding the furious merchant captain and those of his crew who stayed loyal to him.

From the safety of his quarterdeck, Archie watched the merchant ship sink. As the last trace of the ship disappeared under the water, the enchantment was broken.

The instant the sea claimed her prize, a strong wind came to fill the sails.

9

THE CHALLENGE

The idea of keeping Indian slaves in the hold was not setting well with Harper. "But what are you going to do with them?" He asked for what seemed the millionth time.

"I don't know." The answer was the same each time the question was asked. Archie didn't like the idea, either, but he was at a loss for what should be done. After all, he hadn't been captain a full day, he didn't have all the answers. "Feed them well, and find a way to ask if they would like to join our crew, perhaps?"

"Half of them are women and children. I doubt they'll wish to join and I don't know that our men will want them to. Women bring bad luck on a ship. Then there's the old chief. He's just..." Harper frowned, "...old. He couldn't climb the rigging if his life depended on it."

Archie shrugged, he didn't have an answer to this dilemma yet, or to the fact that all attempts at communication with the Indians had been fruitless. Working in the print shop for years had given him the basic knowledge of many different languages. He wasn't fluent in them, but he could manage to get the general idea relayed to the person he was speaking to. The Indians who inhabited the hold were a complete mystery to him. Their language like nothing he had ever heard before. No matter how hard he tried, or which individual he tried to communicate with, they couldn't understand one another. Through the new Spanish crew members, he managed to learn that the merchant ship had captured the Indians in Mexico, intending to sell them as slaves once they reached Spain. None of them had been able to understand the Indians' language either.

Harper watched him for a long moment, and then continued as if there hadn't been a lull of silence, "Speaking of food and new recruits, I have something to report from my brief position held as captain. We had a slight mishap while you were gone to the merchant ship. We'll need another cook." He gave Archie a dour look. "The new cook got his self killed in the battle. One of the cannons came loose after it fired. The ropes broke, and the cannon went a-rollin' and squashed him against the mast. That's why I had them stop firing, we were trying to pull the poor bugger out. He was stuck in there like he was part of the boat."

Archie grimaced. The image painted in his head wasn't one he wished to keep and the thoughts of yet another funeral he had to officiate, along with the bodies of Moreau and a dozen others, was depressing at best.

He caught a scent wafting up through the floorboards that sent his stomach to grumbling. "Do you know who is in the galley? I smell something cooking."

"Ach, yes. Boggs is cooking. He said he felt responsible for the Injuns, since he found 'em and all." Harper shrugged as if it wasn't any big deal.

Archie wondered why he hadn't thought of Boggs as a cook earlier. With the man's wide girth and the amount of belching he performed in a day's time, it was easy to assume that he should have some inkling of how to fix basic meals. If the pleasant scent was any indication that it was true, Archie intended to give the man the position immediately as he had no intention of cooking ever again if he could get out of it.

A scream ripped through the air, surprising Archie and Harper so that they both jumped. Another scream followed the first, and the two tore out of the map room to find the source.

The voice was feminine, and as there was only one place any woman would be on the ship, they headed toward the hold. Archie tripped on the last step, and landed against the old Indian chief, who took a step back and began speaking quickly in his language as if Archie understood. When the old man realized that wasn't working, he gestured wildly to the beams overhead.

Another scream pierced the air, followed by more frantic gesturing. The woman was on deck. Archie and Harper did an about face and scrambled back up the steps.

The deck was vacant. The men who should have been at their stations were not there. Archie spotted Black Caesar by the stack of ropes behind the mast. He was kneeling over someone. Long, tan legs were kicking at his torso in a futile attempt to escape.

"You will stop that this instant!" Archie bellowed, unsheathing his rapier on his way past the mast. He had no intention of letting such vile happenings occur under his watch. He and his crew may very well be pirates, but he would have them act civilized. That meant no rutting around in the rope piles with unwilling females.

He placed the tip of his blade at the base of Caesar's skull. "You heard me." Anger seeped into his words as his voice dropped octaves. "If you do not stand, I will run you through and throw you overboard for the fish."

After a single, still moment, Caesar let go of the girl beneath him. The young woman scrambled away and cowered by the railing. Archie felt Harper move behind him, and then watched from the corner of his eye as the lad made a wide circle around them to check on her.

Instead of standing, Caesar lifted his head, as if gauging the courage of his new captain. The point of the rapier dug into the tattooed skin, and a small trickle of blood ran down the muscles between his shoulder blades and dribbled along his back.

Archie held fast. He was annoyed that Caesar was testing his will, and he hoped the idiot would run himself through and save him the trouble.

It seemed that was what Caesar had in mind. The tip pierced further. So entranced was Archie watching the trickle turn to a thick line, he almost didn't notice Caesar shift.

A ray of sun glinted off of a steel blade at Caesar's side, catching his attention without a second to lose. As Caesar swung his sword around, Archie met it with the rapier. The blades clashed, sending a jarring vibration down Archie's arm.

The two locked gazes over crossed steel.

"T-the Indians are part of the p-plunder," Harper spoke up from behind the mast. "No p-pirate is to steal any part of the l-loot until we reach port and divide our s-shares."

If Archie could have reached Harper, he would have kissed him. He didn't know a lot about the pirate rules, but he thought the theft of booty of over a hundred souls should be a grave offense. It seemed Caesar was taking the words into consideration as the pressure against Archie's blade lessened for a second. Then something dark and sinister moved under the surface of Caesar's eyes.

He struck Archie's blade with even greater force, shoving him backward, and then advanced as Archie teetered near the top of the steps.

He wishes to kill me, Archie thought as he caught his footing and readied his stance. He caught sight of Harper over Caesar's shoulder. He looked stunned that Caesar had no problem committing mutiny.

Well, I'm rather shocked myself, Archie thought in the last seconds before Caesar's thick blade crossed that of his rapier again. The man is insane.

Caesar seemed to be proficient in hacking away with his cutlass, as if each thrust and clash contained every bit of force that his massive body held. Archie was having a bit of trouble matching the power being plunged at him, so he relied on his years of training and decided that wearing the pirate out would be his best option of survival.

The cutlass Caesar wielded would have been perfect for slashing through bodies in close combat, but in a swordfight, it would become heavy and use more energy, the longer the battle waged on. In this fight of one on one, the rapier would reign supreme. It was a light and precise blade, and it would be deadly, if Archie could keep the correct distance away and take enough time to wear Caesar down.

He concentrated on his footwork, taking care not to trip over ropes, as he kept a careful space between himself and the man bent on murdering him. He dodged the majority of the blows, as they were slung in the general vicinity of his middle. If he were a betting man, he would have wagered that Caesar's plan was to slice him in half. Archie managed to place a few well-placed thrusts that got through the blocks, but they still missed their intended marks.

They fought down the length of the ship, and turned to come back up the other side. Out of the corner of his eye, Archie noted that they were attracting quite the crowd. Both pirates and Indians were watching on the quarterdeck, and many were crammed at the mouth of the steps that led below the deck. All were safely out of the way, but still curious to see what was happening.

"Mutiny." Archie heard the word whispered from more than one as he fought his way past the onlookers. Though none had offered to come to his aid, it was nice to know that his crew was of the same mindset as himself. Once this duel was finished—and if he still lived—he planned to have a talk to his men about Caesar's blatant insubordination, and dare any of them to make the same mistake.

Caesar is wearing down, Archie noted. His thrusts were becoming more sluggish, it was a matter of time before he would make the mistake that would win Archie the duel.

Then, it happened. Archie knew they were nearing the center of the ship, but didn't notice the chest of golden coins until it was too late. His heel caught the wooden lid, and he fell backward, landing near the barrel of silver dust. The golden medallions clinked as they rolled around the deck, sparkling in the sun.

Archie struggled to stand. As he gripped the side of the barrel, he realized his rapier lay a few feet away, out of reach. Caesar approached, an evil smile painting his black face. His pointed white teeth sparkled as bright as the medallions.

This is it, Archie thought. The end.

As Caesar raised his blade for the final blow, Archie closed his eyes. What happened next was horrifying. Instead of feeling the cutlass sever his body and end his life, Archie found his head being forced down into the barrel of silver dust. A grip like iron was wrapped in his long hair, making it impossible to move his head.

Archie tried to push at Caesar, but was shoved even further into the mound of silver. His face was covered now and there wasn't any way to avoid breathing it in. It filled his nose and his mouth, choking him as it made its way down his throat.

Adrenaline pumped through his body as he fought, trying to gag and push at Caesar at the same time. The grip on his head didn't lessen, proving Caesar still held more strength than Archie had given him credit for.

He was weakening. All of his air was gone; the blasted silver had taken its place. Just as his mind started to go numb, his ears heard a muffled *thwack*, followed by a loud sound, as if someone had dropped a cannon ball on the deck. His head freed, Archie slid off the barrel and onto the floorboards in a heap.

As he lay there, Archie's eyes opened just long enough to make out Harper. The lad stood nearby, holding an oar. His eyes looked hard and angry as he spoke, his words echoed in the darkness that took over,

"No one breaks the pirate code."

10

THE PIRATE CODE

He awoke with his lungs on fire. The pair of dark, beautiful eyes that stared down at him didn't lessen the pain, but it did manage to distract him long enough that the woman had sufficient time to press a cup to his lips before he could straighten his thoughts and hack up his lungs. He took a sip, sat straight up in the cot, and then proceeded to cough as if his life depended on it.

At least it wasn't ale. Terrible events of late had involved the presence of ale, so as the rum burnt its way down his throat, he took it as a sign that he was still among the land of the living.

"Oh good, you're awake." The relieved voice of Harper caught his ears in the short breaths between coughs.

When Archie finished and began wheezing, the cup was held out to him again.

Why not, Archie thought, taking it and downing another dreg. In a battle of fire, he hoped the rum to win over the silver.

His insides felt raw, as if the shining dust had scraped every bit of him, from his nostrils down to his belly. He looked down into the cup. If the small bits of silver floating around in the ale were any indication, he had ingested his share of the plunder. That thought sent Caesar to his mind, and he would have sprung up from the cot if it weren't for Harper's steady hands pushing him back down to sit.

"Caesar's in chains down in the hold, so there's no need to rise yet. He's not going anywhere." His friend's steady gaze was comforting. A wry smile painted Harper's lips. "Though, you might want to know that the Indians are refusing to stay down there with him, so they've taken to wandering about the ship. I can't say as I blame 'em. Even if I was dead, I wouldn't stay near him." The smile turned grim, and Harper settled on a wooden stool by the cot. Then, as if he decided he'd thought enough about Caesar, the expression left and he asked, "So, how are you feeling?"

"Not well." The sounds coming out of Archie's throat sounded raspy at best. Movement caught his eye. The young woman who first had come with the cup of rum had retreated to the corner of the room. At the sound of his voice, she looked undecided, as if she were wondering whether to offer him the cup again or to stay where she stood. Even though she was thin from being starved on the merchant ship, and her clothes hung in tatters, Archie's first impression was that she was beautiful. Long, black hair framed a face with strong, high cheekbones and a sharp chin, and then swirled like silk to her waist. Her large, almond-shaped eyes regarded him warily, not as if she was frightened, but rather wondering what he was thinking.

"She's stayed with you ever since I clobbered Caesar with the oar. I can't get her to leave, she's stubborn. Seems to think she needs to return the favor for saving her," Harper mumbled under his breath, as if he were afraid the young woman would understand him.

The young woman turned her attention from him and scowled at Harper, giving Archie the impression that she had understood something of his words, but Harper was oblivious of her hard stare, and had turned his thoughts elsewhere. "Smee says he wants to see you in the surgery whenever you've a mind to come down. He says he's too busy to come and give his report."

Nice of him to come and check on me, Archie thought, rolling his eyes.

Harper lifted one shoulder in a shrug and grinned. "He checked on you at first and said you'd live. Then Collins was wailing that the hole in his arm had gone rotten and he's been in the surgery ever since."

Archie opened his mouth to speak, but the burning in his throat kept him from it. He eyed the cup in the woman's hands. The rum wasn't helping matters, but there wasn't anything else to be had. His gaze landed on his barrel of wine in the corner of the room. He detested the idea that sprang into his mind next. If he were to open the cask now, the only thing he would find inside would be grape juice. The open air might ruin its chance of turning to wine and his investment would be lost, but it was possible that the liquid would soothe his throat so that he would at least be able to speak to his crew.

He picked up his empty tankard from the table beside the cot, handed it to Harper, and then motioned toward the barrel.

"Are you certain?" Harper asked, hand poised over the cork. At Archie's solemn nod, he pulled it free and the room was filled with the fruity smell of grapes.

The taste, however, didn't match the sweet smell. Archie forced the juice down, attempting to ignore the rotten aftertaste on his tongue, and concentrated on the soothing sensation it left down his throat.

"Much better." His voice was still hoarse, but sounded better, even to his own ears. He glanced up at Harper, who finished securing the cork back in the barrel. "Are we still on course?"

"Aye, heading with the trade winds toward the Carolinas. If luck stays with us, we'll catch up with the *Anne* yet."

Archie nodded, and then stood up. Finding himself more stable than he expected, he said, "I suppose I shouldn't make Mr. Smee wait any longer."

The woman took a couple of steps toward him, as if she planned to accompany him. "No, you should stay here," he told her, motioning to the stool where Harper sat earlier. "I will be back presently." When she sat, he turned to Harper. "Come on, let's go."

The sight of him will haunt my dreams forever, Archie decided a few moments later. Smee stood in the middle of the room in a blood covered apron, holding an arm that he had just chopped off. The appendage flopped forward at the elbow, as if greeting the two newcomers to the surgery.

Archie's stomach grumbled, threatening to push the grape juice back up. Unaware that his captain was ready to heave up the contents of his belly, Smee sat the arm down in a bucket and wiped his hands on the end of his apron, smearing even more blood about.

Archie tried not to pay attention to the arm, whose hand looked as if it were waving at him from the corner of the room, and decided to look at the previous owner of the appendage who lay moaning on a cot.

"Ach, Collins might make it. He caught a hook in his hand, put a good sized hole in it," Smee said, working the apron around his fingernails in an attempt to clean out the dried blood.

"Just his hand? You appear to have taken his entire arm," Archie said, pointing out the obvious culprit as it waved from its bucket.

"Putrefaction set in." Smee sounded the part of the surgeon, though he didn't look it, Archie decided. He wondered if the putrefaction Smee referred to was gangrene, but he didn't ask for fear of finding out even more that he didn't want to know.

"Harper says you have a report?"

"Aye, three men dead from the battle, not countin' Moreau and those on the longboat. One lad missing an eye, and Collins there, an arm, though his be from the hook, not cannon or musket shot. I wanted ye to know, so that when we reach port, they receive their part according to the code."

"Code? What code?" Archie asked, puzzled.

"The pirate code." Smee glowered as he picked up a thin, leather bound book and thrust it at Archie. "No one breaks the pirate code."

That's the second time I've heard that in the space of a few hours, Archie thought, opening the book. Whatever this code was, it seemed the only thing the pirates respected. He read the heading. "The Articles of Blackbeard, concerning all those souls aboard the *Queen Anne's Revenge* and all other ships under his watch…"

"The Articles are the code," Harper said, looking around his shoulder at the book.

"Yes, so I gather," Archie mumbled, staring at the book. Then he began to read aloud,

"The Articles of Blackbeard,
Concerning all those souls aboard the Queen Anne's
Revenge and all other ships under his watch.

Plunder to be split evenly amongst every man at port. The
captain of each ship will receive two extra shares, and the
first mate and surgeon, a share and a half. The common
treasury will receive two shares, and be held in safe
keeping and given in amounts as follows to those men
who would lose such parts of the body—
A right arm or leg, 500 pieces of gold.

A left arm or leg, 300 pieces of gold.
An eye or a finger of the right hand, 150 pieces of gold.
Any man stealing of plunder or rations, will be branded thief and receive the lashing of twenty strokes, then marooned and given a pistol with a single shot, and left for dead..."

ARCHIE BROKE OFF BEFORE READING THE NEXT SENTENCE. Mutiny to be dealt with by death, by whatever means the captain should choose.

"Delightful," he said wryly, ignoring the blatant stare of Smee as he handed the code back to him. "Might I ask where the common treasury is located?"

"In the captain's quarters, o' course," Smee grumbled. "If ye blasted fairy hasn't stolen it all by now."

"Ah." Archie had forgotten about Miss Bell. If the pixie had any clue that there were bright, shiny coins about, he would have a terrible time making her bring them back, especially since he didn't know how much the common treasury held. Thinking of the coins also brought the plunder to mind that still sat on the deck, waiting to be divided amongst the crew. If Miss Bell had pilfered any of the medallions he had last seen rolling about on the deck, he was going to have a problem on his hands, especially that he now knew what the punishment entailed for such a crime. Twenty lashes and marooning would hardly be fitting for a pixie.

Without saying another word to the irate, blood-covered man in front of him, Archie turned on his heel and left the surgery. He headed toward Moreau's former quarters in search of the common treasury and a lock for the blasted medallions, which he hoped were still accounted for.

As he opened the door to the cabin, he realized that he had made a good choice in not changing to the captain's quarters. In comparison to the cramped room in which he now stood, the map room looked like a spacious castle fit for a king.

Archie sighed and began shuffling through the clutter on the small desk by the cot. Harper had been on his heels since leaving the surgery. "I never figured Moreau to be so careless," he said, peering in from the doorway.

"Most of these papers are written in Dutch, so I believe they belonged to the good Swiss captain who took his tea with Blackbeard. I suppose Moreau hadn't gotten around to cleaning it up. Where do you suppose he put the common treasury?" Archie asked, bending over to peer under the cot. "Ah! Never mind, I think I see something here." It took a hard tug to pull the chest out from its hiding place.

"Come in and shut the door," he instructed Harper. He didn't want Miss Bell around to see the contents, should it prove indeed to be what they were searching for.

As Harper shut the door, Archie clicked the catch and the lid swung free. Hundreds of coins filled the chest. "I believe we've found it." Archie grinned up at Harper, who returned his own toothless smile.

"Aye, now what do we do with it?"

Archie spied a set of locks hanging on a nail behind the door, the keys hanging on another nail beside it.

Call it fate, he thought as he tried each lock, finding both in good working condition. One for the common treasury, and one for the plunder, both so solid that Archie began to relax. There would be no way any man or pixie would find their way into the chests without quite a bit of difficulty.

He locked the chest at his feet and shoved it under the cot as far as he could. He strung both keys on a cord and put it around his neck, hiding them from sight under the ruffle of his shirt.

With the other lock in hand and Harper on his heels, Archie made his way back up to the open deck.

Someone had gathered up the medallions and put

them back into the chest. From the look of the full coffer, it didn't appear anything had been stolen. Archie sighed in relief, catching an odd look from Harper. "No one would dare steal the plunder," he said as Archie snapped the lock shut.

"Better safe than sorry," came the mumbled reply.

"Speaking of safe, what do you plan to do with Caesar?" Harper asked, eyeing the grate over the hold that sat a short distance away.

Archie hadn't decided, though he wasn't going to say it. Several pairs of eyes were watching him now, waiting for the reply. They knew better than he, that an act of mutiny would mean certain death for the first mate. He'd known that Black Caesar wasn't popular amongst most of the crew, but the look of hope that he saw in several faces caught him off-guard.

He didn't care for the man, either. Throwing him overboard as fish bait would be a simple, easy way to rid himself of the mutinous man, but his thoughts kept rambling to the fearless pirate with the fuse-lit beard. What would Blackbeard do? Archie wondered. Surely, there was a reason he kept Black Caesar on board, though Archie had no idea what that reason was. Perhaps he should wait it out, and see what attributes his first mate possessed before he pitched him over the railing. After all, his mum once told him that patience would work through the unknown if you gave it enough time.

His eyes landed on the barrel of silver. Someone had nailed a cover over the top, either to keep the dust from floating away, or to save someone else from dying in it. Regardless, Archie was happy not to be staring at the mound of sparkling powder. Then, the epiphany struck him. The crew would expect retribution, and there was one way that would be agreeable for most parties involved. He would follow the code … part of it, anyway.

"At sunset, Caesar will receive the punishment of twenty lashes. Stealing of the plunder will not be tolerated," Archie announced in as loud a voice as his sore throat would allow. "He will be marooned on the next island we find." *Unless we come across Blackbeard first,* Archie thought. *Then he can deal with him.*

Archie left for the map room, without acknowledging any of his crew's startled faces, including Harper, who stood with his mouth agape. Back in the sanctuary of his own quarters, Archie shut the door and then slumped against it. His nerves were frazzled and his throat felt as if it had hot pokers lining it. He was going to have to drink more of that awful grape juice. He straightened and made his way toward the barrel.

Archie had forgotten the woman sitting on the cot, so when she stood, it startled him enough that he jumped, so high, in fact, that he smacked the top of his head on the ceiling.

He muttered a curse as his hands went up to hold his head.

The woman laughed. It was a pretty sound, Archie noted, through the sharp throbbing of his skull. As if she had known where he had been going, she took his tankard from the table and went to the barrel. The smell of grapes filled the map room again. She brought him the tankard filled to the brim, and pointed to the chair by the desk, which held the maps, indicating that he should sit. He did as he was instructed, and took a small sip of juice, watching as she pulled the stool closer to the table.

The fire in his throat fizzled out and the pain in his head dulled. Archie took a longer look at the young woman who sat watching him. Her eyes held an amused look, and there was a small quirk that tugged at the corner of her mouth, as if she still found the situation humorous, but was trying to be polite.

"Go ahead and smile if you must," he told her. "There hasn't been enough cheer on this ship of late."

As if she had understood him, a wide smile blossomed across her face, showing off pearly white teeth and lighting up her dark eyes. Archie's breath caught. The young woman was pretty before, but her smile made her beautiful.

"What is your name?" he asked. The smile vanished and a questioning look took its place. The language barrier was back. For a moment, he had forgotten that she didn't understand his words and was relying on his gestures. With that thought in mind, he lifted a hand to his chest and introduced himself, "My name is Archibald Jameson." Then, deciding to make things simpler, he patted his chest. "Archie." He watched as she mouthed his name, as if committing it to memory, and then he pointed to her and asked again, "What is your name?"

She chewed on her lip for a moment, and then the smile returned. "Ta-lu-lah."

Well, that's certainly a strange name, Archie thought. His eyes lit on one of the intricate designs of a flower that had been carved in the wood in the wall behind her shoulder. Then he had an idea, he put his hand to his chest. "Archibald Jameson," he said, and then waited a pause and enunciated, "Archie." Then he pointed to her.

At once her hand flew to her own chest as she said, "Ta-lu-lah."

"Lily," he said slowly as he gave her an encouraging smile.

Understanding dawned on her face as she repeated her shorter name, "Lee-lee."

"I am most pleased to make your acquaintance, Lily,"

Archie said, managing to give her a small elaborate bow from his chair, which earned him another pretty smile.

A loud knock sounded from the door. Before Archie could answer, Boggs swung his way into the room, carrying a platter of food.

"Ach, I didn't know ye had company or I'd brought ye extra," he said as he rolled up and settled his tray down in front of Archie. A small belch escaped, causing the tattooed woman on his stomach to quiver. "Beg pardon," he said, as if in afterthought.

Archie fought the urge to laugh. The young woman sitting across from him was staring at Boggs with a mixture of astonishment and intrigue, as if she had never seen such a sight before. "Boggs, if you would be so kind as to escort this young woman back to her people. Make sure they all have plenty to eat."

"Aye, Cap'n," Boggs said, giving the young woman the lowest bow he could manage without his belly getting in the way, which wasn't far at all, "This way, m'dear."

"Leelee," she answered, introducing herself with a wide grin, apparently deciding to trust Boggs.

"Oh. Boggs, you have a new station as the ship's cook," Archie announced as the man was nearly out the door.

"Ach, I figured as much," came the reply as the door shut behind them, leaving Archie to himself.

Definitely one of my better decisions, Archie thought moments later, as he finished off the last of the food on the platter. Boggs will remain as cook so long as I am captain.

The sun came through the window, casting a dull light on the table. The sun would be down soon, and one of his other decisions would have to be carried out, as he had ordered Caesar to be flogged at sundown. Archie wasn't looking forward to it, but he knew he would have to see it done if he were to keep the respect of his men.

This would be the occasion to set an example for his crew, he decided, getting up from his place at the map table. He took one of the paper-wrapped parcels from the tailor out from under the cot. Ripping the paper off, he shook out one of his red coats. The brass buttons gleamed in the dull light. To see justice served, he would need to look the part of a fearless pirate captain and this coat would give him that appearance, even though his stomach was beginning to do flip-flops.

As the sun hovered over the horizon, Archie left the map room and made his way to the quarterdeck. The deck was swamped with both crew and Indians, all come to see Caesar take his punishment. The pirates didn't look pleased, more than likely they had wished to see the bo'sun thrown overboard and done with. The Indians looked more or less confused, with the exception of Lily, who beamed a big smile at him. He refrained from smiling back, choosing instead to keep a solemn face. After all, this was a serious occasion.

Archie spotted Beckett by the grate, peering down into the hold. He was a big, tattooed bloke, the only one on board who was a near match for Black Caesar's height and strength—and he was also one of the few who didn't seem to fear the man.

"Bring him up, Beckett," Archie instructed. The man nodded, as if he had already known the task would be his. He reached down and flipped the grate back, as if it had been made of feathers instead of iron. The grate clanked as it hit the deck. "Easy, man. You don't want to stick holes in the ship and sink us," someone snickered by the railing. Whatever Beckett's muffled reply was, it was met with raucous laughter.

At least they are a jovial bunch, Archie thought, clasping his hands behind his back as he waited for them to come back up.

Caesar looked less than enthused as he shuffled to stand before the quarterdeck. But by the smirk on his face, it didn't seem that he was worried at the oncoming chain of events, though as the boatswain, he was sure to know what his punishment entailed more so than his captain as he was the one who would deal the blows under normal circumstances.

Smee arrived at Archie's elbow. He'd taken off his

surgeon's apron for the occasion, but he was still spattered with blood, some old and some fresh, making Archie wonder if Collins was still living or missing another appendage.

"Here ye go, Beckett," Smee tossed a curl of rope down to the lower deck, saving Archie the trouble of figuring out who would be the one to mete out Caesar's punishment. The cat o' nine tails looked harmless enough, a coiled rope handle with nine separate rope tails with knots tied into the ends. But wielded with force and accuracy, Archie was certain the blows from it would be a rough sentence to endure.

It made sense to choose Beckett, Archie thought, watching as the man set down the rope to strip off his shirt and stretch. The muscles in his back rippled as he tossed the shirt down and picked the rope back up. Seemingly ready enough, he looked up at Archie and waited.

"Black Caesar, you have been found guilty of thievery," Archie intoned. "For this crime, you shall receive twenty lashes."

"Well, get it over with, then," Caesar replied as easily as if he had been asked if he wished sugar in his tea. He faced the mast and lifted the shackles himself, hooking the chain on a nail overhead.

Beckett shook his head and grinned, arching a brow as

if asking if this were to be his cue to begin. Archie nodded. It was time to get this over with.

The first snap sent the nine knots splaying over the blue tattoos on Caesar's back. A *swish* echoed in the air as the rope made contact with skin.

That's one, Archie thought. Other than an instinctive flinch, no movement or sound came from Caesar. After a few seconds, nine lines of red appeared across his back.

One hundred and eighty, Archie calculated, his stomach turning at the thought. That's how many stripes he will have once this is over.

Beckett snapped the ropes again, leaving another set of marks to crisscross the first.

Two. Caesar didn't so much as flinch. Archie's mouth set in a thin line as Beckett snapped again and again.

Three. Four. Blood started to appear from the welts. Caesar had yet to make a sound. The strong, cordlike muscles in his forearms stood out as his arms tensed, the only indication he'd felt anything at all.

Five. Six. Seven. Eight. Beads of sweat popped out on Beckett's brow as he dealt one blow followed by another, and another. It was easy to see that he wasn't enjoying his role as boatswain, but he didn't dare lessen the force of each blow, lest he be accused of taking it easy on the man and be forced to take his place.

Nine. Ten. Eleven. Twelve. Caesar gripped the chain

with his hands, but still stood as straight and still as he had before the beating began.

Thirteen. Fourteen. Fifteen. Sixteen. Black Caesar's back was naught but a bloody pulp. Archie caught himself staring instead at the rivulets of sweat running between Beckett's shoulder blades.

Seventeen. Eighteen. Nineteen. Near silence, but for Beckett's heavy breathing, and the wet, slapping sounds of the rope as it met blood and raw flesh.

Archie lifted his eyes from Beckett to Caesar. The man still stood of his own accord. How, Archie had no idea, for most of his back was bloody, torn, or missing chunks of flesh. The swirling blue tattoos were gone from view. One final time the cat o' nine tails whistled through the air.

Twenty. It was done.

Archie wanted to heave a sigh of relief, but he was captain, so he stood straight and stared ahead as Caesar lifted his chain off the hook. He would see this through to the finish. Each movement the man took was deliberate, as if Caesar were choosing how to move in order to feel less pain. He turned around and faced Archie.

"Half of your punishment has been met," Archie told him, loud enough for all to hear. "You shall be marooned on the next island we find."

Caesar didn't say a word, only gave the slightest of nods and turned to go back to the hold. Smee grumbled something under his breath about his being under-appreciated and left, presumably to tend to what was left of Caesar's back.

"Never did see one make it the full twenty lashes and still walk," Harper spoke up behind Archie, "They've always passed out around ten or so and end up gettin' dragged away."

Archie didn't answer him. Most of the crew were watching, as if waiting for him to speak. Some of the Indians were looking at him, though most were keeping an eye on Caesar as he retreated.

"The plunder will be divided when we reach port, as per the code," Archie said, glaring at his crew. "Any man so foolish as to steal or despoil any of our cargo, gold or slave, will suffer the same fate as Black Caesar. I have no tolerance for idiocy." This last statement was met with a few errant chuckles and mumbled replies before he ordered, "Back to work."

The crew dispersed, some to the rigging, and some below deck. The Indians more or less stood where they were, unsure what they were to do or where they were to go. From the distance they stood from the hold, it was clear they had no intention of sharing space with Caesar, no matter how injured he may be. Under different circumstances, Archie would have put each able man with one of the pirates to learn the ship and work as part of the crew, but over half of the Indians were women and children. They needed a place to stay. Up in the rigging and sliding about on deck would never work for them. They needed their previous space returned.

The hold was the largest place in the ship, too large for a single man to occupy alone when there was an entire tribe that needed a place to stay. There was one solution that Archie could think of. He had to move Black Caesar from the hold and put him somewhere else, safely away from everyone. One place came to mind.

He crossed over to Lily. He met her brown eyes with his blue ones and smiled. He gestured to her and the people around them. "Stay here for now." He motioned toward the deck. Her black hair swung around her shoulders as she nodded. Understanding showed in her face as she turned and said something to her people that Archie didn't understand. As she spoke, all of the Indians banded together in one place. As if they were expecting to be there awhile, the children sat down on the deck and waited quietly.

"Thank you," he told Lily, before he turned to go. "I will return soon."

Archie went to the captain's quarters and retrieved the common treasury, taking it back to the map room. He shoved it as far under his own cot as it would go, and looked about to make sure his deed had gone unnoticed.

As it seemed it had, he left and made his way to the hold, finding Smee and Caesar as the only occupants. Neither of them looked up as he approached. Caesar sat on a stool, his head bent down. Smee stood behind him, placing strips of dry cloth on his back. The fabric immediately spotted red, causing Smee to scowl. The blood had only started to slow from the appearance of the pile of drenched rags at Smee's feet.

"Beckett has a strong hand, that be sure," Smee mumbled, sticking another cloth on before glancing over his spectacles at Archie. "He left no spot untouched."

Caesar chose this moment to look up, too. No emotion showed on his face at all.

"You will be moving from here to another set of quarters. The Indians refuse to stay down here with you, and I cannot blame them a whit." Archie frowned.

"Aye, where have ye a mind to take 'im?" Smee asked.

"Moreau's quarters."

Both sets of eyes widened at that, though they both nodded when the logic of it set in their minds. The captain's quarters were small, out of the way, and currently not in use. It was the perfect place for a solitary prisoner.

Caesar slowly stood. The chains around his ankles and wrists clanked.

Archie walked up to him and stared into his black eyes.

"You owe me your life. Cause me trouble in any way and I will slit your throat and throw you overboard while you sleep; make no mistake," he threatened in a low, deadly voice. Something akin to respect passed under the surface of Caesar's black eyes, and then left as suddenly as it had come.

"Aye." It was simple, but it was acknowledgment and progress of a sort.

It's a step forward so I'll take it, Archie thought, following the two of them from the hold.

They attracted quite a bit of attention on their trek from across the ship as more than one pirate stopped what he was doing to turn and gawk at them as they walked by, though none was so brave to ask why Caesar was moving from the hold, leaving blood to spatter the lower deck with each step he took.

Once he was certain that Caesar had no way of escape, Archie left the two and made his way back up to the deck.

Lily was leaning against the railing. When she spotted him, she stood and walked toward him. Archie's throat felt like it was ablaze. "Take them down. He is gone now," he said hoarsely, pointing to the grate.

He watched as she walked over and looked down into the hold. Understanding what he wanted, she nodded to him and began pulling people over and pointing down into the empty space below. They started down slowly, but then began filing down faster once they realized the threat had been removed.

Content that order had been restored, Archie gave orders to stay their course and retired back to the map room, hoping that soon they would catch up with Blackbeard.

11

ALL GOOD THINGS

Blackbeard watched the approach of the white sails with a sense of impending doom. The British ship had caught him off guard, an uncommon occurrence insomuch as the captain was concerned. He was accustomed to being several steps ahead of any game the British Navy had up their sleeves. He thought he had left Madeira in plenty of time to elude Lieutenant Maynard. He'd even left his newly captured ship behind in an effort to get a head start, but now it seemed to be all for naught and he caught himself wishing that he had waited for the *Roger* and her crew.

The sloop was bearing down on them fast, pinning the *Queen Anne's Revenge* between it and the rocky Carolina shore. The only route of escape would be to cross a shallow inlet nearby and head back out to the open sea. It would be a dangerous wager, no doubt. The better odds lay in turning to fight. One ship against another. Blackbeard was willing to fight, especially if it meant the end of the man who had made no qualms about his wish to place Blackbeard's head on the end of his bowsprit and light his beard ablaze.

"We be outgunned." Blackbeard snarled at the sight of two additional ships that came into view behind the first, British flags billowing between their sails. He didn't know how they had caught up to him so quickly.

Maynard has the devil's own wings to have beaten Moreau here, unless he's sent me mate to the bottom of the sea, he thought, shouting another order, "Hard to port!"

The *Anne* would have to take her chances in the inlet. He knew his ship wouldn't best three of the British Navy's warships. Her best odds lay in the proper pirate manner—run away and live to fight another day.

He looked over the railing of the quarterdeck. Sharp-pointed rocks jutted up from the ocean bottom. They were in treacherous, shallow waters. 'Twould be a miracle indeed if they made it across the inlet and back into open water. Cannons boomed, sending their shots whistling overhead to land in the path ahead of them as if the sloop were trying to cut them off.

The sharp crack of splintering wood echoed in his ears

the second before the *Queen Anne's Revenge* buckled, stopping so quickly that pirates went flying in every direction from the sudden loss of momentum.

Blackbeard cursed, getting back up to his feet. His men had been thrown this way and that, some were curled over cannons, their breath knocked out them and from the splashing sounds, some had landed overboard.

The *Anne* moaned and tilted a bit to her side as she began to take on water.

She's lost. The *Anne* is lost, Blackbeard thought, glancing over to the shoreline that stretched beside them a short distance away. The only way of escape would lie on that white-sanded beach, for his ship was taking on water and would soon lie in the bottom of the shallows, never to sail by his hand again.

"Release the longboats and abandon ship!" He shouted through the din of cannon fire, "Be quick and save yer skins, lads!"

He looked over to find that the first sloop had released their own longboats and were beginning to row toward them. Time was all that was keeping them alive, for once in range, the muskets would join with the rally of cannons.

"Row!" He ordered from his place in the stern of the first longboat. One cannon ball landed a short distance away, dispersing torrents of water everywhere and sending currents that rocked the boat nearly to its side. "Row, ye lazy swine!"

Cannons exploded the water around them, sending buckets of water to drench them. One shot hit its mark in the longboat behind them, sinking it. Gurgling cries echoed in Blackbeard's ears as thirty souls drowned, for only a handful of his crew could swim. He couldn't go back to save them. To do so would mean the death of them all.

Poor devils, Blackbeard grimaced, as the last cries went quiet. He pitied them now, though he knew if he or any of his remaining men were to be captured, their fate would not be so kind.

By some miracle, they reached the beach, losing only the single longboat. At Blackbeard's order, his men split into groups and scurried away. With hope and a bit of luck, a few might manage to escape.

Blackbeard and his own handful of men headed towards a knoll, high up on a ridge. As they neared the crest, he turned back to check on the progress of Maynard and his officers. A small patch of white, far out on the horizon, caught his eye. Taking his first mate's spyglass, he found the *Jolig Roger* had arrived, though the captain on her quarterdeck took him by surprise. It wasn't the man he had left in charge.

Befitted in a bright crimson overcoat, stood the navigator, staring out to sea. Blackbeard chuckled, watching as the ship started to turn.

A shout below him announced that Maynard's men had made it to the beach. Blackbeard handed the spyglass back to his mate and pulled a few fuses from his pocket, then lit them and stuck the ends in his beard.

"Run, run if ye can, in the true pirate way." He smiled, thinking of the lad who had somehow become a captain. "But should fate not be in yer favor, stand and show 'em a fight they'll ne'er forget!" And with that final thought, he turned with a pistol in one hand, a cutlass in the other, and faced them.

* * *

ARCHIE WAS OVERJOYED WHEN SMEE SPOTTED THE *ANNE'S* familiar flag, but the feeling of elation was fleeting and left the following second.

"She's scuttled," Smee announced in a queer tone of voice, before looking through his spyglass again as if to make certain he wasn't imagining things. Without another word, he handed it to Archie so he could look for himself.

Dread knotted in his belly as Archie put the glass to his eye. The *Queen Anne's Revenge* was lying on her side in the inlet, sinking, with no sign of her crew on board. Three naval sloops were sitting a short distance away, as if they were coming as close as they dared in case she were to miraculously fix her hull and sail away.

Archie trained the spyglass on the longboats. There were over a half dozen of them rowing toward shore, filled with the British Navy.

A sudden blast from the sloop nearly had Archie dropping the spyglass. He handed it back to Smee, and began assessing the situation. The sloop was making maneuvers to come after them. In a few moments, the other two would follow suit. Three fast ships against the *Jolig Roger* were not the best of odds, especially with a new captain who hadn't been captain—or pirate—for long.

We'll have to flee and hope to return and look for survivors later on, Archie thought.

As if reading his mind, Smee shook his head. "There be no helpin' them, lad. The *Queen Anne's Revenge* is lost. Best we save our own skins, else we'll be joinin' them at the bottom of the sea."

Having his own thoughts spoken aloud shored up his resolve. Archie gave his orders. "Loose the sails!"

The wind was in their favor and caught the sails. As they made their turn to sail away, Archie caught sight of a solitary figure up on the knoll. He wondered if it was Blackbeard watching them go.

The sloop followed them, keeping parallel to the shoreline. Luckily, they were able to stay just out of reach of her cannons for a while, but then the sloop started to catch up.

"We'll have to head back out to sea," Archie murmured under his breath. "They'll catch us if we stay where we are."

He spotted a dark patch out on the ocean where a storm had kicked up. There would be the best place of losing them, he decided. He gave his orders to lead them into the gale.

12

SECOND STAR TO THE LEFT

The storm had done as Archie hoped. The sloop disappeared from sight moments after they reached the rough sea, leaving the pirate ship to weather the storm alone. The waves rocked the ship and buckets of rain poured down until dusk. Then the gale moved off.

As the skies cleared and darkness fell around them, Archie prepared to plot their course. He unrolled his maps across the table, took a quick look at them, and then went up to the open deck to study the stars.

Most hands had gone below, content to indulge in yet another night of rum and fiddle music. The few left up top were silent as they looked out at the dark sea, watching should the sloop appear again.

Archie stared up at the sky and his breath caught. The sky was bright with strange silvery stars. They were beautiful, set like glistening diamonds in a velvet black sky. The only problem was that none of them was familiar to him. Archie strode every inch of the deck, back and forth, this way and that, staring up, searching for some small constellation that he might recognize.

"Regulus. Where is it?" he asked himself in awe, walking in circles, as he searched for the most familiar, brightest star he could think of. "Nothing is as it should be."

He ran back down the steps to the map room, adrenaline coursing through his veins. His hands shook as he traced the familiar patterns on the maps, the constellations he had known from boyhood. The stars above them now and the ones charted beneath his fingers were not the same.

He flipped the maps sideways and upside down. No matter how he changed them, the stars on the paper wouldn't align with the ones in the sky.

He sat down on the stool by the table and stared at the charts. The stars never change, his brain told him, they always stay the same. That's why they are used by sailors to plot their journey from one destination to the next.

But the stars aren't the same, he thought, those are different constellations. Unlike anything I've ever seen. And if these stars aren't the same, then we aren't in the same waters.

Archie wracked his brain, trying to think of any stories of other oceans where the stars hadn't been known to the sailors. He couldn't think of any. In every instance that he knew, the stars stayed constant.

A bright light at the doorway caught the corner of his eye and he looked up. Leaving a trail of golden dust in her wake, Miss Bell flew to the table and landed before him.

She smiled at him and dipped into a curtsy.

Archie managed a weak smile. "I do apologize, for I am not at my best."

A worried look furrowed across the pretty pixie's brow. Two small tinkling sounds seemed to ask, "What's wrong?"

"I am afraid we're lost. As I don't know these stars, I cannot chart us a heading." The pixie looked confused for a moment, so he added, "I do not know the way back."

Understanding blossomed across her face and she smiled, jumping up from the table to hover above it, tiny wings whirring so quickly that he couldn't see anything of them. She began gesturing with her hands as if she wanted him to get up from the stool.

Come on. Follow me, she seemed to say. *I know the way back.*

When Archie stood, the pixie flew up the steps. The young captain had to run to keep her in sight. Once upon the deck again, he found her hovering over the quarterdeck. When he reached her, she began pointing with her tiny arm up into the sky.

Archie turned to look up at the stars. There seemed to be two stars in the vicinity that Miss Bell was pointing.

"I am sorry, I don't understand. Am I to follow these stars?"

The pixie flew in front of his face, shaking her head. *No.* She lifted a tiny finger in front of his nose.

"I'm to follow only one of them?"

She gave him a definite nod and a pleased smile in answer.

"Which star?" Archie asked, staring back up at the two of them. They were brighter than all of the others. The first reminded him of the North Star, and hadn't the pixie been there to instruct him, that one would have been the one he would have chosen, more for the sake of familiarity than anything else. The other star shone as bright as the first, and seemed to pulsate, as if it were full of energy.

Miss Bell moved to fly beside his face, pointing to the second star.

"Aye, I see it now. We are to follow that star, you say?" He smiled as she nodded. "Very well, I shall chart our course."

She appears to have been in this strange place before, which is more than I can say. It might be wise to trust her judgment, Archie thought.

A streak of golden dust lined the quarterdeck as the pixie disappeared from sight, apparently finished with her good deed and off to find her own mischief.

Beckett approached the quarterdeck. He didn't act as if he had seen the pixie or noticed anything amiss in the sky, though he looked up to the sails. "A good wind is stirring. What be our heading, Cap'n?"

Archie took out his compass and watched the needle jump from one point to the next as if there were no true direction. His mind made up, he glanced back up at the sky one more time. The pulsing silver light seemed to be welcoming them, inviting him to follow it.

"The second star to the left and straight on 'til morning."

* * *

He spent the better part of the night on the deck, charting the new constellations. It was painstaking work, but he kept at it. After all, once they made it back to the Carolinas, he would have an intricate map of strange, new stars that no one had ever seen before.

Part of a map, Archie decided a few hours later, putting his quill down in the inkpot. He frowned at the sky. As the night wore on, the stars had shifted as he tried to capture their location. Some hovered over the horizon and some had disappeared. The ocean had turned black with odd patches of grey, as if the clouds had fallen down into the water. Archie leaned over the railing to take a better look. Bits of silver were down there, as if the stars had moved below them, too. By the looks of the ocean, it seemed as if the *Jolig Roger* were sailing through the sky itself.

Archie had put Beckett at the ship's wheel to steer toward the star they were following, and then he ordered Harper up into the crow's nest to keep watch, should something go awry.

Giving up on his chart, he approached Beckett. "How goes it?"

"The star's moved, though it seems we be getting closer." Beckett shrugged, and then his hand came up to the back of his head, though his eyes never left the star as if he feared it wouldn't be there when he looked back up, "Me neck has a terrible crick in it."

"Here, I will take over," Archie said, relieving Beckett of the wheel. "Go below and get some rest."

"Aye, Cap'n." Beckett heaved in relief, rubbing the sore muscles in his neck as he relinquished the wheel. "Give me a yell should ye be needin' me again."

"I shall." Archie smiled, keeping his eyes on the star. "Off with you, Beckett."

The ship sailed through the night, and though Archie's

neck ached, he never took his eyes off that single, pulsing, silver star. Hours went by until the star was so big that it sat in front of the ship like a giant silver orb. The light was so bright that he was having trouble keeping his eyes open.

Well, now what? Do I continue to sail us through it? He wondered.

The star pulsed. Instinct took over and Archie shut his eyes against the light. Then, the ship shuddered and lurched, making terrible crunching sounds, as if it were attempting to sail through a field of rocks.

The first thing Archie discovered when he opened his eyes, was that daylight had come. The next thing he realized, was that he was lying on the deck, with his head propped up against the railing. He lay there for a moment, taking inventory of his body. He seemed to be unharmed, so he took in the scene around him. The few hands on deck seemed to be in the same state as he. A couple were sitting up, looking befuddled, while the rest were sprawled out wherever they had last stood. Fear knotted in his gut when he remembered Harper.

Reluctantly, he tilted his head up to look up the mast, fearing the worst and expecting to find the rigging empty.

One tattooed forearm stuck out the top of the mainsail. As he watched, the arm moved, and Harper's head popped up. A string of curses rang through the air next, and Archie relaxed.

As he let out the breath he had been holding, it coalesced in front of his mouth in a frosty, white mist.

It was cold. As in dead-of-winter, in the middle of a blizzard, cold. Shivering, he sat up. Crunching sounds behind him caught his attention next. Turning, he spotted icebergs everywhere.

"All hands on deck!" he yelled, jumping up to grab the wheel, which had been turning aimlessly to and fro. Pirates came scrambling from below deck. They were still disoriented, and the sight of the ice didn't help matters.

"We be in the Arctic," he heard one say. "How did that happen? Last I closed me eyes, we sailed the Carolinas."

How, indeed, Archie thought, steering clear of one large iceberg. *Miss Bell has not shown us the way back to the Carolinas.* "Every man to his station," he ordered. "Best we be ready for whatever we find." He nodded to Harper, up in the mast, while addressing those below, "Slow us down, lads, take in the sails."

The crushing sounds of the ice became louder and the ship groaned as it pushed through the frigid sea. Carefully, Archie navigated the ship away from the boulders and into clearer water. Once it seemed they weren't going to hit anything else, he sighed in relief.

"Well, this were warm a minute ago, but now it be as

cold as ice," Boggs announced, kicking open the door to the stairway. In his hands, and balanced on his belly, was a wooden tray with a bowl of soup. The dark-haired woman on his stomach seemed to be trying to do her part as the tray sat precariously atop her tattooed head, bobbing back and forth on its way toward Archie. "Here ye be, Cap'n. Didn't figure ye had time to eat, so's I brought it up. Where on this world are we, might I ask?"

"I have not the slightest idea, Boggs," Archie said, watching as the round pirate rolled up to the quarterdeck and set down his tray.

"It be cold enough to freeze the balls off a brass monkey," the cook grumbled, gooseflesh mottling his bare torso.

As if in answer to Boggs's assessment of the weather, one of the brass fittings holding the cannonballs contracted and a single cannonball shot upward in the air. Luckily, it landed in the middle of a coil of ropes, which softened its landing.

We have to get out of here, Archie frowned. Loose cannonballs rolling about the ship would not make for a happy occasion, especially if one were to knock a hole in the deck or smack one of his crew in the head, for he needed his ship and his crew whole, even though he suspected some of them had naught but air in their heads.

Ignoring the sloshing bowl of soup at his feet, Archie

concentrated on the sky ahead of them. On their starboard side, the water looked clearer and the sun was shining. It at least gave him the impression of warmth. The port side, however, looked even more dangerous than the water they were in now, with towering, sharp spikes of ice that rose up from the blackest waters he had ever seen. He turned the wheel toward starboard and held his breath, hoping that he had chosen well.

Slowly, the *Roger* inched toward clearer water. After what seemed an eternity, the crunching noises were replaced with the soft sounds of water splashing against the hull. The temperature warmed, as if they had moved from one season straight into another. The sudden change of winter to summer seemed to make the crew happier, though most of them were muttering under their breath about magic and enchanted waters.

Suspicious lot, Archie smirked.

A few of the Indians came up from the hold and were looking over the railings. Lily walked toward him. The wind blew her hair over her shoulders. "So where are we?" she asked. The words were still in her strange language, but he understood every word. He looked at her in astonishment.

Thinking that he hadn't understood anything she had said, she gestured around them and lifted her hands up in a questioning shrug. "Where are we?" she repeated.

"I do not know, but it seems to be a strange place, indeed," he answered quietly, watching as her brown eyes widened. Then he turned his attention to his crew, who had noticed something amiss with the young woman who stood on the quarterdeck.

"Drop the anchor, lads! Let's sit here for a bit and gather our wits about us, and enjoy this warm spot we've found. What say you?"

"Aye!" The answer was unanimous. Being as Boggs had been spotted bringing the soup up moments before, the crew was more than ready to pitch an anchor in the water and go below for a bite to eat. The captain and his guest were forgotten and left to themselves on the quarterdeck.

"Are you all right?" Archie asked Lily gently. The girl hadn't so much as moved since she realized that there seemed to no longer be a language barrier.

"Yes," she said, though she didn't sound so sure.

"Would you like something to eat?" he asked, eyeballing the cold, sloshing bowl of soup with a look of distaste. The majority of it was splattered on the deck. "Perhaps something a bit less… mobile?"

She laughed and it was music to his ears. He looked up from the soup to see her face creased in a smile. "No, thank you. I'm not hungry. Do you have any idea of where we might be? This place feels… strange."

"I truly do not know and I must agree, strange is a

most fitting word for this place," Archie said, peering at the ocean over her shoulder to make sure the ice was still a comfortable distance away. As it appeared they were safe, he turned his gaze back to the girl in front of him. It seemed she was doing the same thing as he, for she was watching something over his own shoulder. She glanced back to him.

"What will happen to us when you reach your destination?" Her brown eyes looked at him with no sign of fear. She sought the truth, and from her direct stare, Archie was certain that she would know if he told her otherwise.

"You were taken as plunder and will be sold when we reach port." He hated the sound of those words as soon as they left his lips. They were blunt, sharp things and though they were the truth, he detested saying them, so he added a heartfelt apology in hopes of softening the truth, "I am sorry, Lily."

"I will wish that we never reach port, then." Her smile caught him off guard. It was not the reaction he had expected. "I also wish to thank you for my name."

"Ah. Well…" He shifted from foot to foot. He didn't want to admit the reason for the shorter nickname was that he had thought the name strange and ill-fitting.

"Lily is much prettier than Jumping Water," she said, crinkling her nose in distaste.

I agree with you, he thought. Such a name put him in

the mind of dangerous waterfalls and sharp-toothed beasties that leapt up out of the water to swallow ships whole. But instead of voicing his imaginative thoughts, he gave her a warm smile. "At first, I wished to call you Tiger Lily, truth be known, for you are as beautiful as a flower and as brave as a tigress."

Her smile widened and lit up her eyes, then her expression grew serious. "I would be pleased if you were to call me Tiger Lily. Maybe it will keep me brave when we reach your port."

Before he could answer, he spotted Smee, who had come up to the deck with his spyglass. "Yer blasted pixie is flying about again. Best she keeps her thievin' hands to herself, or else." The old man made a slicing motion under his chin with one gnarled finger, as if warning he would slit Miss Bell's throat should the opportunity once again arise.

"Where was she?" Archie asked, ignoring Smee's scowl.

"She flew in front of me, just as I was headin' up the steps."

Being as the staircase led to the deck, it was easy to assume Miss Bell was somewhere close by. "Very well. I shall keep an eye out for her," he told Smee, who harrumphed and stalked to the opposite end of the ship, spyglass in hand.

"What is a pixie?" Tiger Lily asked, "Is it something like a water spirit?"

A sudden splash of golden dust landed between them. Archie smiled and held his palm out flat. A second later, Miss Bell landed upon his fingertips and stood there, smiling at them.

"This," Archie said, returning the smile, "is a pixie. Her name is Miss Bell."

"Oh my," Tiger Lily said, leaning forward to get a better look at the tiny being who stood on his hand. "I've never seen anything like her before. She is beautiful."

At the compliment, Miss Bell preened at her topknot of blonde tendrils and batted her big eyes.

She's a bit vain, Archie thought, amused. The fairy was busy showing off, walking from his wrist to his fingertips, leaving tiny puffs of golden dust on his skin with every step. Then, she stopped in midstep as if she had heard something, a look of panic crossing her face. Then, she flew off his palm, disappearing across the water.

"Well, that saves me trouble," Smee sounded unusually happy as he placed his spyglass to his eye to look in the direction where she had vanished.

Archie and Tiger Lily walked down from the quarter-deck. Archie planned to escort her below and find them both something to eat, when Smee announced, "There be land o'er that way where yer pixie went. I see a wee bit o' it, but it be an island, nonetheless."

Instead of continuing below deck, Archie strode to Smee and snatched his spyglass. True enough, a small streak of vibrant green sat on the horizon. "We will make preparations to sail," he told Smee. One look at Tiger Lily's saddened face made him add, "But best we use caution, lest we end up at the British Navy's mercy once again." He handed the spyglass back. "Keep a weather eye for anyone on that island. I'll go below and fetch the lads."

"Aye," the old man nodded and set back to his task.

Archie ordered the pirates to their stations and soon the anchor was hauled up and the sails loosed. As the ship came closer to the island, the water below them began to change color. The dark, inky black lightened to the clearest, sparkling shade of blue that Archie had ever seen.

"I don't see nary a soul," Smee grumbled, "Not even a flag, or a ship near her shore."

"It's one side of her, Mr. Smee. Her port may well be in another place," Archie said, trying not to let the hope seep into his voice. While part of him dreaded finding a port, for he had no intention of letting Tiger Lily be sold as a slave, another part wished to know where they were. If it came to it, he would use his own share of the plunder to ensure her safe return.

It is possible none of us will return, he thought,

looking down into the water. As they came nearer the island, the blue in the water sparkled and glistened, as if the ocean were lined with diamonds.

They sailed close enough to the shore that Archie could make out the shapes of birds in the trees without the use of the spyglass, but saw nothing that spoke of anyone inhabiting that section of the island.

This could be the place we leave Black Caesar. He frowned, thinking of the man below deck. As if reading his mind, Tiger Lily stepped closer to him, so close that her shoulder brushed against his coat.

"I hope there is no port in this place," she murmured so low that he barely heard her.

"All will be well. There is nothing to fear," he told her, taking her hand in his.

They were sailing by a small inlet in the shape of a semi-circle. A large, flat rock sat in the center. It was sloped on one side, with one edge that dipped toward the ocean.

Archie's first thought was that a dolphin was lying there, sunning itself. He'd never seen such a creature before, but he had seen pictures of them. The wide tail, which was fanning the surface of the water, seemed that it could belong to such an animal, though he'd never read of one actually choosing to be out of the water.

"Look!" Harper shouted from above them in the rigging, pointing at the rock.

The tail stopped its splashing as its owner sat up. A woman with long, black hair watched them with a look of curiosity painted on her face. Her hair was lying in wet tendrils down her shoulders to her bare waist. But that was as far as she looked human, for there the tail began. Half woman, half fish, Archie thought, dumbstruck, we've found a mermaid!

The pirates seemed to realize that in the same instant as he, only they were more verbal with their thoughts. A clamor rose up, with half of them demanding to sail to the rock, and the other half, being the more suspicious sort, demanding to leave it immediately for the fear of bad luck.

Before Archie knew it, one of the idiots fired a cannon. It whistled through the air and missed its intended mark, landing a distance beyond the rock. A giant splash soaked the mermaid, whose face took on the look of fear a split second before she jumped back into the safety of the sea, disappearing from sight.

"Fool! No man is to fire any weapon without my order." Archie glowered at the guilty man holding the linstock. He walked down the steps from the quarterdeck and stalked toward the pirate, unsheathing his rapier along the way. He pointed the tip at the man's throat. "If the British Navy heard your blast and lie in wait, you will breathe no more, I will promise you that."

The man, who was one of the newest Spaniard recruits, gulped, and stepped away, nodding.

"Any man who disobeys me, I will throw overboard without a word. Consider this your last warning." He gave them the full effect of the cold rage burning in his blue eyes. He returned to his place on the quarterdeck, and glanced at the rock. The mermaid had come back to the surface and was watching them from a safe distance. Even though Archie knew they wished something to be done, the pirates remained silent and still, waiting for his orders. It was the first time Archie felt like a pirate captain. He smiled.

"Sail on, lads. Let us see what other mysteries this island holds."

13

MERMAIDS AND NEVERLINGS

*B*oggs patted the top of his stomach as if he feared he was starting to lose some of his wide girth. "We be runnin' low on food," he informed Archie.

"The men be getting antsy to set foot on dry land, port or no," Beckett chipped in as he ducked into the room, shutting the door to the map room behind him.

"My people want to know what you plan to do with us," Tiger Lily's voice was just as determined as the other two as she crossed her arms over her chest and glowered at him.

Archie fought the urge to beat his head against the table in frustration. Apparently, the three of them had decided an ambush was in order. There was no way that all of them had arrived in his quarters at the same time by coincidence. The only one who hadn't made his demands known was the old man who sat in the corner, whittling on a piece of wood.

"And what of you?" Archie asked Smee, who stopped carving and peered over his spectacles. "What is it that you want?"

"Same as them," he replied, shrugging as he went back to scattering wood chips and shavings on the floor.

A quiet sigh escaped Archie. He'd expected them to come earlier, truth be told. It had taken days to sail around the island, and no port had been found. That they had waited until the *Jolig Roger* came back full circle to the mermaid's inlet was a bit of a surprise to him, and he hadn't anticipated that they would all come at him at once. His gaze rested on Tiger Lily, whose bottom lip jutted out. Had he been a betting man, he would have placed odds that the woman had put the other three up to this ambush.

"We will disembark and search for a means to restore our rations." He gave a pointed look to both Beckett and Boggs. "Best you tell the lads to make preparations. In the morning, we row ashore."

The boatswain and the cook left in happier spirits, followed by Smee, who stood up, flipping the rest of his shavings to the floor. He whistled an upbeat tune as he went out the door.

The only one of the four intruders who hadn't left, still stood in the same place as before, refusing to budge until he told her what she wanted to know.

"Lily," he said softly. He stood to come closer. "I cannot tell you what you wish to hear. If we find anyone on the island tomorrow, the code will be followed."

"And if we find no one?" A glimmer of a wish sparkled in her eyes.

Archie understood, for if the island was truly uninhabited, the Indian tribe could not be sold as the crew's plunder. Still, he didn't want to give her false hope. "If we find no one, we stock the ship as best we can, leave the island, and search for a port elsewhere."

She nodded, not meeting his gaze. "I thought you would say that." She hesitated then, just long enough that Archie spied the small knife hidden beneath her arm. That pause gave him the time he needed, for when she raised it up toward his throat, he blocked her, managing to trap her wrist. His momentum thrust her against the wall, pinning her with his own body. There was no threat now.

Tears welled up in Tiger Lily's eyes as she dropped the knife. It clanked on the wooden floorboards. Archie's brain registered a stinging sensation in the palm that still held her wrist, but he ignored it, because the largest tears he had ever seen began to roll down her cheeks.

"I am sorry," she whispered.

Archie bent his head down and kissed her. It wasn't a possessive kiss by any means, but rather one he hoped would convey his feelings. For above all, he wished her to know what he felt for her and he hadn't the words to tell her just yet. After a couple of seconds, he felt pressure against his lips, and the kiss was returned.

Something was tickling down his sleeve, he broke the kiss and glanced at his hand. A bluish liquid was smeared around Tiger Lily's wrist and was running in dribbles down his own wrist to spatter on the lace cuffs of his shirt.

It took a moment for the shock to set in. His first thought was that the strange fluid came from Tiger Lily. Then, he turned loose of her wrist and the stinging in his palm brought him to reality. Her knife had somehow scored the meaty part of his palm, and that blue color was coming from the wound, where blood should have been.

He realized then it *was* his blood. Stumbling backward, he began searching for his stool. He was lightheaded and knew that if he didn't sit soon, he was going to land flat-out on his face. He squeezed his eyes shut. Perhaps if he didn't look at it, it would go away and be plain, regular-colored blood when he opened his eyes.

He heard a ripping sound, followed by pressure against his palm. "You hold this tight. I will be right back. I'm going to get the doctor," Tiger Lily said.

He managed a weak nod and listened to her footsteps run to the doorway. The door opened, and it became quiet.

What causes blue blood? Archie wondered, refusing to open his eyes and look at his hand. He tightened the grip on the rag Tiger Lily had given him. It squished wet between his fingers and his stomach roiled, threatening to give up its contents. The last time he had seen his blood, it was a perfectly normal red color. And it hadn't been that long ago, he reasoned, trying to ignore the moaning of his belly. When Smee shanghaied me, I had scrapes and scratches aplenty from the pier. Nothing was out of the ordinary then. And all the paper cuts from the print shop? It was red then, too. What has happened to me that my blood has turned blue?

Footsteps returned, though he didn't open his eyes to see who it was. If someone wanted to kill me, now would be the prime time to do it, he thought.

"Let's see what ye have there, lad." Smee's voice sounded curious. He felt the rag being pulled from his hand followed by the sound of a sharp intake of breath. "Saint Brendan," Smee muttered.

There he goes again. Invoking help from the patron saint of whales. Pray tell, what do whales have to do with anything?

"Needs stitches." At the sound of Smee's voice, Archie

chose to open his eyes, though he kept them on the old man's fuzzy white sideburns. "Here." Smee thrust a bottle into his free hand. "Looks ye might need it afore I get to workin' with me needles."

Archie took a long drink, feeling the rum run like fire down his throat. His senses began to numb and he decided to look down and immediately wished he hadn't.

Smee's white head was bent over the hand lying in his lap, but it wasn't the hand he was inspecting. He held one lethal-looking needle between his thumb and forefinger, poking it with another finger to test its sharpness. Apparently it passed the rest, as the finger disappeared into his mouth to suck off a drop of red blood, then popped back out as Smee threaded the needle and readied to sew him up.

"Take another drink, lad, then pass me the bottle," he instructed.

Archie did as he was told, and began wincing at the thought of rum being spilled on his palm to clean the wound. It was going to burn like fire.

"What are ye making such faces about? I haven't even started yet." Smee scowled at him before putting the bottle to his own lips. He gulped down half the bottle, and then set it on the table, his eyes watering as he peered at Archie over his spectacles. "Now ye can cringe, lad. I be ready now."

Deciding that not watching was in his best interest, Archie closed his eyes and tried not to pay attention at the jabs of the needle and the queer feeling as the thread passed through his flesh. A hand came from behind him to squeeze his shoulder in reassurance.

"I am sorry," Tiger Lily said softly. "But I couldn't think of any other way that you would let us go."

Smee harrumphed and grumbled something under his breath. The only word that Archie caught was "women."

A short time passed, before the old man said in a conversational tone. "Knew a man once, I did. He had a bit of silver dust like that on our deck, used to put it in his tea. Said it helped his bowels. Kept him regular, though it turned 'em an odd blue color. Since ye breathed it, looks like yer bowels be safe enough..." he broke off as he dropped the needle, muttering a curse under his breath. The tugging commenced a few seconds later, proving the needle had been located and restrung. A moist, warm breath of air blew against the new stitching as if Smee were inspecting his work before a fresh bandage was wrapped around his hand. "'Tis done, lad. Take care not to pull me stitches free. I'm off to have a drink with the lads."

With that, Archie opened his eyes in time to see Smee walk out the door. He sighed, daring to look down. His hand was swathed in a clean bandage with no trace of strange blood to be seen.

He sighed in relief, feeling better. "If I never see another drop of my own blood, I will be a happy man for the rest of my days," he said, looking at Tiger Lily as she came around, pulling up a stool to sit opposite him. "Remind me that I need to maroon Caesar as early as possible," he told her solemnly.

"I won't forget," she smiled.

"Now," Archie said, prepared to handle the problem at hand, so long as the young woman in front of him hadn't rearmed herself. He took a quick look at her hands, which lay empty and folded in her lap, before he continued, "I wish to ask you why you thought it necessary to kill me to gain your freedom."

The smile left and a frown took its place as she stared at her hands. "My people are from the mountains. We are accustomed to living on land. This new life on this ship has been hard for us, especially our old ones, though the rest of us aren't faring well, either. When I saw the mountains on the island, I knew we could live there if you would let us go free." The words had been coming quickly to this point, but she stopped as she looked up, gazing into his eyes. "I wouldn't have killed you, I only planned to threaten you with the knife until you promised to let us go. If there is anyone on the island, what will become of us?"

The emotion playing in her eyes tugged at his heart.

He leaned forward so that his forehead rested against hers. "I promise you that should we find anyone on that island, you have nothing to fear. Even if it takes the trade of my soul, I will always keep you safe."

* * *

THE MORNING CAME WITH A MIST THAT ROSE UP FROM THE water, obscuring the island, though Archie knew they were close as the mermaid's rock was within sight. Three longboats were lowered into the water, and he took his place in the first at the stern. He ordered any man able to hunt (or fight if the need arose) into a longboat, leaving a handful on board the *Jolig Roger* to keep watch and fish.

Archie glanced back at the ship. In a strange moment of pity, he'd ordered Black Caesar to be tied to the mast in order for the man to get a bit of fresh air. The former boatswain stood there, shackled. His face was emotionless as he stared straight ahead at the mist in front of them.

I hope he causes no trouble while we are gone, Archie frowned. Archie's goal was a simple one, restock the ship as best they could, pray not to encounter anyone, and leave Caesar on the island. After he had talked with Tiger Lily for the better part of the night, he hoped the island to be vacant, though he knew that wouldn't fix all of his problems. Something would have to be done with the tribe of Indians—something that would both protect them and satisfy the crew, no small feat by any means. He didn't have a clue how he was going to accomplish that. However, if they were lucky, they would at least be short one mutinous, evil boatswain once the trip was over and finished.

The mist lifted as they passed by the mermaid's rock. No sign of the dark-haired beauty was anywhere to be seen. Stay gone, Archie thought, do not show up while we are here. He could imagine one of the remaining nitwits on board blasting another cannon as they bobbed along in its path.

He glanced back at the ship. It was shrouded in mist. One figure was barely visible, up in the rigging.

* * *

HARPER WATCHED AS THE FOG ENVELOPED THE BOATS AND listened as the final whispering splashes from the oars ceased. Jameson and the others were gone to the island and the *Roger* was his to command in their absence.

He climbed down the rigging, took a deep breath, and turned to the crew. Everyone was keeping a wide berth of the man tied to the mast. Couldn't blame them, really, as they all knew how evil Black Caesar was. Harper ran his tongue along the rough edges of his gums, the places where his front teeth had once been. He knew first hand of the bo'sun's black heart.

Pirates were pressed against the railings, safely away and mingling with the Indians, crammed in every possible corner. As he watched, the women and children scooted back below the deck, freeing up a few spots.

"Best we do our part," he told the crew, "If the cap'n comes back and we've not caught a single fish, he won't be happy."

Harper wasn't sure if it was fear or respect of Jameson that put the men to action, but whatever it was, he was relieved. They had begun to ready their nets, when a soft, sultry voice began to sing.

"My love sails on the dark, black sea. While I watch from below..." the words were haunting, echoing through the mist.

The voice is beautiful. I haven't heard anything like it since I last heard my Mary sing, Harper thought, as his hand went to touch his tattooed forearm. A soothing sensation clouded his mind as if he were being sung a lullaby.

"My love sails on the dark, black sea. While I watch from below..."

A small part of Harper's brain registered the lack of movement on the deck, as if everyone else were as entranced as he. He felt as if his insides were made of butter, but that didn't matter. As long as the song continued, he would stay where he stood to listen.

"As time goes by, I wait for my love. My love sails on the dark, black sea." A light splash blended with the words and was followed by a smattering of cool droplets that sprinkled across his face.

A beautiful woman, unlike anyone Harper had ever seen, appeared, sitting on the railing. Her hair hung in wet, dark tendrils, framing a perfect, heart-shaped face. Streams of water ran down to her bare waist, as if she had just sprung from the sea, but where her legs should have been, a scaly, grey tail, much like that of a fish, curled to the deck instead.

A mermaid. But not like the evil things in the songs that I know. She's too beautiful to be a terrible creature. She is the most beautiful woman I have ever seen. Harper's hand fell from his forearm as the last bits of Mary left his mind. There was no one else for him in this world. None, but this one who sat before him.

The tail was starting to fade, much as if it had been a dream that hadn't truly been there, and two slender legs took its place.

"One day he shall return, for that I will wait. My love sails on the dark, black sea..." Harper never blinked as he watched her rise and walk about on deck, taking time to look into each man's eyes as she passed.

"Fools." The word stuck out in the middle of the song and shook Harper out of his trance just enough that he noticed Caesar baring his pointed teeth at the woman who had walked toward him. "Have ye no sense enough not to listen to her words? She's bewitched you all."

"My love has returned, has returned to me..." Caesar was struggling, as if he were trying to break free of his bindings to attack the woman. From the angle in which she had stopped, Harper could see the curious expression on her face, as if she were trying to figure out what was wrong with the man before her.

Good luck with that, Harper thought as the woman began singing the song from its beginning. She stood close to Caesar, as if singing it only to him, though Harper felt the soothing effects start all over again and his thoughts were washed away.

"My love sails on the dark, black sea. While I watch from below,

As time goes by, I wait for my love. My love sails on the dark, black sea..."

Caesar's words cut through the muddle in his mind, sounding frantic as the woman circled the mast, continuing her song. "She'll kill us all. Wake up, you fools! Can't you see through her?"

"One day he shall return, for that I will wait. My love sails on the dark, black sea..." The woman stroked

Caesar's muscled shoulder, tracing a scabbed welt from the flogging, and then drew her fingers along the lines of ropes that held him fast.

"My love has returned, has returned to me…"

Harper watched as the woman ripped the ropes free as if they had been only string. She sprang up from the deck and wrapped her arms and legs around Caesar's body, as if in an effort to cover it with her own. The scream that came from the boatswain etched itself on Harper's mind, even in its foggy state. In the next instant, the mermaid leapt from the deck with Caesar still in her clutches, and disappeared over the railing, the ending to her song echoing with the splash.

"My love has returned, has returned to me…

And now he will die in the dark, black sea."

* * *

PIRATES AREN'T A HUNTING LOT, ARCHIE DECIDED, disgustedly staring into the blank eyes of a deer. There was one other, much like the one lying at his feet with its tongue protruding, in the boat behind them. Add three squirrels and a barrel of fresh fruit, and that made up the cache of this hunt. It was pitiful. The dreaded, fearless band of pirates under his watch were complete pansies when it came to searching for food. He'd watched several of them run after game, screaming as if they held hopes that it would surrender should they manage to frighten it sufficiently. The ones smart enough to stay silent were poor shots, missing nearly everything they aimed their pistols at. And some of the game they had seen was slow, moving nearly at human speed through the forest. How they'd managed to shoot not one, but two, deer was beyond his comprehension. It must have been luck, he decided, though he knew if he said those particular words to Smee upon their return, the old man would insist that it had been a blessing from Saint Brendan, keeper of whales. Archie sighed. He was willing to ask Smee's saint for help at this point, however pointless it might seem.

If we never find another port, we're doomed, he thought. We'll starve. I hope Harper and the others had better luck fishing, else our stomachs will be empty before we leave sight of this island. His gaze rested on the *Jolig Roger*, a short distance away. He concentrated on the sides of the ship, looking for any sign that the skeleton crew he'd left aboard was indeed doing their part in trying to obtain fish. No nets were to be seen.

He scowled. Laziness would not be tolerated under his watch. If he found they had done nothing but lounge around on the deck, while he had to go trouncing around after the rest of the non-hunting dingbat crew, they were going to pay—dearly. He squinted up at the railings, but didn't see anyone. He raised his eyes to the rigging, but found it empty, too. That was strange. Though he had left Harper in charge, he still expected to find the lad up by the mast, watching for their return. So far as he could see, there was no one near and he didn't hear anything but the sounds of the ocean as they came alongside the ship.

With fear roiling through his gut, he grabbed the rope and climbed up to the silent deck. The sight that greeted him made him feel worse. He was staring into the barrel of a musket. The fact that Harper was the one holding it was the only thing that made the situation better.

Archie lifted his hand and pushed the barrel away from his face. The lad's hands shook. "What has happened?"

"A mermaid happened." Harper's dry tone implied he had better control of himself than his hands had led him to believe, so Archie took a quick look around. He found that the pirates had banded together in the middle of the ship. They were crouched, back to back, and were armed to the teeth with muskets, pistols, and cutlasses pointed in every direction.

"Only *one* mermaid?" They looked ready for an army of the fishy creatures.

"It only took one." Harper turned and pointed to the empty mast with a circle of loose ropes around its base.

"Where is Caesar?" Archie felt foolish asking the question, since it appeared he was no longer on the boat.

"She took 'im. Came aboard and bewitched us all… all but Caesar." Harper frowned as he said the words, then added, "She seemed taken with him. Next thing I knew, overboard they went."

"I suppose that saves us the trouble of marooning him." Archie shrugged and turned to watch the others that had gone with him, pull up their kills. He pulled an apple out of his coat pocket and offered it to the young woman standing nearby.

"Fruit?" Tiger Lily asked. "I thought you were going to hunt."

"It's coming up." Archie's tone sounded defensive, even to his own ears.

One dark eyebrow arched upward and she left him to peer over the railing. When she turned back, Archie caught the sarcasm in her eyes, before it made its way to her lips. "Three longboats of men to catch two deer and a handful of squirrels. One of my people could do as much in an hour. You were gone all day." She brushed past him and made her way below the deck, not impressed enough with their trip to shore to ask if they had seen anyone.

"Not the grateful sort, is she?" Harper said, watching Tiger Lily's retreating back. "You did well, Jameson. Two deer. The men haven't ever hunted so well."

Archie sighed. He should have known his crew's specialty was plunder and theft, not the honest trade of hunting. Had he thought it through beforehand, he would have taken some of the Indian men with them and left more of the crew on board to deal with the mermaid, but now wasn't the time to second-guess his decision. It was time to sail away from this place.

"Take up the anchor and loose the sails."

* * *

THE WATER HAD BEEN CLEAR OF ICE FOR THE FIRST BIT, BUT soon the sea was full of peril. Sharp peaks of icebergs rose up around them, threatening to destroy the *Jolig Roger's* hull should they come too close. For hours, Archie stayed at the helm, guiding the ship. When night came, he managed to steer them back into warmer waters. The island was no longer in sight, and he felt confident they were on their way home. He relinquished his place at the wheel to Beckett, with instructions to keep their heading and went below for some much-needed rest.

The next thing he knew, daylight was spilling through the round window above his cot and Harper's excited voice reached his ears through the floorboards, "Land, ho!"

Fully awake, Archie pulled his clothes on and shoved

his feet into his boots, and ran up the steps to the deck. The sun was bright, with not a trace of a cloud in the sky. He put his hand to his brow to shield his eyes, and looked up at Harper in the rigging.

The lad pointed ahead, where a small patch of vibrant green showed on the horizon.

"Looks familiar," Smee grumbled at him, as he came up to the quarterdeck. The old man thrust his spyglass at him and glowered. "Beckett's brought us back to the same blasted island."

"I kept the heading, sure and true," Beckett answered, crossing his muscled arms over his chest.

Archie took in Beckett's bloodshot eyes. It was clear the man had stayed up the entire night and spoke the truth, so Archie stayed silent as he lifted the spyglass and looked out at the island, hoping that Smee was mistaken.

Unfortunately, he wasn't. The same shore greeted his eyes, as well as the well-known mermaid's rock.

"The heading was kept? You are certain?" He handed the spyglass back and looked in Beckett's tired eyes.

"Aye." The answer was given without hesitation, and said with such a sense of finality that Archie was certain the man hadn't lied.

A dark shadow flew across the ship, as if something had blocked out the sun. Looking up, Archie expected to see a stray cloud, what caught his eye instead, was a boy sitting on the beam of the mainmast. He wore a green cap with a long, red feather and a tunic made of green leaves. The boy looked at Archie in a suspicious manner before he said in a curious voice, "Who are you?"

It took Archie a second to grasp that the boy wasn't a figment of his imagination, but was truly there. "I am Archibald Jameson, captain of the ship upon which you are sitting. "Who, may I ask, are you?"

"I," the boy began, before jumping to his feet to walk along the narrow beam of the mast, "am Peter." And with those last two words, he did something that amazed Archie. He jumped from the beam and landed before him on the quarterdeck, giving him a neat bow.

"Pleased to make your acquaintance, Peter." Archie returned the bow. "Might I ask how you have managed to find your way upon the mast of my ship and where are you from?"

"Oh, that's easy." The boy grinned, showing a set of small pearly white teeth. "I flew."

"You flew?"

"Mm-hmm," he said, as if bored, and then gestured in an offhanded sort of way to the island a distance away. "I'm a Neverling, of course."

"A Neverling," Archie repeated, more for the sake of trying to let his brain absorb the reality of the boy in front of him than anything else. "Where are your parents? On the island?"

The boy's hands clenched into fists at his sides. "Parents are grown-ups. There aren't any grown-ups on Neverland."

"None? Why not?"

"Because when you're on Neverland, you never grow up."

The statement had Archie imagining the island was inhabited by pygmies, though he doubted that was the case. He didn't get to ask about pygmies or anything else, because someone else's thoughts interrupted.

"Poppycock," Smee grumbled under his breath, "Everyone grows old." Archie hadn't heard the old man arrive on the quarterdeck, but he had been rather preoccupied with the arrival of Peter.

"So, there are no adults on Neverland?" Archie asked, ignoring the glowering old man beside him.

"No." Peter looked at him suspiciously. "No grown-ups have ever come to Neverland before. I'm the only one who knows the way. How did you find it?"

This is going to sound ridiculous, but then again, I am talking to a flying boy, Archie thought. "A pixie showed us the way."

"A golden pixie? About this tall?" Peter made a space between his forefinger and thumb.

"Precisely. She was here until the day we arrived, and then she flew away, looking frightened."

"She'll be punished for showing you the way here." Peter stomped his foot and set his hands on his hips, looking down at the deck with a frown on his young face. "She probably heard the blue pixies coming for her."

Archie felt somewhat guilty about the matter, so he said nothing, and folded his hands in front of him, and watched Peter. The boy must have thought he was waiting for more information, so he continued, "The gold pixies are called Tinkers and there aren't many of them. They keep the seasons in order on Neverland. The blue ones are called Royals. They are pushy. They tell the others what to do."

The scowl that followed led Archie to believe that Peter didn't think much of the blue pixies. Then, to his surprise, the boy lifted up into the air.

He truly does fly. Archie hadn't believed it until now, but there the boy was, flitting about the sails like a bird.

"How do you fly?" Archie hadn't intended to ask the question aloud. Questions kept crowding his mind at an alarming rate, one following another, before he'd had the time to ponder the previous one through.

"With pixie dust," Peter called down as he began flying in more of a haphazard manner. He darted back and forth jerkily before landing back on the deck. He glowered at

Archie. "If you hadn't gotten Tink in trouble, she'd still be here and I could fly better."

"I do apologize. I did not wish her harm." Archie felt guilty, though he didn't know what to do about it. The apology seemed sufficient for Peter because a bright smile lit up his young face.

"That's all right, that means I'll have an adventure. I'll rescue her," he announced and shot up into the air so quickly that it caused Archie to stumble backward into Smee, who muttered a variety of Irish curses. They watched the boy fly toward the island, much like a bird with a broken wing. After a few moments, he disappeared behind the dark, green mountains.

"Well, that was interesting," Archie commented, setting Smee on another rant of wild cursing. Ignoring the man behind him who was becoming angrier with each passing second, Archie lifted his voice to be heard over the din, "Reverse our heading, Mr. Beckett. Once again, we shall attempt to leave this place."

As the ship began to turn, Archie looked back at the island—a mysterious place inhabited by a strange, flying boy and pixies. While part of him wished to find an island with a port, a greater part wondered what other mysteries lay hidden, waiting to be discovered there.

14

WE BE PIRATES

He should never have taken the long way to the map room. Archie's decision to go down the steps and across the length of the ship that took him through the crew's quarters had proved disastrous. In his defense, he hadn't known that his crew would be celebrating their fourth attempt to leave the island. At least, that's what he supposed they were celebrating, though it could well have been something else, such as it being a Tuesday or the fact that Beckett had successfully tattooed an image of an apple on his right bicep. It took precious little to cause a celebration where his crew was concerned.

Archie had seen Boggs dancing, his tattooed woman swaying and jiggling as if in the throes of a seizure, while the rest of his body heaved up and down with the fiddle music. It was a sight that would forever scar his mind. Giving himself a mental shake, Archie tried to forget the wobbling mound of flesh inked into the shape of the portly, half-naked woman as the floorboards of the ship creaked and groaned with each dancing move Boggs initiated. Archie sighed. It was useless. The memory was carved into his brain for eternity.

He went into the map room and shut the door. He filled up his tankard and planted himself behind the table, ready to down yet another vile glass of grape juice. His throat had healed somewhat, but tended to become sore whenever night came. Thus far, the only thing he had found to soothe it was the juice.

He lifted it to his lips, preparing to wince at the rotten taste and discovered something—pleasant. The taste that rolled across his tongue was smooth and sweet.

How on earth did that happen? He peered down into his tankard incredulously. It hadn't been that long since he had bought it on Madeira. A few weeks? A month? It was impossible that the contents of that barrel had changed to wine so quickly. Yet, somehow, it had. And it wasn't just plain wine, either. It was the best he had ever tasted.

He was eyeing his barrel of newly discovered wine when a soft tap at the door caught his attention. He glanced up, wondering who was on the other side. His crew tended to knock so hard, he often wondered why the door hadn't flown off the hinges, but this person seemed hesitant.

"Come in."

Tiger Lily opened the door and stepped inside, offering him a warm smile. "Hello."

He returned her smile and stepped closer, taking her hand in his. "Good evening. How are you?" He lifted her hand to his lips. He had noticed that she had stayed below deck with the others the past few days. He had thought perhaps she was angry with him, and so he hadn't sought her out. He was pleased to see her now, though he wondered what brought her to him so late in the evening—in his quarters, alone.

"I wanted to speak to you."

Ah. Here it comes. There is a reason for this visit and it isn't for the pleasure of my company. Archie felt the strain at the sides of his mouth as he forced a smile and pulled out a stool for her. As she sat, Archie settled himself on the chair opposite her. "How can I be of service?" he asked.

"I have a proposition for you."

Curiosity struck and Archie's brows lifted. "You have my complete attention."

"The food is gone. Tomorrow you will have to go to the island and hunt again."

That's not news, Archie thought. Boggs had resorted to boiling the same deer bones over and over again. The last three meals had been broth. Everything else was gone. The fruit, the squirrels—everything. His stomach grumbled. "If we are at the island again in the morning, yes, we will hunt."

"The island will be there, just as it has been the past three mornings." She'd said it as a statement of fact—as if she expected the sliver of vibrant green to be there once the first rays of sun streaked the sky.

Archie stifled the urge to sigh. It was true. Each time they departed, he gave orders for a different heading and each morning, the result was the same. The island was always there to greet them once daylight came. "What do you propose?" He expected her to offer the aid of the tribe to go and hunt.

"Let us go. In exchange, my people will hunt and bring your ship what you need. Your men can't feed us all. We'll starve." Her dark eyes implored him. Archie knew she was right. The amount that they had brought back from their last escapade hadn't been sufficient for a single day with so many mouths to feed, let alone four days. His crew hadn't begun to complain as yet. Doubling their rum ration had done wonders in that regard, but the Indians hadn't fared as well. The majority of them stayed in the hold despite the fact that the threat of Black Caesar was gone, but the few who wandered up to the deck for fresh air looked gaunt, their eyes sunk into their sockets. If something wasn't done soon, it was going to get worse. Another small part of his brain reminded him of a promise he had made to her, not so long ago. *I will always keep you safe.* That pledge made up his mind for him.

"Very well. If the island is there come morning, your people will go free. You have my word."

Surprise lit up her face first, followed by a smile wider than he had ever seen. She didn't say a word as she jumped up from the stool and wrapped her arms around his neck.

He patted her back. "Do not tell the others until morning—until we see the island," he said into the warm silk of her hair that brushed his face. The last thing he wanted was a mutinous crew, out to slit his throat as he slept.

* * *

WITHOUT HIS USUAL SPILL OF CURSING, SMEE THRUST HIS spyglass at Archie, then crossed his arms over his chest and waited as the captain put it up to his eye. The same sliver of green was there to greet them. It didn't surprise Archie in the least. He handed the glass back, his eyes landing on Tiger Lily by the railing. From the dejected looks of the few Indians on deck, she had kept her word and hadn't told a soul of his promise to her.

She gave him a slight smile, and then turned to look back out across the span of ocean toward the island.

Neverland. Perhaps that was why it was given such a name—the land you could never seem to leave. Archie watched his crew for one thoughtful moment. None of them looked enthused at seeing the island again. Their shoulders slumped and their heads hung low.

"All right, lads. Today providence shall smile sweetly upon us," he announced.

A few muttered groans met his ears next. "I hate hunting. I didn't sign up to go chasin' wild animals," he heard someone say. A quick retort followed from another pirate, "They be too fast to catch." More comments filled the air, leading Archie to believe that perhaps convincing the crew to turn loose of the Indians would be easier than he thought.

"The Indians have offered to hunt for us whenever our food runs low in exchange for their freedom," he announced loudly, to be heard over the din. As he said the last word, complete silence greeted him. Perhaps this is a good thing, he thought, taking in the rather shocked expressions on the faces of the Indians and the pensive ones on that of his crew.

"For as long as we are here?" Harper was the first to speak. "They will hunt enough to provide for us all?"

Taking one quick look at Tiger Lily, who gave a small, resolute nod, he answered, "Yes, enough for us all."

"What happens when we leave this blasted island? If we let them go free, our booty will be gone," Beckett said, scrubbing his beard-stubbled chin in thought.

"We be stuck here," Smee announced in an ominous tone. "It be magic waters we sail in, lads. We won't be leavin' this place. Best we have someone to hunt for us."

"So we vote," a voice chimed in near the base of the mast. Boggs patted his stomach thoughtfully.

Yes, and I know how you'll be casting your decision, Archie thought, amused. Holding his breath and hoping that the others were in the same mindset as their cook, he said, "Yes, we vote. All in favor of having the Indians hunt for us, so long as we are near this island?"

A mumbled aye echoed across the ship, spoken by most of the crew. They didn't sound happy, nor did they look it. Archie smiled. "Any opposed?"

A few unintelligible grumbles met his ears, but none so loud to be considered a vote to counter that of the others. It seemed the majority of the crew were thinking with their stomachs as opposed to their pockets.

"Very well, they shall have their freedom. Ready the boats."

The pirates moved slowly as they lowered the boats. From their expressions, most of them were wondering if agreeing to release the Indians had been a good thing to do. The Indians, however, looked the happiest that Archie had ever seen them. A few of the men were helping the pirates, the jovial grins on their faces at complete odds with the dour ones that moved at a snail's pace. Tiger Lily had disappeared the second he proclaimed them free. Now she was helping the old chief to the deck, with the obvious intention of insuring that he was one of the first rowed to the island.

Once the chief was settled in the long boat, she ran back toward the hold, shooting Archie a grateful, happy smile along the way. Archie watched her complete her circuit several more times, with another elderly or disabled person in tow until they all were in the longboats.

Turning command of the *Jolig Roger* to Harper, Archie jumped into the last boat with Tiger Lily, intent on finishing the details of their transaction before they reached shore.

"We will split everything we find with you. Evenly," she offered, "I will meet you every two days and bring you your share."

It sounded like a good treaty to Archie, so he agreed, and let some of Tiger Lily's excitement rub off on him. He smiled. It would be good to be free of the responsibility of caring for so many. There were at least fifty souls he would no longer have to keep watch over. With the tribe off his ship, he would have only the pirates to contend with.

"I will miss you," he said quietly, so only her ears would hear him.

Her hand came over to hold his. "Every two days I promise I will be on the shore waiting for you to come."

He gripped her fingers. He knew that the days between he would still search the white-sanded beach for any sign that she was near. "Every day that comes, I will watch for you."

The boat was passing by the mermaid's rock. Archie glanced back to the ship. He'd left most of the crew on board, taking only enough men to row the boats. He hoped the mermaid wouldn't return in his absence. He should have stayed on board, but the thought of not seeing Tiger Lily safely to the island was more than he could bear, so he sat there and held her hand tightly in his until the tide washed them close to shore.

* * *

"WHAT ARE WE TO DO WHEN THEY DON'T COME BACK?" Boggs asked, his hands on his hips. "We let 'em go, just like that, and expect 'em to do as they say?" He shook his head, staring into the thick underbrush where the Indians disappeared moments before. "We won't be seein' 'em again. Mark me words."

"We wait," Archie told him, sitting down on the trunk of a fallen tree to demonstrate that he planned to do precisely that. "Tiger Lily gave her word that they would return in two hours."

"Women," Boggs grumbled, sitting on the opposite end of the tree. It groaned, and the end Archie sat on lifted in the air.

Archie grinned. "All is well, Boggs. Have a bit of faith. If they do not return, we shall go hunting—for them."

"I was afraid you'd say that," Boggs sighed, "Between you an' me, Cap'n, I hope them Injuns be honest folk. I'm not as young as I used to be. Can't go runnin' after…"

A scream echoed up the shoreline, cutting him off. Boggs jumped up from the stump, causing Archie's end to splat into the ground. Bones jarred and body aching, Archie stood, catching the last glimpse of Boggs running down the sandy beach, a pistol in each hand.

He's moving faster than I ever would have guessed possible, Archie thought, shooting a fast glance back to the boats on the beach. The pirates had dispersed when they had landed, most of them wandering through the forest in search of food. The handful he spotted were making their way toward him, weapons drawn. Assured that back-up was coming, Archie began his sprint in the sand, following Boggs's rotund figure.

He tailed his cook all the way down the stretch of shore, until he edged around a small inlet. Another scream followed the first. It sounded—young. Archie's first thought was of Peter, for the men who had accompanied him to shore had rough voices from years of life on the sea. The youngest among his crew was Harper, but even his voice didn't hold such a youthful sound.

Boggs turned a corner and disappeared.

"Wait!" Archie yelled, picking up his pace. Though he wished Peter no harm, he also had no desire to lose his cook. Good cooks were hard to come by. He had no intention of serving his men both leadership and their meals. He rounded the bend and bumped into Boggs, who held his pistols before his tattooed belly, cocked and ready.

An enormous crocodile was in the process of hunting his next meal, from what Archie could gather. A smallish, brown animal that looked like a strange, malformed bear cub was trying to escape and didn't seem to be having the slightest luck. A high edge of dirt, that was impossible to climb, rose behind the bear. It was trapped. The crocodile's long tail was swishing back and forth, demolishing the cattails at the water's edge as it advanced on the cub in slow, deliberate steps, as if taunting the smaller animal.

Surely that cub wasn't the one screaming. Archie hoped the croc hadn't already eaten Peter as its main course. He was ready to tap Boggs on the shoulder and tell him to retreat a safer distance from that thrashing tail, when the scream came again—from that strange bear.

In an effort to climb the wall, two chubby hands scrambled in the dirt, searching for handholds and a fur cap slid off, revealing a boy's frightened face.

"Kill the croc," Archie hissed in Boggs's ear. "Hurry and shoot it, man, before it eats him."

"Aye." The word hadn't made it out of his mouth, before Boggs shot both pistols.

One shot went wide, puffing into the dirt wall above the croc, to the left of the boy. The other found its way into the top of the croc's snout, not a killing wound by any means, but enough that the animal stopped its pursuit, wriggling and twisting as it retreated back into the water. It turned to stare up at Archie, as if it knew that he had been the one responsible for the blood coating its scales. It opened its mouth wide, giving Archie a disconcerting view of rows of gleaming white teeth, then it gurgled a low, hissing snarl, and disappeared beneath the surf.

The fur-clad boy stopped clawing the dirt and glanced behind him. Once he realized the crocodile had gone, he slid back to the bottom of the embankment and sat where he landed, looking puzzled as he scratched his mussed, brown head before flopping the bear skin back on top of it.

He hasn't seen us yet, which is amusing as there are quite a few of us up here. Archie watched the boy stare at the water as if he were wondering why he hadn't been eaten.

Archie opened his mouth to call down to him, when someone else beat him to it.

"Hey Beetles, you might wanna get out of there," a voice called from the other side of the inlet. "There's a pile of big people over there watching you."

"Ahhh!" The bear boy yelled in fright, jumping to his feet and tackling the dirt wall with renewed vigor. He made it halfway up, when another boy appeared at the top and dropped to his knees, reaching an arm down in an effort to pull the younger lad up. The one doing the pulling was a tall, skinny boy—clad much the same as his chubby friend below—only this one had a fur cap with two long, floppy ears that danced around his head each time he jerked his friend's hand.

I believe he's wearing rabbit ears, Archie decided. They will both land down there to be eaten if they don't soon hurry up.

"Come on, lads. Let's give 'em a hand up," he instructed his men as he set off around the wide semi-circle of the cove.

"Does this mean they be our prisoners?" Boggs voiced popped up behind him, sounding hopeful, as they ducked around tree branches.

"No, Boggs. We don't need any more extra mouths to feed. We just released the Indians for that reason, you know."

"Hmph," came the unhappy reply, followed by silence.

Well, if that's all he's going to say, it isn't bad at all, Archie thought, looking across at the two boys Boggs wished to capture. They still hadn't made any progress, though they were becoming more frantic in their pulling.

"Hurry up, Beetles. They're coming for us," the tall boy urged, jerking the other boy's arm hard enough that his round torso bounced, back and forth against the dirt. He didn't gain any progress upward. Archie winced, the boy's arm would be sore for days at this rate, not to mention his belly.

"We mean you no harm," he said, slowing the last few steps to make sure they heard his approach. "We only want to help you get your friend up safely. No man should suffer a fate at the jaws of a crocodile."

The tall boy stopped pulling, indecision playing across his face as if he were deciding whether to trust Archie, or to drop his friend and save his own skin. "You know, if you hadn't decided to show off and go hunting that crocodile all alone, they wouldn't have caught us," Archie heard the boy hiss over the ledge, "Now Peter will be angry."

Archie chose to pretend he hadn't heard anything as he knelt down to grasp Beetles's free arm. It took both of them pulling to get the hefty boy over the edge. Once free of danger, he shrugged them both off and rolled a safe distance away from Archie, before getting to his feet. He rubbed his arm and watched Archie with the same distrusting look that Archie guessed had been aimed at the crocodile moments before.

"There aren't any grown-ups on Neverland."

"So I've heard," Archie said dryly, "Yet, we appear to be here, nonetheless."

"You'd better thank him, Beetles," the tall boy said, nudging him in the shoulder. "You'd have been eaten already if they hadn't stopped Tic-Tock." He stopped and looked contemplative for a few seconds. "How did you stop him? He eats whoever he wants."

"*I* shot him," Boggs spoke up from behind Archie.

Archie moved over to let the cook walk through. Boggs stood as proudly as his short, round frame would allow. His head held high, looking down at the two boys before them. "I am the dread pirate Percy Boggs," he informed them in an imperious tone, thrusting out his round belly as he put his hands on his hips. "But don't call me Percy."

Archie bit back a smile, watching as the boys took in the tattooed woman with wide eyes.

"He's painted a woman on his belly—wonder why he did that?"

"I dunno, but I bet she's stuck on there for good."

Deciding now was the time to interrupt, in case Boggs were to demonstrate his dancing moves next and scar their young minds, Archie said, "I am Captain Jameson, of the pirate ship the *Jolig Roger*. Might I have the pleasure of your acquaintances?"

"Oh, sure. I'm Patch, and that is Beetles." The rabbit ears that hung down the boy's head swayed as he nodded his head and gestured to his friend.

"I am pleased to meet you." Archie gave them a low, elaborate bow, which seemed to please them both to no end. As he straightened, two wide smiles were given in return. "Now to satisfy my curiosity, I simply must ask, why is the crocodile named Tic-Tock?"

"Oh, that's because he sounds like a clock." Patch shrugged.

"I beg your pardon?" Archie was certain he had misunderstood.

"He sounds like a clock." It was Beetles who repeated the words, and then added, "You know, tic-tock, tic-tock. It's because he swallowed Peter's clock."

Archie was finding the story intriguing, however improbable it seemed. "And how did that happen?"

"Peter always brings things back from the grown-up land. One time he brought a clock, just to see if it would work on Neverland. Tic-Tock and Peter have never gotten along. One is always trying to get the other," Patch explained. "One day, the croc saw Peter coming back from the grown-up world. Peter was busy looking at his clock and didn't realize he was flying so low. Then the croc jumped out of the water and snapped his jaws just inches away from him. It didn't get Peter, but it startled him enough that he dropped the clock right into Tic-Tock's mouth. The croc swallowed it. Now if you get too close to him, you can hear it ticking, so we named him Tic-Tock."

"A ticking crocodile," Archie heard Boggs say, "that be a new one. How long ago did he swallow that clock?"

Both Patch and Beetles shrugged, as if neither knew the answer and didn't care to know it.

"Well, I was wonderin' how it stayed wound, is all," Boggs mumbled, crossing his arms over his chest, clearly not believing the story that had been told.

"How do you 'wound' a clock?" Beetles asked.

"Well, you twist the knob in the back..." Archie stopped at the blank expressions on their faces. "You do know what a clock looks like, don't you?"

The boys shook their heads. "How are we supposed to

know what it looks like when it got eaten before we saw it?" Patch asked, flipping his rabbit ears over his shoulders to get a better look at Archie.

"You are telling me you have never seen a clock. Never?" He asked again, just to be sure.

Two definite no's, as the boys shook their heads.

"Might I ask where you are from?"

"Neverland." The answer was immediate, leaving Archie no choice but to query further.

"But where were you born before Peter brought you here? Where are your parents?" The questions were piling up in his head faster than he could spit them out now. "And why was Beetles down there with a crocodile?"

"You sure are asking strange questions." Patch wrinkled his nose, looking more rabbit than boy with the gesture. "What's born and parents?"

"I went down there to kill Tic-Tock," Beetles said, crossing his arms over his chest, looking much like a smaller, untattooed version of Boggs, "I wanted to show Peter that I wasn't afraid of him."

"You should have been afraid," Patch frowned, "You like to show off too much."

"I do not," Beetles mumbled.

"Yes, you do," Patch argued. "Besides, Peter isn't even around to show off for!"

Archie rolled his eyes and fought the urge to pull his

hair out, while the two continued to bicker back and forth.

"Go back to the shore and wait for Tiger Lily. I'll be there presently," he told Boggs, "Best we be there, when she returns."

"*If* she returns," Boggs grumbled. Archie wondered if he and the cook would end up quarreling like the two boys a few feet away, but the pirate turned and started back around the inlet, collecting his crewmates along the way.

The boys were oblivious to everything but their disagreement, which had escalated to the point of the two of them rolling around on the ground in a ball of arms, legs, and fur. As he watched the two scuffle, Archie debated just letting them fight it out as he returned with his men. They weren't showing any signs of slowing down.

Archie cleared his throat in hopes that they'd notice. They didn't. The fighting now included various pieces of brown and grey fur being ripped off and thrown into the air. Archie sidestepped the long-eared rabbit hat that came hurtling toward him. At the rate they were going, it wasn't going to stop any time soon and he had a young woman coming to bring supplies. The thought of Tiger Lily made up his mind rather quickly.

"Please do tell Peter I send my regards," he called out over the scuffle.

At the sound of his voice, the two stopped just long enough to answer in unison. "Okay." Then, they went back to their fight and Archie left them to it.

His timing was perfect. When he rounded the corner and the boats came into view, so did Tiger Lily and six men from her tribe.

I'm glad she wasn't joking when she boasted of her people's skill, Archie thought, grinning. Several deer and one enormous black bear lay at the edge of the trees. His men had started carrying the deer carcasses to the boats.

Archie spotted Boggs looking the bear over with an authoritative air, as he walked around the beast, taking it in. Noticing Archie approach, he stopped his inspection and looked up with a wide grin. "We be set, Cap'n."

"Is there enough here?" He already knew the answer, but wanted to hear it confirmed by his ship's cook. Tiger Lily stood nearby, also waiting for Boggs's reply.

"Oh aye, Cap'n. We'll eat like kings," came the easy reply as Boggs left the bear and made his way to Tiger Lily. He took her hand and bent over to kiss it. "My dear, ye be a wonderful woman. The sun itself canna' hold a light to yer beauty. You have eyes the color of old sherry and hair as dark as me Great-Aunt Maddie's."

Archie had never heard such a grand speech from any

of the pirates. He wondered if perhaps Boggs might be working himself up to a marriage proposal. Worried that the pirate might start pointing out other fine qualities not fit to be heard, Archie cut in, "That's enough, Boggs. Best you keep an eye on your bear. 'Twould be a shame if the crocodile would come by and rob you of it while your attention was held elsewhere."

Boggs released Tiger Lily's hand and spun around, as if expecting the giant croc to burst through the trees at any given moment. The young woman forgotten, Boggs took off in the direction of the strongest man on shore. "I need yer help, Beckett. We need to get that bear on the ship."

"I apologize." Archie smiled at Tiger Lily. "I believe he was trying to say thank you, and it got a little out of hand."

A wide grin blossomed over her face, lighting up her eyes. "That's all right. I was enjoying it."

"You were?"

"Oh, yes. It's not every day I'm given such strange compliments. I am glad he liked the bear."

Said bear was being toted to a boat by three men, plus Beckett, who seemed to be shouldering the majority of the weight. They made it to the boat, and heaved the animal in, then looked at the boat with pride, as if they had captured the beast themselves.

Archie rolled his eyes and turned his attention back to

Tiger Lily. "Have your people found shelter for the night? Is there anything you need?"

"They have started toward the mountains. It feels like home here, so we are going to be fine." She stepped closer and reached out, tracing the line of his cheek. "You have done what I needed. I cannot ask you for anything more."

He captured her hand in his and placed a kiss in her palm. "If you need anything at all, you need only ask. If it is in my power to give, it will be yours."

She moved her hand away and took that last step that brought her body close to his. A soft breeze blew her hair toward him, framing her face in a soft outline of shining silk as she leaned forward and pressed her lips to his.

He wrapped his arms around her and held her tight. When the kiss broke, he rested his forehead to hers. "Each day that passes, I will watch for you. And every day I do not see your face, an eternity shall pass."

***

ARCHIE HAD NEVER HEARD ANY OF HIS CREW GIGGLE AS A SIDE effect of their rum ration. He'd seen them drunk more times than he could count, so wasted the majority of them couldn't stand, and those few who could, teetered about on deck like the ship was in the worst of seas, only to end up falling head over heels, sprawled out on the planking. Two unlucky pirates had gone over the railings as a result of not being able to discern where the ship ended and the sea began.

It was after those two unceremonious deaths that Archie started his own code, adding his rules to the end of Blackbeard's in the book.

No man to drink spirits or be drunk whilst on the main deck.

It had worked thus far. Pirates might be a thieving, unruly lot, but they tended to follow the rules laid before them, especially when it held the power to affect their share of plunder. So when Archie heard the high-pitched giggle so close to the quarterdeck, he was a bit surprised. At first, he thought that his rule had been disobeyed, since the sound came so loud and clear.

As it happened, the sound came from below, though not far. I am not sure it is a good sound, Archie decided, taking in Smee's jovial face. The doctor sat on the steps leading up to the deck, giggling like a school girl.

"I say, man. What, pray tell, do you have in that cup?" Archie asked, crinkling his nose as the stench assaulted his senses. The smell was terrible. A rotten, fruity smell. At first, he thought his wine had been discovered, but this was far, *far* worse than his grape juice had ever been. Besides, the smell of his wine had changed as quickly as the taste and filled his quarters with a sweet smell any time he uncorked the barrel.

"Hee-hee," was the only answer given to his question. Smee's red cheeks were a bright contrast to his white sideburns, glowing like stubbled, rosy red apples.

Getting nowhere with the ship's doctor, Archie edged around him, and made his way down the stairs. The smell worsened with each step he took. He reached in his pocket for his handkerchief and pressed it to his nose as he reached the hold.

Boggs stood with a crusty-looking paddle in hand, looking pensive, as he stared down into an open barrel. He seemed oblivious to the stench that surrounded him as he stuck the paddle down and thwacked it on the insides of the barrel. The contents made squishing sounds as he stirred and the reek became worse to the point that Archie began gagging through the handkerchief.

"Whatever it is you are doing, I will beg you to stop," Archie managed between breathless gasps.

"Oh, aye, Cap'n. Sorry to upset your sensitivies, I am," Boggs answered, looking up from the barrel. "It's just that I be trying to figure out how it turned so quick, ye see."

"What's turned?"

"Some of the fruit the lads brought aboard. Ye see, we be runnin' low on rum, Cap'n, and with no port to be found, I figured to make a bit of wine. Nothing much, mind ye, only a bit of an experiment, ye might say, being as your barrel turned so well in such a short time."

Attention piqued, Archie made his way to Boggs's experiment to have a better look. A crusty, brown mash with yellow streaks lay squished against the sides of the barrel.

"What fruit was this, did you say?" Archie asked.

"Not sure, Cap'n. Looked to be something between an apple and a pear. The lads be callin' it 'neverfruit.' Was sweet enough, I gave one a try before I put the others in there and mashed 'em up."

"You're making wine out of a strange fruit that you've never seen before," Archie said, a tone of incredulity seeping into his words.

"Mmph," Boggs replied, shrugging his shoulders, as if it weren't an issue to be bothered with. Then, he added as if in afterthought, "I've had worse. Smee said he would be the first to try it, so as not to poison the lads."

Well, Smee's sudden sense of nobility makes it all better then, Archie thought, shaking his head in despair. He'd seen Smee drunk, but never gleefully so. "I'm thinking it may be a bit strong, even for the likes of our good doctor."

"Aye, I be thinking we might water it down a bit," Boggs said in a thoughtful manner, "But don't tell the lads,

Cap'n. I have no want to be thrown overboard for diluting their spirits."

"Your secret is safe with me, Boggs. You have nothing to fear," Archie said, turning to make his way back up to deck. He stopped at the steps, eyeing Smee. "You shouldn't give him anymore unless it *is* watered down. Whatever the name of your concoction, I believe he's had more of it than he can handle."

"I haven't a clue what I be callin' it yet, other than frightfully stout. Ye have me word, Cap'n. Mr. Smee will no' be havin' any more of it 'til I get it right." Boggs's voice sounded like an echo. Archie glanced over his shoulder. The man had his head shoved down in the barrel, inspecting his creation.

He will be as smashed as Smee, Archie thought, shaking his head. As if his thoughts had been read, another high-pitched giggle came from the steps.

Edging around Smee, Archie made his way up top and found another surprise sitting atop the mast. Peter sat, dangling his feet back and forth, looking bored.

"I was just getting ready to call for you," Harper materialized at Archie's side, looking troubled. "He flew over the ship and landed right next to me on the rigging."

"Hello, Peter," Archie called out. "How are you today?"

"As well as ever, I'd say." A wide grin spread across the boy's face as he got to his feet and walked down the length of the beam. He did so as easily as Harper, as if he'd spent time on the narrow mast, though Archie knew that wasn't the case. The reason for the nonchalant way of balancing on the board was lack of fear. After all, when one could fly, there would be no fear of falling.

Peter demonstrated Archie's thoughts by hopping off the end of the beam and dropping to the deck, so slowly that it seemed he was walking down instead of flying or falling. As he neared, Archie made out a familiar being perched on Peter's shoulder.

"Why, Miss Bell, I am pleased to see you again." Archie smiled at the golden pixie. The smile melted away when he realized that she looked different from the last time he had seen her. Her color had dulled and one wing hung at an odd angle. "What has happened to her?" he asked Peter.

"The water sprites punished her, as I told you they would, but I saved her."

"Oh, no. I am very sorry, my dear." Archie didn't think the apology sufficed, though the pixie gave him a warm smile and made light, bell tones as if saying everything was fine and all was forgiven.

"Will she heal?" he asked Peter.

"Oh, yes. She'll be flying and back to usual by tomorrow. Every wound heals quickly on Neverland, so she'll be good as new," Peter answered, staring at something behind Archie. "Why do you have a boy here? Did he come with you from the grown-up star?"

"Who…" Archie began, as he turned to see what had caught the boy's attention.

Harper stood by the steps, his arms crossed over his chest. His face looked inquisitive, in spite of his rigid stance. Archie guessed that he was as curious of Peter as Peter was of him, though he was attempting not to show it.

"Peter, this is Harper. He is one of my crew, and, yes, he did come with us."

"Is he a boy? He looks like one. He doesn't look like you," Peter said in a conversational tone.

"I am a man," Harper announced, cutting Archie off before he could speak. The curious look had left the lad's face, replaced with a fierce one that glowered at Peter. "I am a pirate, and a part of this ship's crew. I am *not* a boy."

"I think he is right. He just looks like a boy, but he speaks like a grown-up," Peter told Archie, "He has wrinkles around his mouth. It means he's old."

Archie fought to keep from smiling. Those wrinkles were a product of having no front teeth. "Yes, I suppose he is older than you might have thought," he conceded. He heard Harper curse under his breath.

"That's too bad," Peter said, "The Lost Boys would have been happy to have another boy join them."

"The Lost Boys? Who are they?"

"They are the ones that I brought from the grown-up star, but there aren't many of them left. Tic-Tock has eaten a lot of them." Peter scowled. The expression was echoed on the face of Miss Bell.

"Would Beetles and Patch be two of your troupe?" Archie asked.

"Yes," Peter said, jumping up to sit on a water barrel. Looking bored, he searched his pocket and came out with a small, wooden flute. He put it to his lips and gave it an experimental puff.

Archie grimaced. From the scratching, shrill tones, it was obvious the boy didn't have a clue how to play. "One of my men saved Beetles from the croc, just as he was about to be eaten," Archie said, hoping to get the boy to talk instead of blow on his flute.

The diversion worked. Peter's head flew up at the mention of the crocodile and a hard expression came over his face. "No one told me about that. Nothing happens on Neverland that I don't know about."

"Well, it happened just the same, and I assure you that I am not lying. I was there. I saw it with my own eyes," Archie said.

"I told them not to go near Tic-Tock, but Beetles never listens. It was probably him," Peter said darkly as he stood up. In the next second, he was flying to the island without so much as a goodbye to anyone on the ship.

"Well, that was odd," Archie said, watching the boy disappear over the trees.

"I think he's a death guardian," Harper said, catching Archie's full attention.

"I beg your pardon?"

"That boy—Peter. I think he's a death guardian," he repeated. At Archie's silence, he continued, "Me mum used to tell us bedtime stories. In one of her tales, there was an elfin guardian with pointed ears. You did notice that Peter has pointed ears, didn't you?"

Archie nodded. The boy didn't look like an elf, in Archie's opinion, but there was a bit of a point to his ears. He waited for Harper to continue his tale.

"Well, the death guardians were in charge of ferrying souls to the underworld. There was one Mum was fond of telling us, of a guardian who became lonely. His name was Pan. He was given charge of the children who died, and told to keep them safe as their souls crossed over. At first, Pan did as the gods bade and ferried the children to the underworld. But as time went on and years went by, he grew restless—and lonely. He began taking the children to a special place, a place only he knew, so that they would always keep him company—so he wouldn't be alone." Harper's eyes had taken on a far-away look, as if he were hearing his mother's words as they replayed in his mind. He looked more like the boy that Peter had mistaken him for. As Archie watched, the look left and the Harper he knew, returned. "Do you think it is possible that the story is true, Jameson?"

Once, Archie had heard that all stories had a basis in truth. Whether or not that was true, he didn't know. The odds of a bedtime story having roots in their reality was a bit of a stretch for him, but then, so was a flying boy. "I do not know, Harper. I truly do not."

"Well, I think he is Pan, or something like him," Harper said. "After all, stranger things have happened. I need something to make sense."

Archie nodded his agreement. To believe in a fairytale might seem folly, but they were captured in a world where anything seemed to be possible. Perhaps believing was the answer.

15

UNLIKELY ALLIES

*A*rchie had not expected to see one of Peter's Lost Boys on his first trip to meet Tiger Lily. The boy did not look pleased to be there as he helped the Indians tote baskets of supplies to the shoreline.

"Good day, Beetles. I confess, your presence is a bit of surprise. I thought only to find Tiger Lily and a few of her people here this morning," Archie said, giving the short, round boy a polite smile.

"Mmph," the boy grumbled as he set down a basket full of strange-looking fruit, his bear cap falling forward to his eyes. He pushed it back with one hand, and turned to look at Archie. "She said if I was to see you, I was to tell you she's on her way," and with that, Beetles set off, heading back into the woods, presumably for another trip of supplies, though Archie thought he might be trying to escape further conversation.

"Nice of him to help," Harper grinned, "Even if he didn't seem too happy about it."

"Yes, nice indeed," Archie replied, watching as Tiger Lily appeared from beneath the canopy of trees.

"Did you see a boy come through here?" she asked without preamble. "About this tall?" She held out her palm at chest height.

"Aye, and about this wide." Harper held out his hands a good distance from his own waist, indicating Beetles's chubby frame.

"Well, where did he go? He was supposed to come back and help us carry the rest of your supplies to the boats."

"He went that way." Harper pointed to a group of trees in the opposite direction.

"That figures," she muttered.

She looks pretty when she's angry, Archie thought, watching a warm flush creep into Tiger Lily's high cheekbones. Her long, black hair was pulled back in a tight plait that ran down her back. Archie's fingers itched to loosen it and feel her silky tresses between his fingertips. Being as she looked ready to throttle anyone who came near, he held his place and decided to be content to take her beauty in from a safe distance, though he promised himself that as soon as the murderous look left her face, she would be his. Vaguely, he registered that Harper was yammering on about something or other, but his eyes stayed on Tiger Lily. He felt Harper brush past him and heard the lad's footsteps going in the direction he had last seen Beetles.

"What are you thinking?" The angry look had left Tiger Lily's face, replaced with one that seemed to be a cross between confusion and amusement.

"That you are beautiful." They weren't the most poetic words he had ever spoken. Had he given it more thought, he would have taken care to sound more eloquent. But in that second, the truth came free, and he didn't care how it sounded. Silence met his words, so he chose that moment to walk over and press his lips to hers. His hand brushed the tail of her braid, and his fingers had their way with it, traveling up her back, unraveling the soft waves inch by inch until his hand reached the base of her neck. Soon, every bit of the braid was free.

He slid his hand under her hair, feeling the trapped warmth between it and her skin as he cupped her neck and pulled her nearer, deepening the kiss. His other arm came around her waist to hold her close as she lifted her arms, wrapping them around his neck.

A feeling of warmth, unlike anything he had ever felt, rolled out in a wave. It was as if the sun had decided to move into his soul and was warming him from the inside out. There was no one else on this island but him and the woman in his arms.

Just the two of them—and one pesky voice clearing itself near his shoulder. He ignored it as the perpetrator continued, as if he were dredging up every bit of noise his throat held in an effort to become louder. The throat clearing stopped after a couple of seconds, followed by a sigh.

"I beg your pardon, but might you know where Beetles has gone?" The young voice was asking politely enough, but Archie still wanted to choke the owner, regardless of the manners his mother had ingrained in him since childhood.

"I do not." Archie gritted his teeth as he turned, expecting to see Patch or Peter hovering beside him. Instead, his eyes dropped to find a smaller boy, this one covered in grey-furred clothes, with what looked like a raccoon hat perched upon his small blonde head. "Who, may I ask, are you?"

"Runt." The boy looked up at him with clear, blue eyes. He was much younger than either of the boys Archie had seen earlier.

He can't be more than six or seven years old, Archie thought, looking down into small, trusting face. "Your name is Runt?" The name didn't seem one that a parent would bestow upon a child. But then, Beetles and Patch didn't quite seem like given names, either.

"Yes," the boy answered, nonplussed, before he repeated his question. "Do you know where Beetles is?"

"He is coming." Harper materialized out of the underbrush.

"Peter would have been upset if he didn't do what he was told," Runt said in a matter-of-fact voice. "He told him he'd have to help the grown-ups since he went after Tic-Tock."

So nice of Peter to be using us as punishment. The smile that etched Archie's face was a wry one. "Might I ask why he chose us?"

The little boy shrugged. "'Cause you're big, I guess."

"As good a reason as any, I suppose," Archie noted, but Runt's attention had left him and gone to Tiger Lily.

"My mama had pretty, long hair like hers," the boy said as if to no one in particular. "I really miss my mama."

"I told you to stay and help them." Peter was berating Beetles as they both appeared from the underbrush. It was the first time that Archie had seen the flying boy walk.

"I did. I thought they were finished," Beetles grumbled.

Peter looked down at the boy and scowled before glancing back up to Archie.

"You are the one I wanted to see," he announced, hopping off the ground to hover beside Archie.

Archie had the impression that Peter had done so in order to look him squarely in the eye. *He doesn't like to look up to anyone*, Archie thought, watching as the boy lifted an extra inch into the air to look down at him.

"Why, might I ask, am I the one you were searching for?" he asked.

"I want to join forces with you. You and your grown-ups, and the Lost Boys, and me. Tic-Tock has never been afraid of anything until your man stopped him. If he keeps eating my men, there will be no Lost Boys on Neverland. Then, he'll start eating yours. I think he could eat your ship if he wanted to."

Even though Archie doubted the croc had the ability to sink the *Roger*, the thought wasn't a pleasant one. "What precisely do you propose?"

"That your men and mine hunt Tic-Tock together with your pistol things that Beetles and Patch told me about."

"Ah." Archie nodded. He'd wondered how long it would take for the boys to tell their leader all they had learned. The thought of them being around the pistols made him queasy. With the imagination that the children had shown and their lack of knowledge of nearly everything—coupled with his crew's complete lack of caution—such an escapade could spell complete disaster. "Before I commit to such a hunt, I wish to know more about this crocodile," he told Peter, giving the boy the full look of seriousness that lay in his blue eyes. "I will not put my men—or yours—in harm's way before I know all there is to know about our quarry."

"What's a quarry?" He heard Beetles hiss to Runt, who gave him a helpless shrug in reply.

"He means Tic-Tock," Peter told them, flying up to sit on a tree branch a few inches higher up. He settled down, pushing an errant limb out of his way, "Tic-Tock has been in Neverland for forever. Every time we see him, he seems to get bigger. He eats everything and everyone. He's ate lots of the Lost Boys and the mermaids are afraid of him. I think he eats them, too, though they've never said anything to me about him. I just know that they are always gone whenever he shows up."

"Is there a certain place he likes best?" Harper asked, then turned to give Archie a serious look of his own. "I'm asking because I'd rather watch for the croc, than the mermaids."

Peter had listened to the question, and now looked pensive, his small brows furrowed as he mulled over the information that he knew. After a few seconds, he answered. "There is a cove on the other side of Neverland that leads to the caves. I've never seen a mermaid there, though the water would be right for them and there are plenty of flat rocks around those caves where they could bathe in the sun. I've wondered sometimes why I haven't ever seen them there, but I just figured that maybe they liked this side of Neverland better." He shrugged. "Maybe Tic-Tock likes to be around the caves."

"That sounds like the place we should lay anchor," Archie mused. Their encounter with the crocodile had not proved to be as daunting as that of the mermaid, so it did not come as a surprise when Harper nodded.

Peter must have thought that Archie had agreed to join forces, for the boy jumped up from the branch and stood upon it and crowed. This strange commotion must have been a good thing, for Beetles and Runt began to cheer.

Archie traded a surprised look with Harper. Somehow, without their knowledge or Archie's consent, his fearless pirate crew had managed to join forces with a group of children.

16

A-HUNTING WE WILL GO

*H*arper was scowling so hard that Archie wondered if his face was going to freeze in that expression. "I don't like it," he repeated. The scene seemed vaguely familiar to Archie, as the lad had voiced his opinion is much the same way when they had brought the Indians aboard the *Jolig Roger* and settled them in the hold as slaves. He is even in the same place as before, Archie noted. Propped with his bum against the map table and his arms crossed over his chest, with a brown thatch of hair falling into his eyes, Harper looked more like an unruly teen than a pirate who had commanded the ship on more than one occasion.

Archie wondered if the reason for his noticing that Harper looked younger than normal was the fact that Peter had tried once again to recruit him for his own troupe before they left the island the previous evening. The invitation had been rather bold and callous, making Archie wonder if perhaps he shouldn't be trying to recruit Peter as a pirate.

"You'll get old and die if you stay with them," the boy had told Harper in a cold, unfeeling tone, much as if his demise would be imminent the second he stepped back on the deck.

Much to Archie's delight, Harper had answered Peter in true pirate fashion, telling the boy in no uncertain terms, "Shove it, and leave me be, else I'll slit your throat where ye stand. Then we'll see who lives longer, aye?"

Archie suppressed a smile at the memory, for now his young friend was looking murderous once again at the prospect of having to spend additional time with Peter and his troupe of young boys as their forces joined to hunt down the crocodile. Truth be told, Archie could probably have found a way of getting out of the agreement, but after discovering from Tiger Lily that the caves Peter had mentioned were just below the mountains where her people had started to build their village, he began to worry. The thought of the enormous croc being so close to her was unsettling. Better to be done with the beast, once and for all.

So that evening, he had given his orders to leave the inlet and head east. It had taken some maneuvering to get the ship into the narrow mouth of the cove, but once they cleared the rocks, the water cleared from black to the clearest blue waters that Archie had ever seen, free of icebergs and the sharp jutting rocks that seemed to fill all of the other water. It was easy to see why the croc would prefer this part of the island. The cove widened and soon the *Jolig Roger* sat on a still sea as clear and smooth as glass.

They had let down anchor and waited, the few hands on deck watching through the night for any sign that Tic-Tock was indeed present. The night had shown no sign of the massive beast and morning came, bringing only Harper to the map room to voice his opinions on the matter.

"You can't trust him, there's something not right when you look in his eyes," Harper said, a faraway look in his own, as if he were remembering. "If you aren't careful, he'll feed you to the croc himself. I think he would do it just to have a bit of fun."

"Well, we'll have to be careful then, won't we?" Archie replied, a slight smirk popping up to quirk around his mouth as Harper shot him another dark look. "I'm leaving the ship under your command whilst we are gone. With luck, you won't have to deal with Peter and, hopefully, no mermaid shall show her beautiful face while we are away."

"That would be too much to wish for," Harper replied dryly.

"I am leaving half the crew under your watch. Cannons will be more useful against the croc than pistols," Archie instructed. "You have as much of a chance of hunting him here as we have around the caves. So if you see him, blow him out of the water."

"Aye, Cap'n." The lad's shoulders slumped in resignation.

"All will be fine, Harper. You have no need to worry. I have no intention of losing you to Peter's troupe," Archie grinned, watching the fire light back up in Harper's eyes.

Harper had opened his mouth, no doubt to give a sarcastic retort of some sort, when the pounding of feet overhead cut him off, and a cloud of dust came down from the ceiling.

The first thing Archie spotted when he arrived on deck was pirates running in every direction. Ignoring them, Archie searched for the one he had left in charge through the night. Beckett stood on the quarterdeck, with a face gone pale under the dark stubble of his beard.

"Out there, Cap'n." He pointed a few yards out, ahead of the ship. "I don't know what it is, but it be big."

A dark shape moved through the water, a stark contrast of black in crystal blue water. As Beckett had stated, whatever it was, was indeed large—and moved faster than seemed possible, sluicing through the water like a hot knife in butter.

A single, white seagull had been perched on the mast. As the men scaled the rigging for a better look, it flew off and swooped down toward the deck. Upon seeing even more pirates, it changed its mind, swerving over the railing just before it would have smacked into it. The bird flew low over the water for the first couple of seconds, then altered its course and began to ascend higher in the air, en route toward the mouth of the nearest cave.

It had gotten a good distance above the swells when a giant crocodile launched itself out of the water. Jaws open, the seagull flew between the rows of teeth before it disappeared and the jaws snapped together with an audible crunch. The body of the croc smacked the surface of the sea and sent up a giant splash that disturbed the calm water and sent waves to slap at the sides of the ship.

"Tic-Tock," Archie's voice was a hoarse whisper that sounded cracked. "He's here."

As if the crocodile had eaten the bird only because it had come from the ship, it dove back below the surface of the water and swam toward them.

"All hands to quarters! Prepare to fire the cannons!" Archie managed to find his voice long enough to shout his orders. Time seemed to slow down on the deck as he listened to his orders being shouted from one man to the next, as he watched his men move slow as the dark figure in the water came toward them at a speed so fast it seemed unreal.

No ship in the world has ever been sunk by a crocodile, his brain told him. Then a small part of it whispered —but no ship has ever been to Neverland, either. Instinctively, he gripped the railing on the quarterdeck and kept watching.

The blur disappeared at the side of the *Roger* just before she quaked and the sounds of splintering wood filled the air. Had Archie not seen the croc hit them, he would have sworn they had hit an iceberg. Several of his men had lost their footing and were sprawled on the deck. Had he not kept his handhold, he would have joined them. He glanced over the side of the ship where he had last seen the crocodile.

A few of the boards looked as if they had buckled under the blow, but the hull was still intact and the monster was nowhere to be seen. The sounds of splashing on the opposite side of the ship caught his attention. One of his men had been thrown over the rail.

"Man overboard!" The cry went up and blended into another yelled at the same instant as his crew took their positions. "Cannons ready, Cap'n!"

Archie scrambled to the opposite side of the ship just in time to see his lost crewman open his mouth to scream.

In that same second, Tic-Tock emerged from his place under the ship and snagged him, dragging him below the surface before he had even enough time to make so much as a squeak.

"Fire at will!" Archie ordered, watching as the pirate's hand traveled through the water just ahead of the dark shadow beneath the surface, as if a last plea for help. Its owner was most certainly dead in the mouth of the crocodile that was just now within reach of the cannons.

The loud blasts were deafening as the cannon balls splashed all around the croc. One blast hit its mark, and an earsplitting scream rent the air just before a giant, scaly tail sprayed water as it flipped in a giant arc before disappearing back under the surface.

Then, the water colored red.

"We got him," Archie said numbly, as the cannons continued to fire. Even after he gave his order to cease, a couple still fired, as if wanting to make certain the beastie was dead and at the bottom of the sea.

A few moments later the sea calmed; the only indication anything had happened was that now the surface was painted with blood.

"Well." Archie had forgotten about Harper, who had stayed at his side during the whole incident. "I suppose you have less to worry about now," Archie told him. "We have finished hunting the crocodile."

"I doubt that I stop worrying." Archie followed Harper's glance across the railing, where a flying boy appeared, hovering above the red water.

* * *

Harper watched as Peter flew to the ship and circled the mast. Before he could blink, the ruffian had taken his little pig-sticker of a knife from his side and sunk it into the top of the sail, and slit it midway down, and then flew through it as proud as if he had just killed the croc instead of a helpless sheet of canvas.

"Hope you plan to make him stitch it up," he grumbled to Jameson, who stood with his hands folded behind his back, looking up at the mast with no emotion whatsoever playing upon his face. The man stood as still as a statue for several seconds, making Harper wonder if perhaps he hadn't frozen in place as he stared at the boy walking along the beam.

"Cap'n," he hissed, trying to shake Jameson out of his trance.

A single hand flattened, palm-out, behind the captain's back as if ordering silence. Harper rolled his eyes and waited. No way was he going to be the one mending that sail, especially since there had been no call for such an action. Death guardian or no, the scoundrel would have to answer for his deeds. Harper crossed his arms over his chest and waited, muttering low curses under his breath.

"Go below and wait for me." The order came whispered so quiet-like that Harper thought at first he had imagined it. He didn't move, thinking that maybe he hadn't heard him correctly, but then Jameson turned and fixed him with his cold, blue eyes.

"Go below," he repeated.

"Aye," Harper grumbled and walked toward the steps, glancing up at the mast just long enough to realize that Peter was fixing him with an odd stare, one that sent a cold chill up his spine and made the fine hairs on the back of his neck stand at attention. There was no doubt in his mind that the boy known as Peter was also the death guardian from his mum's bedtime stories. Whatever he seemed to be—a boy he was not.

As everyone else was still above from the excitement of the crocodile, he found only one man below the deck.

Boggs was propped up against a wall, clearly hammered from his latest batch of alcohol, that he had dubbed "never-right."

"Ah, Harper. Good of ye to join me." He lifted his tankard up in welcome. "Have a cup, will ye?"

"No, I prefer to have my wits about me, thank you."

Harper couldn't help smiling at the jovial cook who grinned at him and shrugged. "'Tis your loss, lad." The grin left a moment later, followed by a serious expression and a rather loud belch that sent the tattooed woman to quivering upon his belly. "I uncovered a wisdom just last night. I'll share it only with ye," Boggs said in what Harper guessed to be a conspiratorial whisper, though it was loud enough that likely every soul on board would hear this important secret.

"It's in the pixie dust," Boggs confided, pointing a finger to a can with holes poked in the top. "The secret to my never-right. It was r-r-right here all along."

Arching an eyebrow, Harper took a quick glance down into the can and was surprised to see the golden pixie that Jameson referred to as Miss Bell, sitting on the rusty bottom. Noticing the shadow over her prison, she looked up, scowled at him, and smacked the side of the can with one hand in anger, sending tiny puffs of golden dust up through the holes that caused Harper to sneeze.

"Whatever have you done, man?" Harper asked, wiping his eyes with one hand as he carefully set the can back down on the table. "Jameson will not be happy with you. He'll skewer you with his sword when he learns you've captured his pixie." He paused, then added, "How exactly did you do that? I've seen her fly. She's frightfully fast."

"Well, truth be told, 'twas an accident of shworts," Boggs drawled. "She flew into me cup."

"You jest."

"No! No, I wouldn't pull yer leg on such a thing."

Oddly enough, Harper believed him. He had never met a pirate who had the ability to lie whilst being drunk and rarely did ever one stretch the truth when it came to the status of their liquor. If a pixie had just happened to fly into that cup, then so be it. "So what is this secret of yours?" he asked.

"That gold dust fixes the never-right. Here, take a nip out of me cup." The tankard was thrust at him. There wasn't much left in it, only the dregs in the bottom. Refusing to drink anything that had been at Boggs's lips, he bent his head to the open cup and smelled, instead. A surprisingly sweet odor greeted him.

"It appears you are onto something, Boggs," Harper said, handing the tankard back. "But I still say you'd better release yon fairy before the captain gets word that you've been using her like a salt shaker."

"Ach, I will. One shake fixed me whole barrel. I'll turn her free soon," Boggs said in a very unconvincing sort of way.

Harper let the subject drop. He wasn't the captain of the ship. Jameson could deal with Boggs, Peter, and the ruined sail however he saw fit.

Boggs drained the last drops in his cup and bent over to set it down. A large lump rolled on his round belly and he grimaced.

"Are you all right?" Harper asked, "How long have you had yon bulge?"

"This?" Boggs asked, rubbing his wide torso with both hands in an authoritative way. "This belly has been here longer than ye have been alive, lad."

"No, you've got a place right where her bosoms are…"

"Ah. Ye mean me belly pop."

"Belly pop?"

"Aye, one day it just sorta popped out there. It no hurts unless I squish it hard. Mostly just causes gas," Boggs replied, then added with a sly wink. "It fills Nessie out pretty well, don't ye think?"

Harper sighed. Having a strange bulge in the exact place of a tattooed woman's bosoms was an odd coincidence to be sure, but being proud of it was another matter entirely. Instinctively, he covered the tattoo of Mary on his forearm and said a silent prayer in hopes that no strange bulges would mar her perfect image.

Boggs was doing some reminiscing of his own. "Ah, Nessie." Though Harper had not asked for any further explanation of origin or history of his tattooed woman, he continued, "The beautiful Natasha de la Costa, daughter of Juan Marco Velasco, Duke of Cardona. The greatest dancer me eyes have ever seen—and me one true love."

His attention captured, Harper leaned forward to hear more of the tale.

"I was a younger lad when I first lay me eyes on her, but no quite as young as you. I was also a bit… smaller," this followed by a light pat on his belly and a memory that appeared in Boggs's eyes, which seemed to sober him up. "I just arrived at a Spanish port and was looking for the nearest tavern. I seen one up at the end of the street and was fixin' to head there when I heard a scream that stopped me in me tracks. It was then that I turned and seen her. She was standing in the middle of the market spillin' out the longest stream of curses that I ever did hear. The sun was a-glowin' on her hair and lighting on her face. Looked like a beautiful, angry angel, she did." Boggs sighed, forgetting that his audience was waiting for the rest of the story.

"Well?" Harper demanded, "Why did she scream? What did you do? And how did you know she was cursing? You don't speak Spanish."

"Ach, some words are the same, no matter the language," Boggs waved a hand dismissively, repeating a few rude words that made Harper blush.

"All right." Harper was ready to concede the small point if Boggs would continue his tale. "What about the rest?"

"Well, dressed in white, she was. All ready for her wedding day." At this point, Boggs must have felt the need to replenish his tankard of 'never-right.' Harper watched the man stagger to the keg and refill his cup. Such things to recall could be painful, Harper thought, so much that a drink might help numb the pain, so he waited as patiently as he could.

Once Boggs had flopped back in his seat and downed three-quarters of his drink in one long gulp, Harper tried to coax a bit more of his story out of him. "Well, man? You can't leave me hanging."

"Well, Nessie—that was my pet name for her—she was fighting. Scratching and cursing as a man pulled her along. So's I rushed in and clocked him. Knocked him right on his arse, I did. Then I grabbed her hand and we ran away." Boggs's lips twisted in a wry smile. "Didn't know the bugger was her own father and he was a-takin' her to marry her future husband. A Count Viscount-somethin'-or-the-other. 'Twas an arranged marriage, ye see."

Harper gasped. He would never have imagined the rotund cook in his younger years would ever have done something so dashing and debonair. As he sat there open-mouthed and silent for a moment, Boggs stared down into his cup.

After a long moment, Harper asked, "What happened?"

"I found a priest and married her meself." And with that, Boggs downed the last of his cup and teetered back to the keg for more, leaving Harper speechless. Harper glanced down at the tattoo of Mary on his forearm. Her beautiful smile greeted him as it had so many times before, and so he waited for Boggs to return to tell him the end—and wished to be home with his Mary.

* * *

Archie watched Peter strut along the beam as if he owned the ship, only stopping to stare at Harper with a strange expression. Feeling the need to protect his young friend, he had sent Harper below. As the lad left, Archie became the sole focus of Peter's attention, which was fine, as far as he was concerned.

"We were supposed to hunt Tic-Tock together," the boy said, crossing his arms over his chest in a way that reminded Archie of a spoiled young child that had not gotten his way.

"He is dead. It is over and done. That's all that matters," Archie replied. He gave a mock shrug, as if killing crocodiles were as easy as swatting at pesky flies. He wasn't sure why he wanted to get a rise out the boy, but seeing the dark scowl gave him a small bit of satisfaction.

"There is the matter of our sail that needs to be addressed," Archie told him. "For one who has just had his greatest adversary slaughtered for him, you do not show your appreciation well by disgracing my ship. I would have your apology and have it made right."

Peter looked at him darkly. "I would have gotten Tic-Tock without any help from you."

"Proving such ingratitude with such an action is not the way of a gentleman. It is dishonorable," the cold tones in Archie's voice matched the ice in his eyes. "It is bad form, and bad form I do not tolerate."

"I am *not* a gentleman!" Fury was etched in each word, cutting each syllable Peter spoke.

"Then, I am sorry. You will not be welcome upon my ship. Not until you can conduct yourself as such."

Stamping his foot, Peter glowered at Archie, his face flushing red as he took off, flying back toward the island.

Archie shook his head as he watched, then turned his attention back to his crew, every member of which had been silent through the exchange. "Well, get back to it, lads! It appears we have a sail to mend."

A few mumbled curses later, Archie made his way below deck to find Harper. What he found instead, was Boggs, shaking a tin can of golden dust over a barrel.

"What is that?" As soon as the words left his mouth, familiar bell tones sounded frantically. Snatching the can from Boggs, he ripped off the punctured lid to find Miss Bell sprawled haphazardly in the bottom, looking rather cross and not nearly as bright as usual. When she noticed the lid was free, she immediately flew out and hovered near Archie's ear, blasting bell tones into his eardrum that sounded extremely accusatory.

"What have you done, Boggs?" Archie fought to keep the neutral calm in his voice, though he feared he was losing it.

"Didn't mean no harm, Cap'n. I was just fixing my barrel."

The man was swaying like a tree in the wind. Though he was making an apparent effort to stand straight and still, he was failing miserably. "Pixie dust fixes it," he enunciated each syllable, as if trying not to sound drunk.

"Did Miss Bell offer you her services in any way?"

"Er—not exactly."

"Well, then. That means you are stealing and as such, you must recompense her for what you have taken." Archie glanced over at Miss Bell, whose face had taken a beatific expression. "Will that do?"

A small, resolute nod answered.

"My apologies." Boggs sighed. "What will ye have?"

The pixie flew over and inspected Boggs. She made a full circuit around him, then drifted near his round belly, pointing at a brass button on his breeches.

"Oh, no. Not that ye don't. Me breeches won't stay up wi' out it." Boggs backed up an involuntary step.

"Boggs," Archie warned, "Off with it."

With something between a whimper and a sigh, Boggs took a knife from his side and popped the button off. It bounced one time on the floor before it was caught by the pixie. Gathering it close to her, she beamed a huge smile at Archie.

"Are we even, my dear?"

Another nod, and she had flown up the steps and away.

Perhaps she will learn something from this lesson the next time she thinks of stealing from Smee, Archie thought, watching Boggs try to keep his breeches up while keeping his tankard in his hand. And while pirates tended to be a thieving lot every time the opportunity presented itself, he would teach them to be a honorable, thieving lot —even if it killed him.

Harper had gone unnoticed until now. He found the lad propped up against the wall, his forearm before him, staring at the dark beauty whose image was inked in his skin. From the faraway look in his eyes, Archie didn't think he had paid any attention to the goings on of the past few minutes.

"Are you well?" Archie asked.

The vacant look left as Harper answered, "Aye. Has yon ruffian left, then?"

"Yes, Peter is gone."

"And the sail?"

"Still needs mending."

"I'm not fixing it," Harper said, sounding rather sullen.

"Yes, I am quite aware of that, but you might be pleased to know that I believe I may have made our flying friend a slight bit angry."

"Oh?" Harper brightened considerably as he stood, "That pleases me to no end, Jameson. The only other thing that would make me happier would be if you said we were leaving this forsaken place and heading home."

"Be prepared for your happiness, Harper, for we are most certainly going to try."

17

A FAMILIAR STAR

The decision was an easy one to make. Once again, Archie gave orders to leave Neverland as they had so many times before. The only part that held him back and made him hope that the island would be there once again in the morning, was the thought that he hadn't told Tiger Lily of their plans to go. He hadn't told her goodbye, and it crushed his spirit as he began plotting their way through the icebergs. He was more than ready to leave this strange place with its strange, flying boy. What he wasn't ready to leave was his heart and the one who held it. Still, he stayed at the ship's wheel, guiding them through the maze of ice that he had charted. Each spike that rose from the dark water had been plotted on a map, though now he didn't need it. They had attempted escape so many times that he knew the way around them by heart. He only wished there was a way to chart the stars so that he could find his way back to Tiger Lily should this venture prove successful and they find themselves in their own world when the sun lit the morning sky. The stars always seemed to evade him. Constellations shifted of their own accord, just as he was about to set pen to paper, as if they knew of his desire to log their exact location and moved to prove his maps wrong.

I will know the way back, should I ever find the way home, he thought, glancing up into a sky filled with diamond-bright stars. The map he had charted that long night before their arrival was tucked away in a drawer in his quarters. With luck, the stars in his own world had not changed and he would come back to Neverland—he would come back to her.

But for now, he was captain of this ship and keeper of all the souls aboard, so his priority was to get them back into waters they knew. His crew had been rather undemanding thus far, but he knew, as pirates, they wouldn't stay that way much longer. They had already become restless. Harper had been the only one to request going back as yet, but he knew the others would not be far behind him. They would be wanting a port, a way to spend their plunder, and the knowledge that there would be more adventure to be had—in a world they understood.

The night wore on and the water became clearer.

Below him, he heard the sounds of music and thumping. For now, his crew was celebrating their departure again. One loud thump and a muffled splash met his ears, followed by the distinct voice of Boggs yelling out a string of curses that silenced all other sounds for a moment.

His barrel of pixie-dusted spirits has been tipped over, Archie thought, a smile lighting his face as he realized the reason for Boggs's tirade. They can work it out amongst themselves, he decided, listening as angry shouting ensued, followed by several crashes and thumps.

"Fight it out, lads, fight it out," he murmured, looking out across a calm sea. Ignoring the melee beneath him, his thoughts returned to the beautiful Indian woman on the island and the last kiss he had shared with her. "I will be back for you, I promise," he vowed, promising himself as much as her. He couldn't imagine living a life without Tiger Lily.

I'm in love with her. I truly am. The sudden, happy truth warmed him from the inside out, much as Tiger Lily's kiss had done.

Then, the *Jolig Roger* lurched as if something was pushing it up into the air from below. The entire ship lifted several feet out of the water, bringing Tic-Tock front and center into Archie's brain. "Even he could not do this," Archie exclaimed as the *Roger* rose even further out of the water. He turned loose of the wheel and ran to the railing, to look down at the side of the ship. Several feet of wet planks with barnacles came into view, gleaming in the moonlight. A jolt of fear seized Archie and he gripped the railing so hard his knuckles turned white.

Without any warning, whatever had been pushing them up disappeared and the ship slammed back into the water, flipping Archie over the edge.

Saved only by his grip on the railing, he dangled in the open air, his breath knocked out of him. Finally, he gathered his wits and his breath. Just as he opened his mouth to call out for help, he saw one star above the ship that looked familiar. One solitary, shining diamond, sitting amongst thousands of others, reminded him of home. As he watched, it flickered like a dying candle flame, and went out. He had the vague impression that he had just witnessed the way home, and now it was gone.

"Easy now, Cap'n. I've got ye." Beckett's hands gripped Archie's wrists and a second later, Archie was once again safe on the deck of the ship.

"There be something big in these waters," Beckett whispered as he turned loose of Archie. "What be so big to lift the ship out of the water and ye never see it?"

Archie didn't answer, only shook his head. Sailors were adamant believers in stories. Since his arrival, he had heard of monstrous creatures in the oceans, such as squid that could wrap their tentacles around the largest of ships and drag them to the bottom of the sea, enormous scaly monsters with three or more heads that could breathe fire and set the ocean aflame. Archie didn't believe that their sudden ascent was due to a creature below them, but rather that—for some unknown reason—the ship had decided to try to go home, back to its star. A magic of some kind had brought them here. It would take magic to take them back.

"Beckett, take the wheel and keep our heading." Without waiting for an answer, Archie left and went in search of Boggs.

He found the cook sitting by his empty barrel, looking cross.

"I have questions for you, Boggs."

"I didn't blacken Dougherty's eyes, nor threaten to gut Bowen, regardless o' what they be saying, though they both be deserving of it for dumping me never-right." Boggs glowered at Archie, crossing his arms over his chest.

"I have no doubt you are correct, but that is not what I wished to ask." Archie pulled up a chair and sat down across from him. "Boggs, I need to ask how you captured Miss Bell."

"Oh." Boggs uncrossed his arms, becoming instantly friendlier. "She just flew into me cup, Cap'n."

"Just like that. Just flew into your cup."

"Aye, though it happened accident-like. Trying to fix my never-right, I was, and took too big a gulp. The ship sorta took to spinnin' and I was tryin' to keep me feet under me, weavin' this way and that, when I seen a streak of gold flying right at me. I lost me footing then and smacked right into her and into me cup she went." Boggs lifted his tankard for Archie's inspection, as if there would be golden streaks inside the cup as proof that Miss Bell had landed there.

"Why didn't she fly back out?"

Boggs's meaty hand clapped over the top of the tankard, covering it. "That's why. I knew Mr. Smee has a healthy hate for the little golden pixie as stolen his needles and buttons, so's I didn't want her to escape." His dark brows furrowed in confusion. "Why are ye asking me these questions, Cap'n? Has she stolen from ye, too?"

"No, she's not stolen anything from me." Archie shook his head. "But I think she may be the answer to leaving the island. She was with us when we came here, I believe we may need her to return home."

"Well then, seems we need to find us another pixie," Boggs observed dryly. "You made me turn her loose, ye know."

"If we are at the island again come morning, I plan on doing exactly that."

* * *

HARPER WASN'T HAPPY TO SEE THE VIBRANT GREEN OF Neverland. His perch up in the mast didn't help matters as he got to see even more of it than the blokes on the deck. He frowned, staring out across the water. There it was, large as life. The tall mountains that reached toward the sky, their tips covered in fog were the most prominent feature of the island, surrounded by a thick forest, then white sanded beaches and the inlet with the mermaid's rock. They were back at the same cursed island. Again.

He sighed, before calling down, "We're back. Land ho." As if they didn't know that and needed him to say it, he frowned. The hands below began making preparations to sail to the other side of the island, to the somewhat safer cove that seemed void of mermaids. He blew out a slow breath, and leaned his forehead against the web of ropes, watching his crewmates. They moved slowly. They weren't any happier to be back here than he was. For an undiscovered land, it was lacking in plunder and profitable adventure. Unless they were going to pillage Peter's unknown fortress and rob him of his green tights, there was nothing to be had on this island of any worth—at least that he knew of.

So now we go hunting pixies, he thought, waiting for a

few others to join him on the mast. I pray we find them and Jameson's plan works.

His thoughts ran to Mary as they released the sail and he felt the wind catch. He had been gone so long, had she waited for him? He hoped with every fiber in his being that she had. *One day soon, I'll be back,* he promised her, remembering the last smile she had given him. Then, he made himself the same promise. It would be soon.

If pixies were the answer to going home, he would catch an army of them as soon as he set foot on that white-sanded beach.

He made certain that Jameson knew of his wishes to go ashore, since he tended to be the one left in charge of the *Jolig Roger* when they anchored for supplies. There hadn't been any problem with the request, Jameson had turned to Beckett and placed the ship under his watch.

So now they were on their way. Three longboats rowed to shore, filled with pirates bent on capturing pixies. "I hear there be blue ones, too. Wonder if they be more powerful than the gold ones?" he heard Boggs mumble under his breath. Harper fought the urge to laugh as he rowed in sync with the others. He was certain the cook had other plans for catching a blue pixie—one that did not entail going home, but rather involved a barrel of strong spirits and a tin can with holes in the top.

"All right, lads. We meet here at sundown," Jameson

said, as they pulled the boats onto the beach. "Catch what you can."

"Aye." Harper's voice blended in with the others as they set off in search of pixies.

* * *

As luck would have it, Archie ran into Tiger Lily as soon as the crew dispersed. He had forgotten that this was the day to replenish their supplies. Being as they still had plenty, he hadn't thought of her presence on the beach and had planned on heading to the mountains in search of her.

He turned toward the forest and plowed into her, toppling them both over, though he had just enough time to try to land with his arms braced in an effort not to squash her beneath him. It didn't work, and he landed with his body on hers, his face buried in a pool of warm, silky hair.

Her hands were against his chest, though they didn't seem there to push him away. His heart sped up under her touch.

He didn't want to move, didn't want to breathe, but he raised his head up just enough to look into her eyes. What he found there surprised him.

"You didn't tell me you were going to leave again." Her

voice was strong and accusing, but her eyes were what caught him. They looked hurt.

"I promise that I was coming back to you." He shifted his weight off her and onto his elbows. "I would find my way back, whatever it took."

"It still would have been nice to know you were going, instead of standing here watching the ship leave again." Her hands came from his chest to return in a hard shove that knocked him backward and against the trunk of a tree, knocking the breath out of him.

"S-sorry," he wheezed, trying to capture his breath. "I w-would have come b-back because I'm in l-love with you."

Before he recovered, she had jumped up from the ground, ran to him, and covered his mouth in a kiss. He was beginning to think that all had been forgiven when a low, angry voice startled him. Tiger Lily jumped at the sound and the kiss broke.

"No one leaves Neverland." As Tiger Lily moved back, Archie caught sight of Peter. The boy was hovering a few feet away, his fists clenched at his sides. "No one *ever* leaves."

"Well, we shall be leaving," Archie informed him in a matter-of-fact way, "Soon." Of course, that doesn't mean we won't be right back here again the next morning, he added mentally. He didn't dare give the boy the satisfaction of knowing they were stuck there unless they managed to capture pixies and somehow fly the ship back home to their own star.

Peter's face turned red and something dark and sinister seemed to appear in his eyes. Then, he flew off without another word.

"I don't believe he liked the sound of that, but it is the truth."

"I don't like it either, but I understand," Tiger Lily said, nodding at the place where Peter had been. "I think his Lost Boys are giving him trouble since your ship arrived."

"Oh? Why is that?"

"The littlest one, Runt, has been coming to our village. He stays near me most of the time. He misses his mother. From what he tells me, Peter goes back to 'the grown-up star' and gets anything the boys need that can't be found on this island. Runt told me that he wants his mother and told Peter so. He thinks Peter is angry with him because he remembers his mother and none of the others do."

"I see where that could cause Peter some problems," Archie nodded. He didn't think Peter would enjoy giving up his position as leader and role model of his troupe if he were forced to bring parents to Neverland. "I wonder why he doesn't want us to leave?"

"Perhaps he is afraid that they will want to go home if

they see that you can do it," Tiger Lily replied, "And if they go, Peter would be all alone."

"That makes as much sense as anything else." Archie sighed. "I only hope he doesn't take his anger out on the sails again. The men weren't happy about his last visit. If he tries anything like that again, they'll be ready to fight."

* * *

Harper ducked under an outstretched branch. A few hours had gone by and so far he had had no luck whatsoever in finding a pixie. Blue, gold, or even polka-dotted, for that matter. He was getting more frustrated with each moment that passed. No one else had any luck either, from what he could tell. He had bumped into a dozen or more of his crewmates, and none of them had seen so much as a sprinkle of fairy dust.

I believe Peter was lying when he said there were blue pixies on this cursed island, he thought as he edged around a briar patch. There is probably only one pixie, and that is Miss Bell. He let out a string of curses when one briar caught his forearm and raked along its inner flesh. His tattoo of Mary now had a line of tiny dots crossing her as droplets of blood welled up from the scratch.

That, naturally, set off an even more elaborate string of

cursing. A few moments later, feeling somewhat better that the briar patch had been sufficiently cursed, he calmed down and began searching again. "If I were a pixie, where would I go?" he wondered. He didn't know much about the tiny fairies, other than Miss Bell's attraction to shiny objects. In a forest of green, he didn't see anything there that would capture her attention. Trees and rocks. That was all that was around him. Perhaps, he should work his way back to the ocean. The water sparkled if the sun hit it just right, maybe that would be shiny enough for her liking.

His stomach grumbled, informing him that he had forgotten to put anything to eat in his pockets for this excursion. His empty belly had him turning around to head back to the boats. With luck, he might find some kind of foodstuffs there, especially if he had the fortune of crossing paths with any of the Indians. If not, he would suffer and wait until sundown.

All thoughts of hunting for pixies left his mind as he trudged back toward shore, so it came as a surprise when one zipped under his nose and flew in the direction that he was heading. It happened so quickly, that he froze for a couple of seconds before reality sank in.

"I've found a pixie!" he yelled as loudly as he could, running after the trail of golden dust that seemed to be heading toward his own destination. He hoped the others were close by to help capture her, for now that he caught sight of her, he realized that he hadn't planned on how he was going to catch her.

She is so fast, what if I can't keep up? His lungs were on fire as he ran after her, barely jumping in time to avoid tripping over an exposed root. Just when he thought she was out of reach, the pixie slowed and turned, as if making sure that he was following.

That's odd, he thought, using his last burst of energy to try to close the gap between them. Then, she veered to the right. He nearly lost his footing trying to make the curve, but he stayed with her.

I've caught up, he thought, as she zipped through a patch of leaves on a low branch ahead of him.

I'm nearly there.

* * *

ARCHIE HEARD HARPER'S SHOUT AND JUMPED UP, RUNNING toward the sound of his voice. He had only called out once, so when Archie reached a grove of trees, he stopped, unsure of which way to go.

"That way." Tiger Lily's slender arm came from behind him, pointing to the left. "I'm certain of it."

He took off again with Tiger Lily close behind him,

and was rewarded with the brief sight of Harper ducking into the shadows of the trees ahead.

A few seconds later, he was at the exact spot where Harper had disappeared. The branches above them were arched, giving them a clear view of Harper, who stood facing them—a few yards ahead.

"Did you catch it?" Archie asked, noticing that Harper's face held a rather surprised expression. "Did you catch a pixie?"

Harper opened his mouth, but no sound came out. He took one step toward Archie and fell. A ray of sun came through the trees, glinting off the silver-gilded hilt of a small knife that had been sunk into his back.

Peter stood in the place where Harper had been a second earlier. He fixed Archie with the darkest look that Archie had ever seen, leaving no doubt that Peter was indeed the death guardian that Harper had warned him of.

"No one leaves Neverland." The words came out low and lethal, echoing against the trees before he flew past them and disappeared.

Dark, red blood pooled around Harper's body. He had landed with one arm outstretched. Mary smiled up at Archie from her place on his forearm. The smile first brought his tears.

Then the anger came.

18

THE PAN

Archie stared at the sail-wrapped body lying before him on the deck. It felt surreal. He kept expecting to see Harper up in the mast, letting out sails or pulling them in. He never imagined that he would see his friend bound in one, lying at his feet, and waiting for a funeral. Tiger Lily had offered to give Harper the honor of burial in her people's way, but Archie had refused. He would not leave the lad forever on an island that he had wished to escape. While he might not be able to take Harper's body back to his beloved Mary, he would do his best to give him the tribute he deserved as a pirate.

Smee stood beside him, seemingly lost in his own thoughts. Archie wondered if he was thinking of his recently finished job of inspecting Harper's wound and preparing his body for burial. Archie was certain the inspection was more of a cause of curiosity than anything else, for the lad was dead and stitching him up would not bring him back.

"A clean kill. Upward thrust into the kidney," Smee had muttered, looking at the wound in Harper's back, then at the small knife whose blade was crusted in dark blood. "Killed before, the boy has. Best ye take care that he doesn't do it again."

"If anyone dies, it will be Peter," Archie retorted, crossing his arms over his chest. "Peter is no more a child than I am. He will pay for what he has done." The feeling of rage was washed away by waves of nausea as he watched Smee put stitches in the lad's eyes, mouth, and nose, and then laid a shining copper coin on each sewn eyelid. "Is that necessary?"

"Be quiet and let me work. Ye want the lad delivered safe to the other side, aye?"

Though he had heard of paying the ferryman, Archie hadn't been sure why having every orifice on one's head sewed shut would ensure their safe delivery to the otherworld, but he had done as Smee said and waited for him to finish. At the last, he crossed the lad's tattooed forearm over his chest, then placed the other arm over for good measure. "So as he can keep the lass close to 'is heart," Smee said gruffly, wiping at his watering eyes. As Archie watched the old man stare at the lad's neatly wrapped body, he knew that Smee had done the best that he knew by Harper. Now it was his turn.

The wind had caught the sails, pulling them farther from Neverland. Beckett was at the wheel, navigating around the icebergs. "Hope yon wee bugger flies over here to tell us we can't leave again. Feed him to the fishes, I would, for what he did to Harper," he grumbled.

Several others chipped in with various threats and suggestions of what they would like to do to the deviant who killed their fellow crewmate.

He had a family here and didn't know it. Every man aboard was willing to fight for him. Archie gazed across the clear sea, free of icebergs and out of sight of Neverland.

"This is the spot." He nodded to Beckett and gave his orders to release the anchor.

Once the ship had stilled, he took a deep breath, willing his own spirit to quiet. The effect was catching, as silence enveloped the ship and those who wore hats, took them off in a motion of respect for the dead.

Archie had officiated over more funerals than he cared to admit in his brief time as captain, but he had never spoken for one who had been a close friend. He allowed himself a long moment to reflect on the memories he had, from the first day he had met the young man who reminded him of a stuttering squirrel to the fearless one, bent on catching a pixie to return home. Archie smiled as a sudden realization came to him, Harper had never stuttered again once he had whacked Caesar with that oar. That act had given the lad courage.

May I have the same strength, Archie thought, stepping up to address his crew. It was time.

"Today we lay to rest a fellow crewman into the briny deep. Jonathan Harper was quick and sure-footed on the rigging and swift to lend a hand to any man in need." Archie stopped, glancing down at Harper's still form. "I am proud to call him the truest friend that I have ever known. I was with him the day he had the image of his true love inked upon his arm and I know of his plans to save every coin that he could in hopes to someday marry his love." Archie felt the ice etch into his words as he spoke. The coldness seeped into his voice. "That will never happen now and she may never know of the love he held for her in his heart."

He walked over to a small sea chest that held all of Harper's belongings. He bent over and flipped the lid open. Hundreds of bright coins filled the chest to the brim, glinting in the afternoon sun, and on the top of the pile of riches, sat a worn and creased picture of a beautiful young woman.

"Harper will never make it back to her," Archie said quietly, though he knew they all heard every word. A moment passed as he chose his next words, for he knew as soon as he uttered them, they would change the course of not only his own life but those of all aboard. "For that I will have revenge. Peter will pay for his crime. Who is with me?"

The answer that met his ears was deafening as the silence disappeared and a hundred pirates yelled their reply, "Aye!"

A wry smile came to Archie's lips. His crew looked like a murderous lot, indeed. Teeth bared and rage in their eyes, most of them waving a cutlass or a pistol in the air in addition to their verbal response.

"Aye," Archie repeated. The word felt strange upon his lips, but seemed to fit the occasion. He gestured to the sea chest. "The man who brings me the flying boy known as Peter, will have Harper's gold as his reward."

Several appreciative murmurs met his ears, though most seemed content enough to hunt Peter down without the added bonus of treasure. Then, Beckett spoke up behind him. "Will ye be wanting him brought to you alive, Cap'n?"

Archie turned to Beckett, fixing him with his cold eyes. "You can bring him to me in any manner you wish."

Beckett grinned at him. "Aye, dead it is, then."

A few moments later, over a dozen men had lifted Harper's body to the railing, some having only enough room to squeeze in one arm to help the others that crowded in beside them. As Archie watched, they eased him over and the white-wrapped body disappeared into a frothy sea. The only trace of Harper now lay in a sea chest with a crinkled photograph. Archie bent over and picked up the picture and tucked it into his own pocket. If, per chance, one of his men brought Peter to him alive, he wished to have some small part of Harper with him to exact his revenge.

* * *

THEY SPENT EVERY DAY ON THE ISLAND, SEARCHING. AS IF Peter knew they searched for him, he flew in front of them, taunted them, and then would disappear.

Two men had been shot as their crewmates had been aiming their pistols at Peter and missed him. As luck would have it, neither man's wound was life-threatening, though it didn't improve the mood of any of the pirates. Unable to catch the one they wanted, they began capturing the Lost Boys instead.

Archie drummed his fingers on the map table while eyeing the boy sitting across from him. Patch, the boy with the rabbit ear cap, was regarding him with wary caution.

An impasse, Archie fought the urge to smile. So far, the

boy had only answered his questions with queries of his own.

"Will you tell me where Peter is?" Archie asked yet again, certain that he had asked this same question a dozen times.

"Will you tell me why you want him?"

Archie rolled his eyes and repeated the same answer. "Because he killed one of my men."

"Mmph," the boy shrugged and continued to stare at him.

The door opened and Beckett appeared. "Beg pardon, sir, but we got two more. Where do you want them?"

"In the hold with the others," Archie replied, and Beckett left, shutting the door behind him. Archie caught himself doing a mental headcount. There were six boys down there, plus the stubborn one before him. Perhaps, he was going about this all wrong. So far, he had been asking questions, maybe he should be letting some of his information out, instead.

"Patch, I wish to tell you of my plans," he began as he tipped his chair backwards on two legs, leaning back to the wall to prop his booted feet on the table. "You see, my men and I wish to leave this island and Peter doesn't want us to go, so I need to talk to him and explain the situation." It was a lie, a large one. Ever since Harper's funeral, leaving the island had been the last thing on their minds.

A few had even made the comment that they had seen pixies, but none of them had made any moves to capture them. Even Boggs had refrained from making another batch of his never-right in hopes of capturing a flying boy instead. And as far as explaining went, Archie's only explanation would be to Peter, and it would come at the fine point of his rapier. He struggled to keep the neutral expression on his face as Patch shifted on his chair.

"I don't know where Peter is," the boy admitted. "None of us do."

"Then where do you meet him? Surely you have a certain place that you can find him," Archie insisted. His men had been searching Neverland for days and kept finding hidden coves and new inlets around the beach each day, as well as niches in trees that were large enough for them to crawl into and explore, and they hadn't even gotten to the caverns in the north. For an island, it was large and mysterious.

"No, we just wait. He always finds us. We don't find him."

Deciding this line of questioning was useless, Archie excused himself and left the boy sitting at the table and went up to the deck to get a breath of fresh air. The evening sun had cooled, and the boats were coming in from the island. Frowning, he noticed several empty seats in the first boat.

"There be six o' our men missing," Boggs announced as soon as the boat was tied to the ship. "No idea where they be. Never heard any shots, be like they just disappeared."

"Lovely," Archie grumbled, staring across the railing to the island that seemed more cursed with every second that passed. "No sign of them anywhere. You are certain?" He reached over the railing to give Boggs a hand up and over the railing.

"Aye, they are gone," Boggs grunted, heaving his round torso over the side of the ship and doing a quick, sideways two-step to keep his footing. Then he added, in what Archie guessed to be his most dire and disastrous tone, "They be vanished."

As if in answer to Boggs's statement a lone voice yelled out from the island, "Ahoy!" It was just loud enough that it startled Boggs into tripping. He landed on the deck with a loud thump. Archie twisted around to look back out to the island, avoiding Boggs, who seemed to be sprawled in every conceivable direction. Noticing the spyglass tucked in Boggs's belt, he bent and snagged it, then jumped out of the way, pressing the glass to his eye.

On the white-sanded beach, stood one of the "vanished" pirates, waving his hands in the air in an attempt to be noticed.

"Boggs, take the boat back out and get him. It's Dougherty."

"Ach, leave it to Dougherty to be the one I gotta go save," Boggs mumbled irritably as he crawled back over the railing. "I should've blacked more than his eyes."

Five more bodies followed Boggs to help row and Archie watched as they set back out to shore. Once the missing pirate had been collected, they rowed back. Archie set to helping pull each man up. He noticed that Dougherty was the last to come up and that the man didn't seem anxious to be on the ship again.

A man with pinched features and a generally mousey look, Archie couldn't decide whether it was Ben Dougherty's usual appearance, or if the strange expression upon his face was a product of fear. It also didn't help that the bruises around his eyes had gone to the greenish stage of healing, giving him the look of a man gone seasick.

The man stood before him, looking squeamish. His eyes darted everywhere but to Archie's face.

"Well, man, let's have it. Where have you been and what has happened?" Archie demanded, crossing his arms over his chest.

"The boy Peter caught meself and five more, then tied us up. He sent me free to give you a message," Dougherty's voice came out in a near squeak. "He says he wants his men free, else he starts killing ours, one by one."

"Oh, will he now?" Archie's voice dropped octaves and came out in a whisper.

"A-aye," Dougherty stammered. "He w-wants 'em back by nightfall."

Archie glanced up into the evening sky. The sun sat on the horizon. Within a couple of hours, night would come—and with it, more dead sailors, unless he worked quickly.

"Did he say where to bring them, or am I just to shuffle them off on the beach anywhere I choose?"

"He said to bring them to the place where you saw him last. Said you would know where that was."

Archie knew very well the place he had seen the flying boy. It was the place where Peter had murdered Harper in cold blood. The look on Archie's face must have been a sight, for not only did Dougherty look away, but so did Boggs.

"We will do as he asks," Archie muttered, though he didn't say all that he wished to say. *We will do as he asks—for now. Once I have my men back, he will pay for what he has done.*

* * *

It was nearly dusk when they arrived in the dark canopy of trees. Expecting to find Peter hovering in the same place as before, Archie had come armed to the teeth with a troupe of his men behind him. Pistols and cutlasses were aimed in every direction, but what they found was their men, bound against a tree.

"These ropes be familiar," Beckett announced, hurrying over to untie the men at the tree.

"Yes, I believe they are ours, though I hadn't realized they were missing," Archie said, taking in the lumps on each pirate's head. Three out of the five were still unconscious, slumped against one another. The two who were somewhat lucid were talking nonsense about cannons.

Seeing no threat anywhere around them, Archie took to untying the ropes.

"He's on the sh-ship," one man managed, leaning his head back against the tree in an effort to focus on Archie's face. "The boy is on the ship."

"With... the... cannons," the other added as Archie turned to look back in the vicinity of the ship. He knew that he wouldn't see anything, due to the dense foliage of the forest, but the urge to turn to look was too great. "He said to tell you he would know if you didn't do as you were told."

"What do you want us to do with these boys, Cap'n?" Boggs asked, the line of Lost Boys behind peering around his round frame to see what was happening.

"We have our men, we will release his." Archie nodded, waiting as Boggs untied the ropes around each boy's wrists and set them free. As soon as the ropes fell, they scattered, disappearing into the forest. Only Patch stayed just long enough to mumble a quick thank you, then he vanished behind the others.

"We might oughta kept 'em for safe-keeping," Boggs grumbled.

"No, he kept his part of the bargain. We will keep ours."

The entire trek back to the longboat, Archie worried about the safety of the ship. In his haste, he had taken the majority of the crew with him to the island, leaving a skeleton crew aboard the *Jolig Roger*. It had been a foolish, ill-thought plan to take so many with him. With the ease that Peter had shown in taking a half dozen of his men, Archie had no doubt that he could best the few, unsuspecting souls he had left on deck.

Let them all be safely on board and whole, he hoped, taking his spyglass out to look at the ship, which, thankfully, was still afloat where he had left it.

Beckett's tattooed body was the first thing that caught Archie's eye. Flanked by the last rays of sunlight, he stood tall and imposing on the quarterdeck, looking every bit ready for any fight that would come his way. Archie's worry disappeared as they rowed back to the ship.

"Is all well? Did you catch yon flying fiend?" Beckett asked, reaching over to give Archie a hand onto the ship.

"All is well enough. We never saw him. How is everything here? Anything new to report?"

"Nay. All quiet here."

Archie nodded. "Keep your watch. If anything should happen, let me know. I will be below."

He hadn't intended to do it, but he began walking each inch of the ship. Something told him that Peter had been on the ship, even though no one had seen him. He wouldn't have given an idle threat, his mind reasoned logically. Had we not released his men, he would have found a way to make us. He's been here. I can feel it in my bones.

Step by step, he searched each deck and each room, finding nothing amiss until he came to his own quarters. A wave of anxiety rolled over him as he opened the door and found the contents of his map table lying on the floor.

Paper was strewn over every inch of the room. Maps had been pitched here and there and more than a few of his charting instruments had been flung in every direction. Most disconcerting was the small knife that had been sunk into the wooden surface of his table, as if it had been put there as a signature. That knife said more than if Peter had been there himself to announce his presence. It was a small blade, nearly a twin to the one he had used to kill Harper.

Archie felt his breath catch. No one on deck had heard

anything. Beckett had been watching, but he hadn't seen even the slightest sign of Peter.

His name isn't Peter; it's Pan. Harper's voice popped up in his mind, reminding him of his friend's story of the death guardian. Archie began picking up his maps and started putting his quarters back together again. All the while, Harper's voice kept echoing in his head. *His name is Pan.*

* * *

A week passed by with no sign of Peter. The search commenced every morning, though in an attempt to keep the focus on Peter, Archie had given his orders that no Lost Boy was to be captured. Each evening, his men came back empty-handed.

Then, it happened. As Archie walked along the beach to meet Tiger Lily, a single boy appeared, as if he had been waiting for him. But it wasn't Peter.

"Hello, Runt," he greeted the youngest of the Lost Boys. "How are you?"

"Not good," the boy replied. His small face was scrunched up in an expression that looked like he was ready to cry.

"What is the matter?" Archie asked. He was more than ready to offer assistance to the smallest of Peter's troupe, especially since the boy stayed with Tiger Lily most of the time and held his own special place in her heart.

"I'm supposed to give you this," he said, thrusting out a rolled up sheet of paper that had been somewhat creased by his small hands. As Archie took it, two large tears escaped and rolled down Runt's cheeks.

"Whatever it is, I'm sure everything will be all right," he tried to reassure the boy as his own heart dropped at the sight of the familiar scroll with his own handwriting.

"It won't." Runt shook his head, sending more tears free to track down his face. "It won't be all right ever again."

Trying not to concentrate on the distraught boy in front of him, Archie focused on unrolling the paper. His hands shook as he realized that he held his map of the stars—the same one that he had charted on that fateful night before their arrival. The map that had been tucked away in his desk because he had valued it above all the others. It was the one that he had planned to use to bring him back to Neverland one day, the one that would bring him back to Tiger Lily. In his tidying of the map room, he hadn't noticed its absence—had not realized that Peter had stolen it.

Archie looked up from the map to Runt's tear-streaked face. The boy was staring at the back of the map.

Perplexed, Archie flipped the map over, and found the reason for Runt's intense gaze.

There, on the back of his map, was another map, drawn in the shape of Neverland.

Runt's next words sent chills down Archie's spine.

"Peter said to tell you that the X is where you will find Tiger Lily."

19

THE MAP

Smee glared at the back of the map as if the parchment contained the secrets to the greatest evil on earth instead of a crude drawing of the island. "What, in the name of Saint Brendan, does he expect ye to do with this?"

Archie sighed. The odds of his figuring out Peter's strange map were about as good as discovering the reasons behind Smee's obsession with the patron saint of whales. Both mysteries would probably remain unsolved. Still, he answered as best he could. "I believe he expects me to follow it in some fashion."

"Are you going to follow it?"

"If it leads me to Tiger Lily—yes."

"Mmph."

"Yes, that's my assessment of the situation as well,"

Archie said before taking the parchment from Smee's hands and giving it another inspection. Though crude, the map depicted the correct shape of Neverland as far as he could tell, each inlet and cove that they had visited were recognizable. There were also a few shown that Archie had never seen.

"Was the boy certain that she had been taken?" The look on Smee's face told Archie that the old man did not believe Runt's story.

"Yes, he was certain. But to be sure, I checked with her people. They haven't seen her in over a day and have been doing their own searching. They haven't found any trace of her, which worries me. They can track anyone. There is no other explanation. Peter has her."

"Well, what are ye going to do? It says clear as can be at the bottom o' the page that ye haven't much time to be dawdlin' about." Smee leaned forward and placed a gnarled forefinger at the place he spoke of. Though it wasn't quite as clear as Smee made it out to be, the words *You have two days* were printed in a childlike scrawl, along with two more at the bottom. *Come alone.*

Two days until what? Archie wondered. Would Peter kill Tiger Lily as quickly and easily as he had Harper? And if so, why? She had never done anything to him that Archie knew of. The only conclusion that Archie could come up with was that Peter had taken her out of amusement, because he knew of Archie's feelings for her.

At that thought, Archie wanted nothing more than to rush to her aid, to follow the cursed map wherever it led him in hopes that it would lead him straight to her side, but his previous escapade with his men and the Lost Boys as prisoners made him wary. Now he wished to think every angle through as thoroughly as possible. As for coming alone, he didn't plan on taking any of his crew with him, but if they happened to just show up in an effort to win Harper's gold, he wasn't going to stop them.

He traced his fingers over the map, much the way he had when charting the stars that lay on the other side of the paper. One thing worried him more than anything else. His map was torn. While Peter's map of Neverland was complete, the paper on either side of his drawing had been ripped free, as if Peter had wished his drawing to be the only focus of his map.

"The *X* is where you will find Tiger Lily." Runt's words ran through his head, so he repeated them aloud in hopes that Smee would make some sense of them.

"That is all that he said?" Smee asked, scooting his bench closer. Once settled, he adjusted his spectacles on the end of his nose and took on a scholarly appearance as he studied the map on the table. "I see no Xs," he muttered under his breath. "The lad be a poor map maker, that be sure."

Archie didn't bother stating his agreement, but rather sat and stared at the drawing, wishing the phantom x would appear. Silence enveloped them. Several long moments later, Archie jumped and pointed at the map. "There it is."

The sudden commotion made Smee fall back, nearly off his stool. He placed one gnarled hand over his chest and glared at Archie. "Do *not* do that again. Ye nearly gave me a heart seizure."

"It's here, hidden in the trees at the bottom of this mountain." Archie was standing now, fingertips trembling as he pointed to the drawing of a grove of trees not far from the Indians' village. Hidden between two of the branches, near the trunk of one tree was a small, barely discernible *X*.

"I hate to be the one who tells you this, lad, but there be no way he left her so close to her own people," Smee said darkly, "Not alive."

Archie hated hearing the words spoken aloud, but the truth was that he had thought them, too. "It could be a trick. He's tricked us before. He seems to have a great fondness for games."

"Aye, I s'pose so." Smee scratched his bearded face. "Hope, we will, that he is only making sport of us again."

Yes, hope we shall. Archie looked down at the map again. He didn't believe Peter would kill Tiger Lily, to do so would take away his fun. Still, his heart hurt at the thought of not being able to protect her.

Let her be unharmed, he sent up a silent plea, hoping that in the first rays of the morning sky, he would find her safe.

* * *

By the time dawn broke, Archie's nerves were a frazzled mess. The thought of finding her hurt—or worse—gave him the worst sense of dread that he had ever felt in his entire life.

The row to shore that normally took a half hour at most, stretched on for so long that he wondered if they would ever reach Neverland.

As he set foot on the white-sanded beach, a new problem arose.

"Best ye let us come with ye, Cap'n," Boggs said, patting the pistols strapped to his sides. Then, he nodded to the other five pirates who had helped row the boat. Each of them gave him a grave nod, agreeing with Boggs. "Ye never know what ye might find and then ye will be needing us."

Come alone. The words echoed in Archie's head, over

and over. He had the funny feeling that if he did not follow the instructions exactly, that Peter would somehow know and then Tiger Lily's fate would be sealed.

"No, stay with the boat," Archie decided, shaking his head. "If I do not return within the hour, come and look for us."

"Aye." Boggs sighed, flopping back down on the seat of the boat. He landed so hard that the wood made an audible crunch as the boat squashed down into the sand.

Archie smiled in spite of himself. Should everything work out all right, it would take quite a bit of time to extract the boat from the shoreline.

After nodding a quick farewell to a disgruntled Boggs, Archie set off into the shadow of the trees. It did not take long to find the spot that had been marked on the map. Archie's heart sped up as he neared the place. His palm slick with sweat, he placed his hand on the hilt of his rapier, expecting to find the worst. Instead, he found nothing.

There was no sign of Tiger Lily. Letting out a few low curses, Archie stalked around the circlet of trees several times over before he stopped and pulled the map out from his coat.

The parchment crackled as he unrolled it and lifted it up for a closer inspection. He squinted at Peter's drawing, trying to take in each branch and limb that had been scrawled there. The sun streaked through an opening in the trees and lit up the back of the map, sending his own written details to shine through the back. Various stars mottled the drawing, making Peter's workmanship even worse than it had been before.

Frowning, he stepped under the shadow of a giant tree to avoid the sun's glare. If the map had been drawn true to form, he was standing under the tree where Tiger Lily should be. The X was hidden between two branches, high up in the tree. With a sinking feeling, Archie looked up, hoping that Peter hadn't placed her above him in the giant oak.

A flash of white caught his eye in a forked branch. It was a piece of parchment, not unlike the one he held in his hands.

"A fine place to leave me a note," Archie grumbled, looking at the slip of paper that seemed impossible to reach. The tree was old, half-dead, with splintering branches that popped out like dried-out tentacles. It would be treacherous to attempt to climb it.

Several ideas jumbled through his head, one after another, each crowding out the one before it.

If I had a pistol about me, I could shoot the limb holding it. Maybe the wood is rotten enough that it would break. No, the branch is too thick for that.

He tapped the hilt of his rapier with his fingertips. No

way to throw it at the branch and hope to knock it free. With the luck he had had of late, he would either get his blade caught in the tree branch or skewer the paper—both instances that he would wish to avoid.

Letting out a sigh of frustration, he looked at the trunk of the tree. It was enormous, but the bark was rough and uneven. It might be possible to climb it, but Archie was betting that it wasn't going to be pleasant. He laid his map down on the ground and walked around the base of the tree, searching for the best spot to climb.

"I detest heights," he cursed. Finding what he thought to be the best spot, he sat down and took off his shoes. Perhaps, climbing the tree would be like the ropes of the rigging and be easier without them.

Barefoot and heart thumping, he stood up and began to climb. After a few seconds, he realized that it wasn't as hard as he thought it was going to be, so he calmed and began focusing only on reaching the branch that held the paper.

He didn't realize that the branch just below it was rotten—until it was too late.

With a loud snap it broke and sent him falling back to the earth. He landed solidly on his back. The force of the fall left him gasping for air. He watched in a surreal way as the slip of paper came free and floated in slow motion, landing upon his heaving chest.

"Bloody hell," he managed to croak as he snatched the paper off and sat up. His heart had been hammering before, but now it was ready to beat its way out of his body. He sat for a long second, forcing himself to take a single, long breath—then he opened the folded paper.

It was another map, much like the one that lay crumpled beneath him, only this one was different.

He means to send me on a wild goose chase, Archie thought, incredulous, as he looked at the section of paper that had been ripped from his own map. Once again, Peter had charted his own rendering of Neverland, and on the opposite side of the island near the coast, sat another blasted *X*.

"At least it looks easier to reach," Archie grumbled, slapping his shoes back on. He gathered up his maps, stood, and made the trek back to the longboat.

* * *

"Ye think perhaps we should have brought Beckett along with us this time?" Boggs asked as they rowed along on their way to the next spot.

"Why ever for?" Archie answered with a question of his own.

"Because he be a sure shot with that musket of his. He could take out the wee bugger that keeps sendin' us in circles and we would have Miss Lily back safe and sound-like."

"A fine time to tell me that Beckett is a good shot, Boggs," Archie said. "It would have made hunting a lot easier had I known this sooner."

"Didn't think about it until the Indians done offered to do it for us." Boggs shrugged.

Archie rolled his eyes. Out of all the pirates accompanying him, the one who might prove the most useful was standing guard on the deck of the *Jolig Roger*.

"Beckett's not used to moving targets, anyway," Smee muttered beside him, giving Boggs his usual grumpy stare.

"Aye, that may be, but I'm sure he'd like to try," Boggs replied, nonplussed.

Water sloshed over the side of the boat, covering Smee's feet. He harrumphed and crossed his arms, not impressed with Boggs or the trip to shore.

Archie had thought having the ship's surgeon along a good idea in case Peter popped up with any other surprise that would leave him out of sorts or missing air. Now, as he looked at the crabby old man, Archie wished to trade him for Beckett, but there was no way to do so without turning around and rowing all the way back to the ship.

The sun was resting just over the horizon. It was too late to go back now. There was nothing to do but press onward; one day remained to find her.

He opened his map and laid it out on the flat of his lap. From the placement of the *X*, whatever he was supposed to find was ahead.

Fate smiled down upon him a few moments later as he spied a fluttering piece of paper held down by a rock, lying close enough to the water that it was within his grasp without ever leaving the boat. He leaned over and snatched it.

"Well, where we be headed next?" Boggs asked in an airy tone, as if he regularly rowed his captain anywhere he wished to go and that their current trip was naught but a joy ride.

Archie ignored him, concentrating on the piece of map. As if he planned on being difficult, Peter had placed the *X* in a cove to the north of the island, in a place that the *Jolig Roger* would be unable to sail. To get there, would take a smaller boat. He had nearly told Boggs that they would be heading north, when he spied the childish scrawl at the bottom of the page. There wouldn't be any help on the next excursion, from Boggs, Beckett, or anyone for that matter.

Come alone—or she dies.

* * *

"Best ye wait til morn. There be no way one man can

row in these waters in the dark, ye'd end up smashed against the rocks," Beckett advised as the ship neared the cove. It was well past midnight. "The water's not near as calm as the other spots we've laid anchor."

Archie nodded his agreement. He knew Beckett was right, even though his heart wanted him to go right then. The *Jolig Roger* was rocking back and forth with each swell. A smaller boat would be crushed, along with the fool who would attempt to row it. A fat lot of good being dead would do to rescue her.

He sighed. "I will leave at first light. Keep a watch out, Beckett. If anything should go amiss, call for me."

"Aye, Cap'n."

He trudged back to the map room, hoping to find some rest. Sleep eluded him. He spent the wee hours of morning, tossing and turning on his cot, wishing for day to break.

At some point, exhaustion seeped in and he found himself waking to a frantic beat on the door.

"Cap'n," Beckett's voice came through the wood as clear as if he were already in the room. He burst through the door a second later, too impatient to wait for a reply.

"What is it? Have we run aground?" Archie flipped his legs over the cot and jumped up, expecting the worst. "What is it?" he repeated.

"The tide has risen o'er the night and the water be calmer this morn," Beckett said in a matter-of-fact way.

"That's it?"

"Aye, I thought you might want the report afore ye go."

"You came here to tell me the tide has risen?"

"Aye, but none so much that it should give ye any trouble getting into the cove. If anything, it might make it a wee bit easier to get around some of those sharp rocks that come up from the sea bottom." Beckett paused. "Are ye certain none of us can go with ye?"

Ah, there's the reason for coming. "None can come, but I thank you for your concern, Beckett. If I were to not follow Peter's exact instructions, I fear the worst will happen to her."

"Well," Beckett frowned, "it be easier to show him the blade of a cutlass or the tip of a pistol and be done with these games."

"If it were only that easy." Archie slid on his shoes. "It seems Peter knows our plans before we do and as he is the only one who knows where Tiger Lily is, I would need him alive."

A cloud of dust fell from the beams overhead, followed by the sound of pounding feet.

"Something is happening." Beckett's eyebrows raised for a split second, before he turned and rushed up to the deck with Archie on his heels.

The first thing that met Archie's ears was the shouted curses that seemed to come from every direction. He caught a glimpse of green before it disappeared behind the sails. A volley of pistol shots rang through the air, peppering the canvas.

"Cease fire!" Archie yelled, looking up at the canvas that now resembled a piece of limp Swiss cheese. The sail was ruined. He hurried to the opposite side of the ship, expecting to see some trace of Peter, but he had disappeared.

"There! There he is." Archie wasn't sure who had shouted the words, but everyone's attention had moved toward the cove, where the flying boy had turned, as if expecting Archie to follow. Then, he vanished behind the rocks.

* * *

BECKETT HELD HIS TONGUE AS HE HELPED LOWER THE SMALL rowboat, but once he was certain that his captain had rowed far enough to be out of earshot, he let out a string of curses that shocked the rest of the crew into silence—no small feat as the majority of them had quite the colorful vocabulary all their own.

"Curse this blasted island and every soul upon it!" He finished his rampage and grasped the railing to the ship so hard that his knuckles turned white. The polished wood beneath his fingers creaked under the pressure, threatening to splinter as he watched the small rowboat disappear behind a tall column of rock.

"He be gone now, out of sight," Smee said, spyglass to his eye. "He should have taken some of us with him." He retracted the spyglass and placed it in his pocket, giving Beckett a cold look, as if the situation were his fault. "I don't like it. This is fool's errand."

"Ye aren't the only one who doesn't like it, but he gave his orders. I won't disobey 'em."

"Ach! The lad isn't thinking straight, only thing in that brain of his now is *her*. Mark me words, no good will come of it."

"He is captain, and he gave his orders," Beckett said, letting go of his grip on the railing and turning his back to the island. Silently, he agreed with Smee and wanted nothing more than to release another boat, fill it with men, and wreak havoc on the one who had been causing them so much strife, but he would obey his orders. Keep the ship and the men safe. He looked up at the sail, tattered strips of canvas fluttered in the wind. Deciding that he had best do the part of keeping the ship safe, he opened his mouth to give orders to replace the sail, when the ship lurched and he found himself lying flat on his back, looking up at the sky.

His first thought was that the ship had run aground on rocks, but that thought was chased away by the recollection that they were anchored, safely away from any of the jutting boulders near the cove. He jumped to his feet and scrambled to the railing.

Something had hit them.

And it sat beside the ship, glaring at Beckett with two dark, intelligent, hate-filled eyes.

"Ready the cannons!" Beckett shouted, watching as the dark form turned and began swimming toward the cove, fast for a crocodile with naught but a stub for a tail.

"Cannons ready," the reply echoed back up the line of the ship.

"He's near the rocks." Smee had arrived at his side and was looking through his spyglass again. "Close to where I saw the cap'n last."

"No way to fire without trapping the cap'n in that inlet," Beckett muttered, taking the glass from Smee to see for himself. Sure enough, the crocodile was taking the exact path the captain had taken, as if it were hunting for the man itself.

"What be your orders?" One man yelled from the other end of the ship, linstock in hand, ready to touch to his cannon's fuse.

"Half of you stay with the cannons, but don't fire unless he returns." Beckett nodded to them. A wry grin painted his beard-stubbled face. "The rest of you buggers, release the boats and follow me. We are going to hunt us a croc."

* * *

THE MUSCLES IN ARCHIE'S ARMS WERE ACHING BY THE TIME he pulled the rowboat up on the shore. Even though the waters had calmed, he still had been tossed dangerously close to the rocks more times than he cared to admit. Had he tried his rescue attempt any earlier, he wouldn't have made it.

He took one long, deep breath before he took out Peter's latest drawing. If the map were true to form, his next clue to Tiger Lily's whereabouts would be waiting for him a short walk away. Unwilling to waste any more time, he folded the map and thrust it back into his pocket and set off across the beach.

The next slip of paper was stuck on a stick at the mouth of a cavern, waving in the breeze like a small, white flag of surrender. Carefully, he unfolded it, finding yet another map. Trying to squelch the feeling of hope, he knelt to the ground and placed each of Peter's drawings end to end. Every piece of his map was now accounted for. Unless Peter had managed to filch another map without his knowledge, this last drawing would lead him to Tiger Lily. Folding up all of the other tattered pieces of parchment, he stuck them back in his pocket and concentrated on Peter's latest work.

A twisting, turning trail began at the mouth of the cavern, where he now stood and led into it. Archie grinned. He was close.

20

END GAME

It started out dimly lit, which was the reason he hadn't thought to construct a torch of some kind. At least that was what Archie was busy telling himself, though he knew the true reason was that he had been in a rush and hadn't thought this last bit of his journey through.

I'm close now, I know I am. I can feel it. If only the light will hold out. Archie squinted at the drawing before he turned another corner. The squiggles on the map seemed accurate, with each turn leading him farther into the cavern. The air became cold and stale and darkened with each step he took.

Two twisting turns later, it was pure blackness. Archie put one hand out to steady himself and found the damp, cold rock of the cavern wall. His heart began pounding.

There wasn't any way to see anything. Not what lay ahead, much less the map. At this rate, he would have to turn back and find a source to light his way. He didn't want to do that. While he thought he had enough time left to find her, something in his gut was telling him that he didn't and that time was running out.

He slid one foot in front of the other in an effort to make progress. One step down, he thought, trying to still his beating heart.

"Take deep breaths, take deep breaths," he chanted as he took another step into the unknown. This step held more peril than the one before as the floor dipped. Then, he lost his footing and landed on his arse. This set off a loud tirade of curses that bounced against the walls and echoed back and forth. Words that his dearly departed mum would have washed his mouth out for, were now blasting his own eardrums before they made their way down the length of the cavern, likely to a trapped Tiger Lily whom he would never find.

"Saint Brendan," he hissed a moment later, hoping that those words would follow those earlier and mark the cursing as Smee, just in case his beloved had indeed heard his rather colorful vocabulary.

He sat there on the cold, stone floor for another few seconds, listening as the last of the echoes quieted. He was torn as to whether he should stand up and try to continue his trek in the dark, or turn back and run as quickly as he could to the entrance to find light. There wasn't a choice to be made, really, he would have to go back.

With a heart that felt like lead, he stood up and began to turn. Then, the most unexpected thing happened. Miss Bell arrived, as if out of thin air. Her beautiful, golden light illuminated the darkness just enough that Archie could see a bit of his surroundings—and the unhappy look on the pixie's face.

"You have no idea how happy I am to see you, my dear," Archie exclaimed, his spirits rising. He chose not to query his small friend on what troubled her, but asked her assistance instead. "I need your help, Miss Bell. Can you light the way for me?"

The tiny pixie didn't answer with her usual bell tones, but gave him a small, barely discernable nod, as if she did not want to help him, but would do it, since he had asked her nicely. She turned, and began to fly forward, turning her head to see if he was following.

He stayed close behind her, taking care to step in the path left by the fading golden dust left in her wake. She wasn't as bright as usual, which left Archie to wonder if perhaps Boggs hadn't been using her as an ingredient in his never-right again. He made a silent promise to find the biggest, brightest button on the entire ship as payment for her help once this escapade was over and done. He held the map up in front of him, hoping to catch the next turn that he needed to make before they missed it. To his surprise, Miss Bell turned a quick right, moving in the direction that he was getting ready to point out. It was as if she already knew where he wished to go.

Puzzled, he stayed silent and kept the map before him, in case she missed the next twist or turn, but she didn't. Several moments passed as they traveled deeper into the cavern, with nothing but the faint echo of his footsteps as proof that anyone was there at all.

What if I am too late? He wondered. It seemed that the pixie lighting his way was getting slower with each passing second. *How does she know the way? She hasn't missed a single turn.*

The sound of running water mixed in with the echo of his footsteps caught his ears. "Please, we have to hurry," he implored the pixie who was now barely moving in front of him. At the sound of his voice, she stopped and hovered where she was. "Please..." He stopped when he saw the impossibly fat tears running down her cheeks. Without so much as a single tone, she flew back in the direction they had come from, and disappeared.

I will find out what is wrong when this is finished, Archie promised himself, thanking his lucky stars that Miss Bell hadn't left him in complete darkness. The tunnel they had been following along had widened, and somewhere ahead of him—there was light.

He ran, slipping and sliding on the slick, rock floor. He rammed halfway into the wall, making another turn. He vaguely registered the pain that shot through the muscle of his shoulder, but pushed it from his mind and concentrated on the sound of the water. It was loud, but the sound seemed to ebb every few seconds, as if it were mimicking the ocean's tide.

You have two days.

The tide is rising, Cap'n. Beckett's voice echoed in his head. Coupled with Peter's warning, it pushed Archie faster. He had to find her soon. He glanced down at the paper crushed in his fist just long enough to discern one final turn before the *X*. It was up ahead, just around this last straight stretch. He ran as fast as his legs would carry him, flung himself around the final bend, and found himself falling end over end.

He landed in an unceremonious heap, several feet below where had last stood. Body aching from his tumble, he sat up slowly. Finding nothing broken, he took in the scene around him.

He was in a giant room of sorts, with slick, wet walls that vaulted upward to an open ceiling that showed a bright, blue sky. The sound of the ocean ebbing in and out had been an astute deduction, for mere inches away from his outstretched legs was the water coming in from a large opening in one wall, filling the room with more water with each surge.

In the center of the room, tied to a jagged rock, was Tiger Lily. The water had risen to her waist, but she was alive and staring at him with an expression of profound relief. Archie shot to his feet and began searching for the quickest way to her.

The water was riddled with rocks, making the most direct route impossible. With the way that the water was beginning to churn, he knew he couldn't swim to her for the certainty of being bashed against the rocks.

One flat rock ran the length around the room, serving much as a ledge, above the water. On the other side of the cavern, the rock jutted out and ended, mere feet from the stone where Tiger Lily was tied.

"Are you all right?" Archie called out.

She nodded. It was then that he realized the reason for her silence. A rag had been tied around her mouth and was cutting off her voice. She managed to give a strangled sound in response.

"Worry not, my love, I am coming!" With that, he ran toward her.

In his hurry, he slid on the slick ledge and barely caught his footing. Knowing if he landed in the water, all would be lost, he forced himself to concentrate and slow his pace. He began again.

The ledge was deceptive. Though it looked straight and level, there was just enough of a tilt to it that an unsuspecting person could fall. Add in the slick green algae, and the odds of plunging into the dark water increased.

"Slow down, slow down," he chanted to himself, watching the water that threatened to flow onto the ledge. He glanced up to make sure the tide hadn't taken her under. It hadn't, though it had risen several inches.

You have two days.

I will make it in time, Archie promised himself, I *have* made it in time. I only have to set her free and escape this cursed cavern.

"Mmph," Tiger Lily's strangled cry and a frantic splash, snapped him back into frantic mode. He had almost started to run toward her, when he realized she was trying to warn him.

Peter hovered before him with an impish, sly grin on his face. "You are very good at reading my maps, Archie."

Archie gritted his teeth, "You may call me either Captain, or Captain Jameson. You have no right to call me by name."

"Why?" Peter asked, glancing over his shoulder at Tiger Lily, "I've heard her. She calls you Archie. She has called for you often the last day or so. I've sat at the top and listened to her cry." He looked up at the opening in the ceiling. "I didn't think you would make it before the tide came in," he admitted, then fixed Archie with a cold, dark stare that Archie had never before seen on the face of a child. "I hoped you wouldn't."

"My name is my own and only those I call friend have the honor of using it. Let her go. I've played your game and I won. I followed every map, obeyed every rule," Archie said, feeling the coldness creep into his voice. "Let her go or I shall kill you."

"No." The dark look hadn't left Peter's face. If anything, it had intensified. "You haven't won, because I'm not done playing." He took the knife from his side. The sun glinted off the blade. "I challenge you to a duel, *Archie*."

"And if I don't accept?"

"She'll die—as will you."

Archie looked over at Tiger Lily. The water was rising and there was no other way to get around Peter. If fight he must, he would have to do it soon.

He unsheathed his rapier, the thin blade made a tinny metallic echo as it came free. He poised the blade before him and gave a small bow for the sake of formality. "I will accept, on the terms that you fight as a gentleman and that this is the last of your games."

"I agree to your terms," Peter nodded. "And I have my

own. If you win, she goes free. If I win, you never try to leave Neverland again."

There was no choice to be made. The only thing that mattered was Tiger Lily. "Agreed."

The first strike came the instant the word left Archie's lips, sending up a crackling spark as metal met metal. The force behind it caught Archie off guard and he took a step back, before countering with a strike of his own, which Peter deflected. The boy moved quickly, delivering blow for blow.

Peter had a definite advantage as his feet never hit the ground. He flew to and fro, effortlessly dodging each of Archie's thrusts. Archie, on the other hand, was slipping and sliding on the ledge.

"Bad form," Archie managed after one staggering blow that he nearly missed.

"What's bad form?" Peter paused, his knife poised.

"Having bad form is my way of implying that you do not fight as a gentleman. You are flying, which is putting me at grave disadvantage. A gentleman would make certain that his fight is fought fairly."

Peter's face went scarlet with anger before he said in a calm voice. "Then I won't fly."

Archie hadn't expected this, so when the boy landed on the slick rock before him, he was surprised. He smiled and gave an elaborate, deep bow. "And that, Peter, is what I would call 'good form.'"

Peter's reply was to send another stinging blow against his rapier that made his arm numb. Archie countered with his own, happily noticing that Peter was now sliding about as much as he. The duel was now fair—or more in his favor now that the young ruffian wasn't flitting about in the air.

They fought the length of the ledge, with Archie advancing on Peter, one blow at a time. The boy countered each thrust. It seemed Archie wouldn't be wearing him down anytime soon, so he concentrated on trying to push Peter back, trick him into taking one fatal misstep that would either make him fall or land him in the water.

The clang of the rapier against the knife echoed back and forth against the rock walls. It sounded as if war was being waged by an army, instead of two souls locked in a single, deadly duel. Archie registered that the ledge had left the wall and they were now on the section that jutted out into the water. There was at least an inch of water on this new section of rock. The sounds of sloshing mixed in with the echoes as they fought.

I must hurry, there isn't much time left. The tide will soon cover her. Archie began fighting with renewed vigor, which seemed to catch Peter by surprise. The boy stumbled once, and retreated a few quick steps, as if to regroup. Archie closed the gap between them and poised his rapier for a quick thrust at Peter's heart.

Instead of blocking the movement, as Archie had expected him to do, he spun around, took a step off the end of the ledge—and flew.

Archie's rapier had found its mark, but not in the boy who was now flying high above. The jarring sensation of the rapier sinking into flesh felt surreal at first. But now, as he looked into Tiger Lily's wide, shocked eyes—he was horrified.

His heart felt as if it was the one that had been pierced. "No, no, no," he whispered as he pulled his blade from her chest. As it came free, she slumped forward against the rope that held her fast. The hilt of his rapier made a dull clang as he dropped it to the ledge and leaned across to take the rag away from her mouth. Realizing that he needed his rapier to cut her free, he snatched it back up and cut through the ropes, before throwing it back down again.

"No, no... no..." he whispered again as he knelt, cradling her body to his, feeling the last bits of his heart die as she took one shuddering breath—and went still. He laid her down on the ledge, watching as the water brought her hair up to float around her face in dark, silky tendrils. She looked like a sleeping princess, but the narrow hole in her chest belied that she would ever wake again. Overcome by emotion, he bent and brushed a kiss to her lips. For the first time, it wasn't returned. She was gone—and the fault was his.

The sound of a blade scraping against rock cut through the muddle in his mind. Instinctively, he reached behind him for his rapier. When his hand found nothing but water and slick stone, he remembered the forgotten, flying boy, and turned.

Holding Archie's rapier, Peter hovered just above the water's surface, poised as if he had fought with such a weapon before.

Fury roiled over Archie as he stood and grabbed his blade. He ignored the sting of pain as the metal bit into his flesh. He gripped it tighter in his hand, bending the metal down. "You will pay for all that you have done, even if it takes my death to make it so," the words seeped out in a low whisper.

Peter's eyes went wide at first. Then, a dark look passed over them, giving him the appearance of being much older than the boy he seemed to be. "No, it won't take your death. Not yet. I find myself enjoying this far too much." With a quick, forceful jerk, the blade was ripped from Archie's hand, slicing through the tender flesh between his fingers as it came free. Then, before Archie had the chance to move, Peter swished the blade through the air, straight at his still uplifted hand.

Time slowed as Archie watched a ray of sun catch the silver blade, causing a sparkle to run from the hilt and travel toward the tip. In the instant the gleam touched the tip, the blade found his hand, severed it, and sent it flying through the air.

Blood poured from Archie's wrist, trapping his attention as it oozed from a stump and covered the lace cuff a gory, dark blue. This isn't happening, he thought, taking an unsure step back, watching as the blue blood ran down to his elbow and began dripping into the water in an increasing stream.

A laugh caught his attention, and his eyes left the empty place where his hand had been, so where it now was, in Peter's grasp. The boy looked jubilant, as if he had done some grand thing.

"My blade, if you please," Archie said coldly, trying to ignore the fact that his vision was now clouding and his body was weakening with each passing second. He stumbled forward and lifted up his uninjured arm to retrieve his rapier, daring Peter to take that hand, too.

Peter lifted an eyebrow, as if he was thinking of doing exactly that, but then he pitched the blade down, and flew off, disappearing through the opening in the ceiling. He hadn't thrown the rapier to Archie, but to the ledge, where the water had risen so much that it splashed near Tiger Lily's body.

Archie turned back and staggered toward her. The current was moving the hilt of the rapier back and forth. He was having difficulty focusing on it. His vision kept darkening each time the water surged.

He slipped as he bent over to pick it up and found himself on his knees by Tiger Lily. Instead of finding the rapier, his hand felt the cold silk of her hair that floated in the water. His vision cleared only well enough to watch his rapier wash over the ledge with the next surge in the tide. As it disappeared under a blanket of hazy, white foam, his vision left and the darkness closed in. He felt warm.

It's over now, Archie thought. The pain left as the water covered his face. A single thought passed through his mind as his hand found hers.

I will die with the one I love.

21

NEVERMORE

Runt stood on the deck of the ship. He had been there when they brought his body on board. He'd caught a glimpse of the captain's face. It was white and pasty and had the look of the dead.

How will I join this crew if Captain Archie is dead? Runt watched, horrified, as they carted the captain's body below.

The sullen-looking, old man they had called the doctor looked even grouchier than the one other time Runt had seen him. He brushed by Runt as if he hadn't noticed his presence and followed the others down the steps.

It was quiet for the rest of the day. He stayed on the deck, wanting to help in some way, but didn't know how to go about it. The ship was a strange thing with hundreds of ropes stretching up to the huge pieces of canvas that billowed in the wind.

"Come up here, boy," a large man with rippling tattoos said from the deck above him, "I will teach ye how to sail the ship."

He did as the man asked and climbed the steps to the upper deck. "I am Beckett," the man introduced himself, "What be yer name, lad?"

"Runt." It came out in a nervous squeak, making Runt feel even more self-conscious as he stood in front of the hulking man before him.

"Well now, Runt. If ye wish to be a pirate, ye must know all there is to know about the ship, aye?" the man named Beckett said, giving Runt's shoulder a quick squeeze, before motioning to the big, round wheel in front of him. "What say ye take the wheel and bring us out to sea, eh?"

"Aye-aye, Captain," Runt said, taking the spokes of the wheel in his hands.

A chilling scream rent the air, sending gooseflesh along Runt's arms. He gripped the wheel and looked up at Beckett with wide eyes.

Beckett was looking toward the steps, where the scream had seemed to come from. "Nay, lad, I am not the cap'n of the *Jolig Roger*. I only be watching over her 'til her true cap'n is fit to handle her again."

Runt had been looking at Beckett's tense face, when he noticed something just over his shoulder. With a sense of dread, he whispered only loudly enough for Beckett to hear, "He's here. Peter is here."

Beckett whirled around as the gravity of his words hit him, and began barking orders to every man in sight. Runt cowered next to the wheel, hoping to escape Peter's notice.

"Ye stay close to me," Beckett said, as he stepped in front of Runt, blocking his view.

Runt hid behind Beckett's legs, hoping that Peter hadn't caught sight of him. He didn't want to be one of the Lost Boys anymore, but he wasn't feeling brave in this particular moment, either. He had been brave when Peter took Tiger Lily away. He had stood up to him and told Peter to leave her alone, but it hadn't worked. He had been too small to do any good. Now, he wanted to be invisible, but he still wanted to watch, so he peeked around Beckett's legs, just in time to see Peter fly past, so close that Runt could have reached out and touched him. He was carrying a long, pointed knife—one that looked like the one Runt had seen before at Captain Archie's side.

"He forgot this," Peter announced, throwing the long knife at the big pole in the middle of the ship. It made a loud thwack as it sunk in, the shiny handle moving back and forth.

Without another word, he flew upward, disappearing into the clouds. Several long moments passed as they watched for any sign that he would return.

"I guess he came and did what he meant to do," Beckett's words sounded hard, but he shrugged as he turned and offered Runt a hand up from his hiding place. "Let's make ye a pirate, lad. I feel we be needin' all the help we can get."

* * *

Images came and went in a jumble, mixing and twisting so that nothing made sense. Archie wanted the darkness back—wanted the peace that it brought. The colors came in blurs, though the blue always seemed dominant, the cursed blue that always reminded him of blood. Some flesh colors reminded him of the faces of his crew or of the mermaid he spotted at their arrival. Several times over, he thought he was staring into the face of Smee, but then the blue would take over and the pain would come alive.

Each time, he wished for darkness. He wished for death—but it wouldn't come.

"Come on, lad. Ye have tried to give up for three days now, but yer spirit be too strong. Best ye open yer eyes and deal with it, eh?" Smee's voice broke through the darkness and shattered it. "If ye do, I promise the pain will go away sooner."

Archie's eyes opened a slit as he tried to focus. Smee's white sideburns came into view first, followed by his bulbous nose, and his spectacles. Two shrewd, watery blue eyes were looking at him.

"Ah, there ye be," Smee said in a conversational tone, as if his captain had been misplaced instead of at the brink of death. "If ye would like to sit up, I'll get ye a drink. I'd imagine ye need one," he turned, presumably to pick up a tankard of rum. Then, Archie heard him mumble, "I know I do."

Archie sat up, body aching and throbbing, though the worst of the pain was coming from his left arm that had been tucked under the covers. That brought his memories back and he remembered his last thought. "How is it that I am not dead? Or is it that I *am* dead and stuck in this cursed place for all eternity?" His voice was raspy as he took the offered tankard from Smee. He took a long drink, noticing that the old man had taken pity on him and filled it with wine.

Smee sighed, settling down on the bench across from him, his own tankard clasped in his hands. "Ye aren't dead, lad, though I thought ye to be when we found ye floating in the water. Lucky for ye, Beckett wanted to go hunt a croc, else ye would have been dead, sure enough. Ye lost a hand and more blood than I ever saw from a single man, but ye must have a purpose to stay alive, 'cause ye are still here."

Archie slipped his wounded arm out of the covers. The sight of the wrapped stub was a shock, even though he had expected it to be there. The worse part was that the air above it ached, as if his hand were still there, only invisible and hurt.

"They say those who lose a hand or a foot will have its ghost to haunt them, unless it is buried proper-like," Smee said, as if he had read Archie's mind.

"That will be difficult to do, as the last I saw, it was in Peter's possession." Archie grimaced, taking another gulp of wine.

"Eh, no, he doesn't have it," Smee said, fidgeting on his stool. Catching Archie's cold stare, he continued, "He flew around the sails a bit yesterday, so as to make sure we was watchin'. Then he flew a ways out, and waited for the croc. When the big beastie came to the surface, the boy threw it to 'im. Yer hand got eaten, lad. Won't be any burying it, I'm afraid."

"Lovely."

The two sat in silence for the next few moments until

they had both drained their cups. "Beckett has a report to give ye, whenever ye want to hear it. Ye also have a new man that wishes to join the crew. If ye want me to send 'em down, I will," Smee said, standing.

"Send them."

Smee waited, and when it became apparent that Archie had nothing more to say, he left, shutting the door to the map room. No one ever shuts that door quietly. It must be worse than he lets on, Archie thought, swinging his legs over the side of the cot.

Without thinking, he placed his left arm down to grip the side of the cot. His wrapped stump thunked against the wooden rail, sending currents of pain that radiated all the way to his elbow.

Archie gritted his teeth until the pain subsided. Then he stood, struggled into his breeches and coat, then fumbled with the fastening on his belt. At last clothed with the help of his single hand, he sat down in the chair behind the map table to wait.

He had expected Beckett to arrive first, but a moment later Smee came back into the map room, carrying a small wooden box. "I haven't told Beckett to come yet. There be somethin' I wanted to give ye." He sat the box down on the table, and flipped open the lid.

"This belonged to Blackbeard. He bought it on

Madeira, but forgot to take it with him. I found it at the tavern when he left. I suppose he meant to use it, should he ever lose a hand. I doubt we ever see Blackbeard again, and ye are the captain of this ship. It's yers, if ye want it."

Lying on a pad of black velvet, was a gleaming silver hook.

Archie didn't realize Smee had left again until the door closed behind him. As he lifted up the hook, the light caught the thick, white scar on his palm. A memory of Tiger Lily raced through his mind. A bargain for her people's safety, a cut to his hand, and a chaste kiss, rushed through him, sending tears to his eyes.

She was gone, and it was his fault. One solitary tear trekked down his cheek. He fixed the gleaming hook onto the stub, ignoring the stabs of pain that radiated in his wrist as he clamped down the leather strap. He would take this gift that Blackbeard had left—and in doing so, he would vow his revenge. If the death guardian wished someone to battle until the end of time, he would be there to do it. He would not rest, nor ever leave Neverland, until Peter had paid for what he had done. He glanced down at his scar. He would have it to remind him of Tiger Lily. He took Harper's drawing of Mary out of his coat pocket. It was ragged now, water-stained, and ruined, but he could still make out her beautiful face.

He undid the fastenings. Curling the picture around his stub, he replaced the hook, trapping the image of Mary between his skin and the leather. He tightened the strap, hearing the paper crinkle as it became part of him.

Now, on each hand, he would have a reminder of what had been taken from him. Feeling the last bits of his heart harden, he stood. Without waiting for anyone to appear, he made his way to the deck.

The first thing that caught his eye in the dwindling daylight, was his rapier, stuck fast in the mast. Without a word, he jerked it free, and slid it back into the sheath at his side. Then, he stalked to the quarterdeck, watching as his crew moved to stay out of his way.

"You have a report?" he asked Beckett, who looked rather shocked to see him.

"Aye, Cap'n," Beckett managed, then took a breath as if collecting his thoughts. He continued, "The lads came back from hunting a short while ago. The Indians refuse to hunt for us anymore. They found the girl's body and they aren't sure who to blame. They be makin' noises that anyone who comes to their village is an enemy."

"Leave them be. We will provide for our own. No man is to approach them, we will honor their wishes," Archie said. It was the least he could do for Tiger Lily's people. If they wished to be left alone, he would make it so, even if it meant several disastrous trips before his men learned to hunt. "Smee said there is a man wishing to join our crew, send him up."

"Aye, Cap'n. He is right here." Beckett motioned to a teenage lad that had been waiting by the railing. He had been silent and Archie hadn't seen him until this moment. "I've been teaching him the ship. He's nimble and quick on the ropes. The only man I've seen any better with the mast was Harper."

At his friend's name, Archie's eyes narrowed. A breeze came, ruffling the boy's blond hair. He squinted at him, giving Archie the vague impression that he had seen this boy somewhere before. "Are you one of Peter's men?" he asked without preamble, mentally ticking off each of the young boys in Peter's troupe that he had met.

"I used to be, but I'm not anymore."

"What is your name?"

"Runt."

Archie had opened his mouth to say that such a thing was impossible, but no words came out. The anxious expression on the lad's face was an exact replica of the one he had seen on the young boy's face as Runt handed him the first of Peter's maps. In a matter of days, he had somehow gained a decade of age.

"It happened after the first day. He fell asleep a young boy, and woke up as he is now," Beckett explained, "The island's spell wore off when he left. He's as old as he should be, from my way of thinking."

"Won't Peter be missing you?" Archie asked. "If one of my men were to disappear, I would search until I found him."

Runt shook his head, "No, I told Beetles to tell him that I was leaving. Besides, he's gone after Wendy now." At Archie's questioning glance, he continued, "He told me that since he took away Tiger Lily, he would bring me someone new. He found someone named Wendy in the grown-up place. He was going to bring her here to be our mother." The lad frowned, as if he found the thought not to his liking, "I don't want to be a Lost Boy ever again. I wish to be a pirate."

"Will you tell me all that you know of Peter and his whereabouts?" Archie asked, "To become one of my crew, you must tell me all you know."

"I will tell you." Runt nodded. "Every single word of it."

Archie motioned to Beckett. "Bring the book. Let the lad make his mark. He will join our crew."

"Aye, Cap'n. While I go, is there a heading ye wish for us to sail? The sun is nearly set." Beckett turned to head toward the stairs.

"No, we won't be leaving. We will wait here for Peter's return, however long it should take."

Beckett nodded and left, returning moments later with the leather bound book.

"Make your mark and join our crew." Archie pointed to the empty space under the last scrawled name.

"Aye."

Pirate words sounded odd coming from him, Archie thought, fighting to suppress a smile. "Welcome to the crew of the *Jolig Roger*, Runt."

The words that came out of the lad's mouth next, chased away every hint of a smile and darkened his heart even further. "Thank you, Captain Archie."

"No, that is not my name." A fresh wave of darkness washed over his heart as he fixed his newest crew member with his cold, blue eyes. "The one you knew by that name died in the cavern with the one he loved. There is nothing and no one left for me in this life." He lifted his left arm, letting the last rays of dying light catch the silver on his new hand. "Now—and forevermore—I will be known as Captain Hook."

The End

* * *

What other untold stories are in Neverland? Find out!

Sign up for my newsletter and be the first to receive news on my latest releases, exclusive excerpts, free stories, and more –
http://www.krthompson.net

THE ADVENTURE CONTINUES!

READ ON FOR AN EXCERPT OF THE NEXT
BOOK IN THIS EXCITING SERIES...

22

THE SEA WITCH

*T*HESPA, QUEEN OF the water sprites and ruler of all the Never Sea, returned to the human world with a profound sense of dread. As the leader of the watery half of Neverland, not much worried her.

At least, it hadn't until the humans began forgetting about magic and the sprites began dying.

This trip back to the human world wasn't one she had made out of choice—necessity brought her here. She'd come to find someone to believe in her, possibly several someones, depending upon how successful her quest proved to be. Then, she'd bring them back with her as a sort of insurance so she'd never have to come to this wretched place again.

Fish won't do, she decided, staring at the wide-set eyes

of one particularly ugly pufferfish. She stood on a wide piece of coral, deep beneath the waves of this warm human ocean, and looked around. More unintelligent fish, crabs, and other sea creatures milled about, none looking particularly pleased or excited to see her. The only ones who showed any interest in her at all were the ones who stopped just long enough to see if she was a small, sparkly bit of food.

This could take forever. Her wings dipped down in dejection. *I wonder how long it took the pixie to find that flying Peter-boy?*

One of the golden pixies, Tink, had been the first to bring someone to Neverland. When that proved successful, she'd brought a handful more. Her Lost Ones, the pixie had named them. They were, Tink explained, the ones the human world wouldn't miss.

Thespa crinkled her nose in disgust. As a creature of the sea, she didn't care for humans. Though they resembled water sprites and had legs to walk about on, they lacked a graceful set of wings that could take them through both water and air. And they most certainly didn't have any magic. Humans were meant to be above the sea, not below it. Still, the idea of taking someone or something to Neverland that wouldn't be missed *did* appeal to Thespa. She sighed, wondering again how long it took Tink to find her Lost Ones.

She started to fly from her perch and try a new place when something stopped her. Literally.

Thespa looked down and scowled, kicking the errant strand of seaweed that had twisted itself around her foot. The bit of green plant gave way at her vicious kick, but left a long green streak of slime down the length of her leg as a parting gift. This, of course, did absolutely nothing to improve her mood.

She was so aggravated that something extremely important had escaped her notice—the gaping jaws of an eel headed directly at her. Her anger disappeared in a fleeting second, but it was too late to move.

Then, a hand wrapped around her an instant before the monster's teeth snapped.

Nonplussed at missing its small, sparkly appetizer, the eel swam off in search of another easy, unsuspecting meal.

Once the hand opened, Thespa let out an uneasy breath and looked up into a pair of wide, silver eyes, framed by long locks of blond hair.

At first, she thought she'd been saved by a human, but then she spotted his long tail and realized he was as much a creature of the sea as she—and he was exactly who she'd been searching for.

Read more...

ALSO BY K.R. THOMPSON

The Keeper Saga:

Hidden Moon

Once Upon a Haunted Moon

The Wolf

Wynter's War

Charmed

The One

Under a Dark Moon

Blood Moon Rising

Wynter's End

The Untold Stories of Neverland:

Pan

Hook

Nerida

Jack

Shifter's University:

Shifter's University

Forest of Lost Souls

The Chronicles of a Blue Fairy:

Dragon Kept

Anthologies:

Once Upon a Spell

Tales of Red

ABOUT THE AUTHOR

K.R. Thompson is a USA Today and New York Times bestselling author.

An avid reader and firm believer in magic of books, she spends her nights either reading an adventure or writing one.

She still watches for evidence of Bigfoot in the mud of Wolf Creek.

Connect with her on her website - http://www.krthompson.net

Or on Facebook - http://www.facebook.com/thekeepersaga

Printed in Great Britain
by Amazon